HEARTS
UNDER
SIEGE

Will the truth bring them together?

Brady Fitzpatrick has spent a decade burying the pain of a broken heart while working for SIEGE, an information-gathering spy agency. That it kept him away from his family as well as his best friend Molly has been an unfortunate side effect. But when his brother, also an agent, is killed during a foreign op, Brady is drawn into a web of intrigue that threatens the lives of everyone he loves...

Molly Byrnes has loved Brady forever. As his best friend and a de facto member of the Fitzpatrick family, she holds them together in their crushing grief. But as a member SIEGE's ground team, she doesn't buy the official line about Brady's brother's "accidental" death and launches her own investigation—only to uncover a shocking secret that she and Brady must get to the bottom of before their target finds them.

Tangled emotions land them in bed together, opening Brady's eyes to the incredible, fearless woman who's been there for him all his life. But after a lifetime of disappointment, how can Molly trust the possibility of a future with him...or if they can count on any future at all?

HEARTS
UNDER
SIEGE

Damschroder

NATALIE J.
DAMSCHRODER

Other books by Natalie J. Damschroder

Entangled Publishing, LLC
2614 South Timberline Road
Suite 109
Fort Collins, CO 80525
Visit our website at www.entangledpublishing.com.

Edited by Nina Bruhns
Cover design by Fiona Jayde

Ebook ISBN 978-1-62266-494-8
Print ISBN 978-1-62266-609-6

Manufactured in the United States of America

First Edition February 2014

This book is dedicated to Andrew Jacobus,
my brother, my first hero.
Thank you for being the kind of man I can point to and say,
"That's the goal."

Chapter One

SOUTHERN CONNECTICUT
THANKSGIVING

"You missed the turn."

"Dammit." Dragging himself out of his own head, Brady Fitzpatrick scowled at his best friend. Molly Byrnes smirked back at him and shoved her feet up onto the dashboard, her fingers dancing across her knees like they were a keyboard. He checked behind him and did a U-ie in the middle of the empty street. "Why didn't you say anything?"

"Because when I said something two turns ago, you growled at me." She pointed to the left. "There."

Brady made the turn and tried to remember what they'd been talking about, before he'd gotten lost in his thoughts. Right. True love. She'd razzed him for believing in it and said it wouldn't make a good pickup line. For who-knew-how-many miles, he'd brooded about the job offer from SIEGE, and how true love fit into it.

He cast another glance at Molly, who was now humming

something unfamiliar. Probably an assignment for the composition class she hated, judging by the dark look on her face. That explained why she'd let him brood for so long.

"Check that, would you?" He motioned at the crumpled directions stuffed into the cup holder between them. "I thought we'd be at the station by now."

Molly heaved a sigh, dropped her feet, and pulled out the paper, comparing it to their location. "Couple more miles on the right, looks like." She went back to playing her knees. "So anyway, women aren't going to fall all over a guy just because he walks up and tells her he believes in true love."

"I'm not talking about picking up chicks," he protested. "I'm talking about relationships like my parents'." He squinted against the glare of the sun off a sign, trying to see if it was for the train station. His parents had moved from Massachusetts to Connecticut a few months ago, while he was at school, and he didn't know the area yet.

"Your parents are, like, the exception that proves the rule."

"Well, yeah, my parents are awesome." Molly's parents couldn't go five minutes without sniping, a whole day without a knockdown, drag-out fight. That was why she'd come down here with him for Thanksgiving instead of going home. "And they're not the only ones."

Molly snorted. "Name another couple you know who's been together longer than three years."

"There's—" He stopped. No, Sheri and Dave had been married less than two years. His aunt and uncle had just separated. Who else did he know? He couldn't believe he was going to lose this debate when it had barely started. Though it kind of answered his question about love versus work. "Anyway—" His phone rang, and he snatched it off his belt, ignoring Molly's derisive laugh. "Hello?"

"Did you get her yet? Where are you? Why didn't you call me?"

His brother. The reason he and Molly had ended up on this

topic in the first place. "Geez, Chris. Chill. Her train's not due for another half hour."

"Dad said the trains are early sometimes." There was a tiny snap, and Brady knew his brother was biting his nails. He was really gone over this girl. "Make sure she knows I would have gotten her if Mom hadn't — "

"Don't worry, I know the story." Brady rolled his eyes. "I'll make her feel so welcome she won't even miss you."

"Okay, good. Hey, wait!"

Laughing, Brady shut the phone and dropped it into the console. "Chris is freaking out that we're going to miss the train."

Molly shook her head. "He really wanted to be the one to pick her up. What's her name again?"

Spotting the station parking lot up ahead, Brady flipped his turn signal and slowed the car. "Jessica. Sounds like a princess. Just his type."

"Yeah." She snorted again. "True love."

"Maybe." He parked and they stepped out into the sharp November air. Brady threw an arm around Molly when she shivered and hunched into her denim jacket. The sun was warm, but the wind, light as it was, still bit. They bickered as usual, crossing the lot and climbing the steps to the train platform. Brady glanced at his watch. Still a good twenty minutes until the train was supposed to arrive. He scanned the nearly empty platform almost automatically.

And then he saw her.

His gaze touched the woman, and an invisible fist slammed into his solar plexus, knocking every atom of oxygen out of his lungs. His vision narrowed, the edges fluttery and thin, and all he could see was…

Her.

She sat on the bench against the wall of the ticket office, bent over what looked like a hardbound journal. Sleek blond hair hid her face, but as he watched she swept it back behind a perfectly shaped ear with a long-fingered, graceful hand. Her cheek curved sweetly, a lush pink mouth pursed in a bow, and when she blinked, her eyelashes glided through the air in slow motion.

True love whispered through his mind, and he knew, without a flicker of doubt, that she belonged to him.

Molly elbowed him, and the world came rushing back. The roar and clang of a train entering the station, the cold breeze in his face, the buzz of his phone at his waist. But still, he couldn't take his eyes off her.

She looked up. Bluish-hazel eyes, full of sparkling humor, met his. It filled him with euphoria and a sense of rightness. He had to meet her. Now.

"Fitzpatrick!" Molly yanked at his arm. "What's wrong with you?"

He ignored her and stepped forward, trying on a smile. The cold made it stiff. God, he probably looked like a dork. "Um, hi."

She beamed, her perfect lips seemingly unaffected by the temperature. "Hi. Brady?"

He blinked. She knew his name?

"Uh…yeah. I'm—"

"Chris's brother, I know. He texted me that you were coming." She marked her page with the ribbon attached to the book, twisted her pen closed, and slid both into her bag before standing. She was the perfect height, a couple of inches below his.

Brady didn't know what to say. His brain wasn't processing this. She knew him? She couldn't. He'd remember if he'd met her before. Unless she'd been, like, fat or something. He squinted at her, and she laughed. No, he'd definitely remember that dancing trill. He'd remember thinking ridiculous words like "dancing trill."

Molly shoved him aside and took over.

"I'm Molly Byrnes. Sorry we made you wait. Brady didn't

believe the train would be early." She held out her hand, and Brady's destiny shook it. The two women turned to walk toward the steps, Molly taking the handle of a small rolling suitcase he hadn't noticed. They were talking animatedly, as if they—

Crap.

The second punch in the gut didn't have the same sense of wonder and joy. This one brought depressed understanding. This was Jessica. Chris's girlfriend. His *brother's* girlfriend. Fuck!

Molly glared at him over her shoulder, motioned toward the parking lot with her head. But Brady's feet felt cemented to the platform. How could this be happening? Everything lined up. They'd been talking about true love, and there she was. And he'd been struck, just as his father had always described feeling when he saw Brady's mother for the first time.

Okay, not *everything* lined up. There was that decision he had to make by the end of the year, the one that would dictate the direction of his entire life. The job offer from SIEGE—Strategic Infiltration of Enemy Group Enterprise—was one any guy would frickin' die for. The chance to do real good in the world. To fight terrorism in the information age. Protect his family. Be a hero. But he wouldn't be able to tell anyone about it. That was the part holding him back. He'd have to lie to his family, to Molly, for the rest of his life. He wasn't sure he was capable of that. But his original plans looked stable, responsible, and positively coma-inducing in comparison. He'd been weighing the options for weeks.

But shit, now instead of two paths in front of him, he had, like, ten. Okay, half of them were blocked, but there were always ways around obstacles, if you looked hard enough. He just had to look. Hard.

"Fitz?"

He blinked again. Molly stood at the top of the steps, this time frowning in concern. "You okay?"

"Yeah. Fine." He shook off his inertia. *Maybe it's not*

serious, her and Chris. The thought galvanized him enough to follow the women to the car, but he still reeled internally, from the dual shock of finding his soul mate, and literally five seconds later losing her to his brother. But those two hadn't known each other that long. Chris had never had a long-term girlfriend. Three months was his record, as far as Brady could remember. Maybe he still had a chance.

"Is it a long drive to the house?" Jessica asked as they reached the car, and a buzz went down Brady's spine. He closed his eyes for a second, but of course she didn't keep talking. She'd asked a question. He realized Molly was staring at him from the back end of the car, Jessica standing next to her, waiting for him to answer. Also, probably, to open the trunk. Sheepish, he hit the button on the remote key and hurried to lift the suitcase into the empty space. Jessica thanked him, and this time the sensation down his spine was more like warm honey. He suppressed a shudder and slammed the trunk, testing to be sure it was latched, and hoped Jessica hadn't noticed his reactions. He peeked and found both women looking at him from the side of the car now. Crap. He still hadn't answered her question.

"About half an hour," he managed as he moved to the driver's door, and cursed when the key missed the lock and nicked the paint. Dad would notice that. He managed on his second try, and then, as he opened his door and reached for the unlock button, realized he should have opened the other side first, held the door for Jessica. Too late now. She'd already climbed into the back seat.

Pull it together, man. He leaned his forearms on the car roof for a moment. He sucked in a deep breath, letting the cold air clear his mind. He was acting like a doofus. Even if Chris wasn't serious about Jessica, even if they broke up soon and Brady had a clear field...well, she wasn't going to want to have anything to do with her ex's dweeb little brother.

The phone buzzed again and Brady snatched it up. "What?"

"Did you get her?"

He blew out a breath. "Yes. We got her. We're on our way."

"Let me talk to her."

Brady hesitated. "Doesn't she have her own phone?"

"Don't be an ass, Brady, just give her the phone."

Brady lowered his arm but didn't open his car door. Handing over the phone was like handing over *her*. But that was stupid, she wasn't his to hand over. God, his stomach hurt.

The window slid down, and Molly, leaning across the seats, scowled up at him. "What's the deal?"

Brady handed her the phone. "It's Chris. For…Jessica." His voice practically cracked on her name, and he stayed where he was until Molly handed the phone back a few moments later. He swallowed hard a few times and sucked in lots of air, trying to clear his head enough to drive. Nice start to a relationship, killing the woman he loved. Not.

Finally, he was in control—mostly—and they were on the road. Molly kept a constant stream of conversation going, twisted to face Jessica in the back seat and digging her bony knees into Brady's side. He thought she was doing it on purpose, but any time he looked at her, she seemed oblivious, totally focused on Jessica.

Luckily, the back roads of Connecticut weren't as busy as the highway. Otherwise, he'd have crashed them for sure during one of his peeks into the rearview mirror. The watery sunlight cast Jessica in a kind of glow that made his chest hurt. When she laughed at something Molly said, her teeth flashed, straight and perfect, no overbite or crooked canines. He had no idea what they were discussing. All he could think about was the sweet perfume filling the car, how soft her skin had to be, what she'd taste like when they kissed.

She's your brother's girlfriend, he told himself sternly when his fantasies dug beneath her off-white wool coat and cashmere scarf, wondering what kind of body they hid. Even if she and his brother weren't a serious couple, he couldn't make a move on Chris's girl!

Not until they broke up.

That would be too late, though. She'd be back at grad school in New York, and Brady would be up at UMass again, with almost an entire year of college left. He could transfer. He'd do it in an instant. He loved New York. But it was his senior year, and what if all his credits didn't transfer? That would be stupid. He couldn't damage his future over her. Then what would he have to offer? Plus, she and Chris might not break up before the end of the year. How would he tell SIEGE his decision with that still up in the air? If he said yes to their job offer, he'd have a hard time combining that kind of work and a new relationship. He didn't even know what their rules were about that kind of thing. He wasn't sure he could handle it. Too many secrets to keep track of. Too easy to make mistakes when you were new at both.

But so what? It would be worth it. He could always quit the stupid job, five-year minimum commitment be damned.

His thoughts spun on and on, counterpart to Molly and Jessica's barely heard conversation, until he suddenly realized they were on his parents' street. He'd retraced his route without even realizing it. He pulled in behind Chris's old Nissan and shut off the car.

"I'll let them know we're here." Molly leapt out and dashed up the walkway.

Brady's heart pounded as he met Jessica at the trunk. "I've, uh, got it." He raised the lid and reached for her bag.

"Thanks." She brushed a few strands of hair off her face. "You've been awfully quiet. I'm sorry if we—"

"It's Molly," he interrupted, then felt himself blush at his rudeness. *Blush*, for cripes sake! "She never shuts up. It was nice to be able to tune her out for a few minutes, let someone else pick up the slack." When she laughed, his shoulders dropped a fraction and he felt looser, less tense. "Seriously, she's my best friend, but she knows how to keep a conversation going. I didn't have anything to add." *Since I wasn't paying attention.*

"Thanks for picking me up and everything." She looked toward the house, then back at him, her smile blinding him to anything else again. "I'm a little nervous about meeting your folks."

"Don't be, they're cool." He lifted his eyes to meet hers as she brushed at her hair again, blown back into her face by the breeze. Her light fragrance wafted toward him. It was something Brady couldn't identify, but it made him think of hunger. Heat swelled in his chest, reminding him of fifteen years ago, when he'd been five and begging his parents for one of the puppies their neighbor was selling. Longing. That's what it was.

Jessica didn't look away immediately, but paused, and her eyes seemed to refocus, really seeing him.

Sizzlesnap.

She looked startled, then scared, then nothing, her expression a pleasant mask. But a thrill of excitement went through Brady. *She'd felt it, too*.

"Jess!"

She spun, and the connection disappeared. Disappointment replaced thrill. Brady shut the trunk and picked up the suitcase, stopping to watch Chris engulf Jessica in a hug, then kiss her as if they hadn't seen each other in a month instead of three days. Jessica accepted the kiss, no hesitation, and Brady wondered if he'd imagined the moment of connection. If he'd just wanted it so badly he'd projected it onto her.

But no, as he followed them across the yard and up the steps of the old colonial that was Rick and Donna Fitzpatrick's new home, Jessica glanced over her shoulder, then quickly back to where his mother stood in the doorway, beaming at them all. He wasn't imagining the wariness that was now in Jessica's expression.

Hope took root, a tiny glimmer deep in his heart. He couldn't betray his brother, for God's sake. He could not go after Jessica. But if *she* wanted *him*…well, nothing he could do about that, right?

A few minutes later, he'd escaped the annoying greetings in the foyer to bring Jessica's suitcase upstairs. He was standing next to the guest room bed, telling himself he had no right to even *think* about opening the case, when Molly appeared in the doorway.

"What the hell are you doing?" she hissed in a loud whisper, glancing down the hallway before coming in and grabbing his arm. "Get out of here."

"What?" But Brady let her pull him down the hall into the bedroom they were sharing, the one with his and Chris's old twin beds. His parents were letting Chris and Jessica use the double bed in the guest room, and Brady fought a surge of jealousy, thinking about it.

"Will you get a grip?" Molly let go of him and shut the door. "I can't believe you."

"What?" he said again, but he knew she wouldn't let him get away with it. She'd known him since kindergarten, grew up in his back yard, almost literally, as their houses had backed up on each other. She'd known when he spiked the punch at Chris's high school graduation party, and when he'd lied to the head cheerleader, telling her he was the starting running back for the homecoming game so she'd go to the dance with him. Hell, she'd known all the way back in third grade that he hadn't done his homework because he'd been catching frogs in the creek down the street. And she hadn't needed evidence or first-hand knowledge to catch him in his lies. She just knew him that well.

Still. He wasn't going to come out and tell her what was going on with him. Someday she'd be wrong. Why not today?

"She's *Christopher's*," she accused.

Okay, not today. He flopped onto his bed, arms out-flung, and wondered when the throb in his chest would go away. "I know she is."

"Then why did I find you about to dive into her unmentionables?" She stepped up onto her own bed and sank down, cross-legged, clutching a pillow on her lap. It was a familiar pose, and it eased something in him. He didn't know why.

"I wasn't," he protested half-heartedly.

"You were thinking about it."

He said nothing. The ceiling had no cracks. Not like their old house. But there were brush strokes in the paint. He concentrated on finding patterns.

Molly sighed. "She's way out of your league, dude. Even if she weren't taken. By your *brother*. Whom you worship."

"I don't worship him." That was true, at least. He had, of course, when they were little. Okay, not so little. But once Chris had gone off to college, Brady got a taste of being out of his shadow, and finally realized he wasn't less than his brother. He had talent on the football field—maybe not enough to start, like Chris had since freshman year, but enough. He got good grades and was his class salutatorian, something Chris had missed out on. His mother had said he'd found himself, and in doing so, he'd been able to see his brother as just a guy. They'd had a much better relationship in the last few years because of it.

But this…

"If Chris finds you ogling his girlfriend," Molly started, and Brady cut her off with a slice of his hand.

"I'm not going to ogle her." He felt her tension subside and should have left it at that, but his mouth kept going. "She deserves more respect than that."

"Brady!" Molly slammed the pillow beside her and scrambled off the bed to loom over him, hands on hips. "She's not available! Do you seriously want to screw up your entire life over someone you met an hour ago?"

"No." But maybe he didn't have to screw everything up. Maybe he could—

"Stop it!" She slapped his forehead.

"Ow!" He glowered at her, rubbing the sting away.

"Seriously, Brady, get her out of your head. What the hell

are you thinking?"

He sighed and rolled his head so he was staring at the ceiling again, not her accusing, piercing blue eyes. "I can't help it," he admitted. "She hit me. Right here." He pressed the heel of his right hand against his breastbone. "The instant I saw her. Just like Dad when he saw Mom. It was—"

"Don't say it." But her tone was softer, more understanding. She sat on the bed next to his hip and took his hand onto her lap. "Oh, Brady. You know this will end badly, right?"

"No, it won't. She felt something, too," he told Molly. "I saw it. Maybe they aren't serious. Maybe she's ready to break up with him already. You know girls do that—hang on even when they know it's over."

Molly didn't argue, which surprised him. She hated generalities, especially about her gender.

"Okay, maybe they'll break up. And then what? You go to school in different states."

"I could transfer."

"Oh, for Pete's sake, you're not going to transfer." She tossed his hand away and stood. "Let her go. You know you have to."

But he didn't know that. This kind of thing happened all the time. And, all right, most of the examples he thought of were from TV shows. But they had to be based on real life *some*times.

An hour ago, he'd been facing the hugest decision of his life. Jessica's effect on him made it seem as easy as ordering a sandwich.

"Dinner!" his mother called from downstairs, her tone muffled by the closed door, her annoyance at their disappearance nevertheless clear.

"Coming!" Molly called back. She grabbed his hand and hauled him off the bed. "Stop thinking about it, at least. You know Chris will notice."

"Yeah, I know." That was the first thing she'd said that he

couldn't find a way to dispute. Chris was keenly observant, a talent that had snagged him a lucrative job with a business consulting firm, one of those companies who sent in a team to a company that wasn't doing well, identified their problems, and advised how to fix things. He would definitely notice if Brady acted weird.

So over dinner, Brady forced himself to make jokes, tease his mother about her cooking, needle Molly about anything and everything, and insult his brother to Jessica, acting as though he was making a play for her. It was exactly what he would have done if he hadn't been into her, so everyone responded normally.

"So, Jessica," his father said halfway through the main course, and Chris groaned.

"Come on, Dad, can't you skip the interrogation?"

Rick Fitzpatrick grinned at his son. "Certainly not. This is the first girl you've dated longer than three months. It's even more important now!"

Brady stared at his father, then at Chris and Jessica. It had already been longer than three months? *No.* They were holding hands. While they ate. Jessica was left-handed, or good enough not to make a mess, anyway, and their fingers kept toying with each other's, and...no, that wasn't good.

"What are your plans after graduation?" his father asked, taking a bite of mashed potatoes.

"I'm getting my degree in interior design, so it's whatever I can get in the field."

Brady shoved his fork into a piece of meat, not really aware what kind it was. Her voice was killing him. Soft and sweet, but not girly or weak, it sent a constant stream of shivers down his spine. He was getting back cramps, trying to hide those shivers.

"My goal," Jessica continued, "is functional design, like in classrooms and training centers. Day cares and special-needs schools, places like that."

"So not just decorating?" his mother asked, clearly

interested. And why not? Jessica was altruistic, like his parents were. Most of their family vacations had been spent doing Habitat for Humanity, Help for Haiti, going wherever the most recent disaster had occurred and hauling debris, distributing water, whatever was needed. His parents' jobs had made that stuff possible, and here Jessica was, planning a combination of marketability and benefit to others.

She was perfect.

"What are your grades like?" his father asked.

"Pretty good," she responded, but Chris shook his head.

"She graduated summa cum laude from college and has a three-point-eight right now."

"Impressive."

That came from Molly, and Brady kicked her. She only smiled, not looking at him.

"Where do you want to go after you get your degree?" she asked Jessica, who turned toward their end of the table to answer. Brady lost her words in the impact of her beauty, and didn't pay any attention to the rest of the conversation. His parents were a lock. It wasn't going to matter if Chris and Jessica broke up, and if Brady moved in. They wouldn't consider him betraying his brother, they'd be glad he kept her in the family. Brought her into the family.

The fantasy was playing out in his head when he realized his father was giving a stamp of approval, tongue in cheek.

"Glad you feel that way, Dad." Chris cleared his throat significantly.

Alarmed, Brady jerked his head around, wanting to stop him. To change the conversation, throw out a joke that would make everyone laugh and forget what Chris was about to say.

But of course that wouldn't work. Because what Chris was about to say was more important than anything Brady could do. He could see that in the way Chris's hand closed around Jessica's, in the soft smile she gave him, in the sudden anticipation in the air. Molly leaned toward Brady and put a hand on his arm, a clear attempt at comfort. But there was nothing to comfort him over. Not yet.

And then the world fell apart.

"Mom. Dad. Brady. Jessica and I are getting married."

. . .

"No, idiot, pi doesn't have anything to do with it! Where's your head?" Molly stared across the dorm room at Brady, knowing full well where his head was. Inside whatever Jessica fantasy he was spinning today.

He lay in his standard sprawl across Molly's bed while she curled in the chair at the desk and quizzed him for his differential equations course. Finals were this week, and in three days they headed back to Connecticut for Christmas. For the first time ever, she wasn't looking forward to the holidays. And that damned woman was the reason why.

She sighed. She'd already been worried about Brady for a couple of weeks before Thanksgiving. He'd gone all broody and quiet, like he was considering something major. But he'd still been Brady, even stuck on Serious. Then he walked up on that train platform, and *boom*. Good-bye Broody Brady, hello Lovesick Nutcase.

She let him wallow for a minute, mesmerized by the baseball he was tossing up and catching, over and over. He probably had no idea the ball was the one signed by Nomar Garciaparra after she'd caught his home run. If she yelled at Brady, he'd assume it was because of the signature, not because it was one of her few sentimental prizes. She and Brady had gone to that game together, just the two of them, and while they were often just the two of them—like now—it wasn't often that she could pretend their relationship was more than it was.

Amusing, how she was constantly telling him to get over Jessica, when anyone else would tell Molly to get over him. But a decade of habit was hard to overcome. *He'd* only met Jessica once, a month ago.

She couldn't stand it. Pushing out of the chair, Molly leaned and caught the ball as it dropped. "Get over it," she told Brady for the umpteenth time, and he didn't ask over what, so she knew she'd been right. He was moping over Jessica again. "They have a February wedding," she reminded him.

He sighed and rolled upright. "I know. And he's totally gaga over her. I can hear it in his voice when he calls. Which he does, twice a week." He ran a hand down his face. "We used to talk once a month, if that. Now he just wants to go on and on about her."

"That's natural." She watched Brady carefully, trying to gauge how he *really* felt about his brother's fiancée. She wanted to dismiss it as a crush, but couldn't. He'd kept it up over three weeks without exposure, without seeing Jessica again. That was something different. Something more.

Dammit.

"I don't think I can do this." He looked up imploringly. "What am I going to do? I can't stand the thought of watching her marry him. Of seeing them together at every holiday. Of…" He trailed off, staring into the distance.

"Oh, honey." She stepped forward and cradled his head to her stomach. He wrapped his arms around her hips and buried his face against her. The familiar surge of love and need followed, but she stroked her hand soothingly through his shaggy, dark-brown hair and gave him what he always needed from her—comfort and friendship.

"It'll be okay," she told him, and hoped she was right.

But back in Connecticut three days later, tension skyrocketed.

Molly thought she was the only one to feel it. At least the Fitzpatrick parents were oblivious, babbling about traditions they could pass on to Christopher and Jessica and their eventual kids, about wedding preparations and when they'd get to meet Jessica's mother—her only close living relative. Chris acted natural—affectionate with Jessica, indulgent with his parents, and good-natured with Brady.

At first no one, including Jessica, seemed to notice Brady's increasing withdrawal. Molly covered for him pretty well, and without much hardship. After all, she'd preferred the Fitzpatricks to her own family for her entire life. If she participated boisterously in the family cookie baking, sang vivaciously while they decorated the tree, it all fit with past behavior.

And then Molly overheard Jessica and Brady having a private conversation in the back hall. Chris and his father had run to the store for more wrapping paper, and Donna was down in the basement doing laundry. Molly carried empty popcorn bowls into the kitchen and heard Brady and Jessica murmuring at the base of the back stairs, right outside the room. She didn't think anything of it at first, but as she was about to pass the doorway, the murmuring turned into sighs and the unmistakable sound of a kiss.

Molly froze, stunned. And then it was too late. She should have kept walking, making her presence known before they'd done anything. If she did it now, they would know she'd heard.

Cracks crazed the surface of her heart. She'd always known Brady didn't love her that way—that pain was different, a softer, more constant suffering. But this sharper, more acute pain wasn't for her. It was for Brady, who was making himself vulnerable to a woman who wasn't going to decide in his favor. For Chris, who'd be devastated if he found out about this. For Rick and Donna, who just wanted both their sons to be happy.

"I should say I'm sorry, but I'm not," she heard Brady say.

Molly closed her eyes and leaned against the rough pine paneling of the kitchen wall, resigned to having to listen to this.

"It's okay." Jessica's voice was high and breathless. Molly wanted to stab her through the heart. "I've known, well, since the day we met. That you—"

"—have feelings—"

"—for me. Yes. But, Brady…"

"I can't help myself, Jess. I love you. If there was any chance, any way, you could love me back, I had to do this now."

Now? Why now? Molly held her breath through Jessica's hesitation, then as she repeated Molly's silent question aloud.

"It doesn't matter." Brady sounded impatient, almost desperate. "I have to figure some things out before the end of the year. This is one of them. Jess," he pleaded. "I need to know how you feel."

"Your brother," she protested.

"I love him, too. And I never want to hurt him." Brady's voice cracked just enough that Molly knew he meant it. "Please, Jessica. Be honest with me."

For long moments, there was only breathing in the little space of the back hall. Molly's hands tightened on the bowls she held. If Jessica said yes, if she said she cared about Brady… God, what a mess this would be. And the tiny spark of hope that Molly never fed, never admitted even existed, would be crushed forever.

"I can't," Jessica wheezed, and the tightness around Molly's heart lessened. "I love Christopher. I'd never betray him. And even though there's…something…between us, it's not worth throwing away what I have with your brother. We just—"

"I get it." Sorrow drenched Brady's words, and Molly ached to go to him, to comfort him, to ease his pain any way she could, regardless of what it would do to her own heart. She pushed away from the wall, but he wasn't done speaking.

"I can't do this, then."

"What?" Jess sounded confused. "Do you mean the kiss? I don't want—"

"No, not that." Disgust didn't quite overcome the sorrow, and Molly was glad to hear it. Glad to know her best friend wouldn't commit adultery with his brother's wife, or even allude to the possibility.

"What, then?"

"Anything. I can't do these family get-togethers. I can't see you, spend limitless hours watching you with my brother. Not when I think he's the wrong man." His voice held conviction that injected fear into Molly's battered heart. Whatever had been bothering him since fall semester, whatever he had to figure out…Jessica's answer had resolved it for him.

"He's not wrong," Jessica said, her soft tone no less convicted.

Molly imagined Brady nodding.

"Okay. But I still can't do it."

"But…the wedding?"

"I'm the best man, of course I'll be at the wedding. After that, though, forget it."

An uncertain pause, then, "If you have to."

"I do."

"Okay, then." After a moment, Molly heard light footsteps going upstairs, and Brady entered the kitchen.

He didn't notice Molly standing there, and she had to hold back a sob. That kind of utter defeat should never be seen on the face of someone so young. He walked across the kitchen to the island, where he braced his hands wide and hung his head. A tear fell to the butcher block, then another, staining the soft wood dark. After a couple of minutes, he raised his head and spotted her in the reflection of a copper pot. He turned, and there was nothing in his eyes. Not pain, or sorrow, or even determination. Not the Brady she knew.

Molly didn't move, afraid that this might be one of those defining moments, the kind that didn't occur in every life, when someone could look back and say, "That's when everything changed." Then, with perfect clarity, she recognized that it was. That none of them, even her, would ever have the same relationship with Brady again.

And she was right.

Chapter Two

"Yes, we do piano tuning. What's the model?" Molly grabbed an order pad and started taking notes, keeping an eye on the teens goofing off with the guitars. She knew them, trusted them for the most part, but that was because they knew her, too, and knew she was a hard-ass. "Earliest we can get to you would be next Wednesday. That okay?" The front door chimed as her cell phone began blasting "Smoke on the Water." She ignored the phone and watched the older man wander to the sheet music section while she finished scheduling the piano tuning. She'd just hung up when the kids approached to pay for the picks and strings they wanted, and then silence rode behind them as they went out into the chilly October night.

Her cell rang again. The old man looked up, his eyes sharp, glancing down to where the driving beat of her favorite Deep Purple song demanded her attention. Instead of answering, though, she thumbed the unit to silence it and waited for the man to approach.

He carried a few sheets of music to the counter. *Andante* and *March in D Major* by Bach, for cello. "No *Ode to Joy*?" she asked, and the man shook his head.

"Too pedestrian," he commented, his voice smooth and cultured. CIA, she guessed, though she never knew if she was right. She took the music from him and went into the back room, a little alarmed to hear her cell phone go off again. Someone really wanted to reach her. Why didn't they call the store? Urgency gripped her insides, and she quickly found the box the man was here for, under a stack of plastic bags. She slid the folded papers he'd handed her with the sheet music into the file cabinet and shoved it closed, locking it before heading back out front. The man stood right where she'd left him, patiently holding his hat and apparently reading the calendar hanging next to the curtained doorway to the back room.

"Winterbourne Garden."

"What?"

The man nodded at the calendar. She twisted to look, saw the flowering vines or whatever on the picture, and nodded impatiently. "Yeah, I guess." She handed him the box a little too abruptly and reached for her phone.

"Ah." The man tipped her a nod of thanks, raising the box a little, and left, thank God. She snatched up her phone. All the missed calls were from Jessica.

Brady.

Panic made her fingers stiff as she hit the combination to return the call, not bothering to check the voice mails Jess had left. The phone rang four times before she answered, and every ring was a new horror, a new shaft of fear into Molly's heart.

Ri-iing.

Killed in action.

Ri-iing.

Terrorist prisoner.

Ri-iing.

Explosion, too few parts to identify.

Ri-iing.

"Hello? Molly? Hello?"

"Yes! Jessica. It's me. What's wrong? Calm down." Jessica was hysterical, sobbing so hard Molly couldn't understand a word she was saying. Her fears coalesced into a giant fist compressing her lungs until she could barely breathe. "Who is it, Jessica? Who's…hurt?"

Rick, Donna, Chris, Brady. *Please don't let it be Brady, God that's selfish but ple-ease don't let it be Brady!*

But Jessica couldn't calm herself, and Molly had to wait her out, pacing behind the counter, Fitzpatrick names pounding in her head with each step, Fitzpatrick faces flashing behind her eyes as Jessica cried and coughed. Rick was sixty, with no history of heart disease, but that didn't mean a heart attack couldn't happen. Donna could have had a stroke, or fallen, or had a complication from her diabetes. They could have been in a car accident. Christopher…and Brady…

No. She couldn't think it.

"Jessica," she said softly but firmly, her own desperation well hidden. "You have to calm down. This isn't good for you."

"I know. I'm sorry." The cries became more muffled, compressed. Choked back, rather than controlled.

"Tell me, hon. What is it? What happened?"

A long, deep breath, then, her voice quavering but finally clear, "Christopher. He's…oh, Molly, he's dead."

Even preparing herself for the worst couldn't keep shock from cascading over her. Heat swept from her head to her feet, and guilty relief—*not Brady*—made her sway, her vision dimming around the edges, lights flashing. She leaned on the counter. "Oh, Jess. Oh, no. What happened?"

"I don't know. They won't tell me. I don't understand— some guy came to the house and told me— told me he was— he'd been killed. He won't leave until someone gets here. But he won't tell me any more." She broke down into sobs again.

Shit. Molly was in Boston, Jessica in Connecticut, hours

away. "Did you call Rick and Donna?" They might already know. They often sent someone to the parents and spouse at the same time. God, they were going to be devastated. And Brady...

"Yes," Jessica said. "They're on their way over. They should be here—oh. They just pulled in." She sounded calmer already.

"Did anyone call Brady?" Molly's voice broke on his name. She closed her eyes, sucking in air to combat nausea.

"I can't reach him. His voice mail says he's out of touch for a few days, and his secretary said she didn't know where he was." Anger strengthened Jess's voice, and Molly knew she would be all right, for now. "How the hell can his secretary not know where he is?"

Because she wasn't his secretary. But Molly couldn't tell her that.

"I told her it was an emergency! She told me to leave a message. As if I could relay something like this that way." She started to cry again, but not as hysterically.

Molly had to sit down. There were no stools or chairs behind the counter, so she sank to the floor, her back to the shelves under the register, and tried not to fall apart. "I'll find him," she assured Jessica. "Are Rick and Donna there?" Jessica's mother had died of breast cancer a few years ago. An only child, she only had her in-laws now.

"Yes, the...whoever he is just let them in. He's talking to them, but I can't hear what he's saying. I have to go." She hung up abruptly.

Molly slowly closed her phone and rested her head on her knees. They shook, and so did her hands. It was the adrenaline. She had to sit here for a minute, let it dissipate. Let her body recover.

Then she had to find Brady and tell him his brother was dead. She pressed a fist to her mouth to hold back her own sobs. It was somehow vital that she hold together better than Jessica. Grief surged now, as if it had been waiting its turn, and she couldn't keep it back. Tears burst from her eyes and she let go, burying her face in her voluminous skirt, crying for the loss, for the hole it would leave in the Fitzpatrick family—for what it would do to Brady.

It was going to kill him. He'd blame himself, even though he had no clue that Chris wasn't the business consultant he'd always presented himself to be. He'd blame himself because he hadn't been there. Hadn't seen his brother for years, except for the occasional lunch or dinner when they were both "on business" in the same town. Brady refused to go to Chris and Jessica's home, refused to attend any family gatherings...had even missed his aunt's funeral three years ago. His parents went down to DC every once in a while, his mother totally baffled by his distance from the family, his father stoic about it. Molly had told them why he did it, when Brady refused to and she couldn't stand to watch his parents suffer in confusion. Of the two of them, Rick seemed to understand best, maybe because Brady had described his first reaction to Jessica as being just like Rick's to Donna. But Donna didn't know why Brady couldn't put it aside, couldn't stifle the love he felt for his brother's wife, so that he didn't lose them all. So they didn't lose him.

The worst part, for Molly, was Brady pulling away from her, too. She'd known, that day in the kitchen, that he would do it. It had been slow and painful because she fought it, and they'd had ingrained habits and routines at college. But once they graduated and he moved to DC, it had become a lot easier. She'd stayed in Massachusetts to get her master's before spending a few years traveling the world with various orchestras, rock bands, and opera companies—and hated every minute away. She'd been preparing to open the store here in Boston when SIEGE—Strategic Infiltration of Enemy Group Enterprise, a government-sanctioned, privately owned information broker—had recruited her.

They weren't close anymore, she and Brady, and she'd never stopped regretting it. Most of their communication was via e-mail. Once in a while, he took or made a phone call, and their connection was still there, tenuous but strong enough that she knew it would never be lost completely.

And knowing how much he loved his family, staying away to avoid hurting them as much as to avoid his own pain, she'd kept him updated on family news. She hadn't yet told him the latest, knowing it would devastate him. But this—this was so much worse.

The door chimed, jerking her back to awareness. She'd forgotten the store was still open. Dragging herself to her feet, wiping the remnants of her tears from her face, she almost expected a solemn, dark-suited facilitator to be standing there. But no, it was a young woman in slouchy cargos and a snug hoodie, hair pulled into bunches all over her head, dark rings of makeup around her eyes. She could be an operative or a carrier, but not a facilitator.

She turned out to be none of the above, just a music major looking for a certain CD that Molly didn't have. She held on to her patience by her fingernails while she processed the special order and ushered the woman and her boyfriend out, locking the door behind them. After rushing through her closing procedures, she stuck a sign on the door saying CLOSED FOR FAMILY EMERGENCY and did a quick bank drop on her way out of town.

Six hours, eighteen phone calls, and one about-to-explode bladder later, Molly arrived at Brady's apartment in DC. He wasn't going to be here—the phone calls had helped her pinpoint his location in South America—but she'd need things from his stash before she caught a plane. She'd taken off with a full tank of gas, a bare-bones duffel bag, and nothing else. Who knew how long it would take her to zero in on Brady? He was supposed to be out of communication for another week.

His "secretary" had offered to set up a communication bridge, but Molly didn't want him to find out alone, far away, via strangers. Despite the separation of the last decade, she was going to be there for him when he got the worst news of his life.

. . .

Brady pulled the hood of his all-weather coat higher over his head and hunched against the thunderous rain. Fuck this weather. Fuck this country. And fuck the fucker who was following him.

He'd been here a bit too long, his cover growing shaky over the last few days, but there was one piece of information that would make the previous week and a half worthwhile. Without it, the rest of the intel was file-filler and not much else. His contact had set up a meet for three hours from now. His cover only needed to hold until then. But his shadow had appeared this morning, and he—or she—was good. Too damned good. Brady had been moving around the city all day, trying to lose him. Taxis, buses, quick dashes down alleys, and always the bastard remained just a few steps behind.

Time to change tactics. Stop moving, see what the guy did.

Brady entered a tenement building SIEGE occasionally used for a safe house and ducked into the elevator. His shadow entered the foyer a second before the doors closed. Brady hit the fourth floor—high enough for the elevator to reach before the shadow did via the stairs. As soon as the door opened he hurried to an apartment across from the stairs that he knew was empty, jimmied the lock, and slipped inside, watching through the tiniest crack. Three breaths later the stairwell door opened and a small, black-clad figure glided through and paused, eyes on the barely open door Brady stood behind. It had to be a woman, someone that slender, but he couldn't see a face past the jacket hood. He narrowed his eyes. A jacket very much like the one he was wearing.

She reached for the door, her body tensing and angling sideways, presenting a smaller target. Brady wasn't going to wait for her attack. He yanked open the door and swung, his fist slapping into her palm.

A door opened down the hallway. Brady twisted his hand around the woman's wrist and yanked her into the room, spinning her to try to pin her against his body. She used the momentum to slam them against the door, bouncing off and putting distance between them. Her hands went up. No time to assess if she had a weapon. He went for a leg sweep but she leapt into the air and rode him to the floor, trying to pin his wrists with her knees. Her indrawn breath poked at his brain, but instead of analyzing it he rolled, using his superior weight to reverse the pin. She bent her leg and narrowly missed the jewels, her knee digging into his groin. He grunted and closed his eyes in reflex, and, oddly, she froze. He opened his eyes, his gaze landed on her face, and—

"Molly?"

Shocked beyond belief, he jerked back and onto his feet. He'd have reached down to help her, but she stood first.

"What the *fuck* are you doing here?" He couldn't even engage his brain enough to consider possible reasons.

"I came to find you."

Still not processing. Barely reacting. Someone could come through that door behind him and take him out right now, and he wouldn't even have the capacity to know it was happening. "Why?"

Instead of answering, Molly walked past him, opened the door to check the hallway, then reclosed and locked it with the state-of-the-art deadbolt installed by SIEGE rather than the flimsy one he'd jimmied so quickly. How did she know how to do that?

The answer to that was obvious, but made absolutely no sense. She was a *musician*, for cripes sake. Or music teacher. Or whatever. Something that created a total disconnect with her presence in this country. And the skills she'd displayed a moment ago.

"Brady, sit down."

He didn't move. "You took me down."

She sighed, and it wasn't Molly. Not the Molly he knew. There was no exasperation or affection in the sound. Only... sorrow? He refocused on her rather than on her presence, and fear, an unfamiliar emotion, shot through him. Her normally brilliant blue eyes were flat, her always milky skin so pale the shadows under her eyes looked like someone had punched her. Her mouth dragged down at the corners, deep lines etched on the sides.

Something was very wrong.

"What is it?" He stepped forward to close his hands over her shoulders, and when she seemed to droop under them, he tugged her into a hug. "Molly, you're scaring me. What's wrong? Why are you here?" His brain ground back into gear, enough so he couldn't stop to let her answer. "You've been following me all day. How the hell did you stick to me like that? Why didn't you just approach me? Why didn't you call me?" But the last one, at least, he could answer himself. "Okay, right. I'm not in contact. They'd have needed to set up a bridge. But that doesn't explain...anything." He let her go. "I'll shut up now. You talk."

Her movements stiff and weary, the opposite of her grace and speed when she'd first hit the room, she eased down onto the end of the bed, one of only two pieces of furniture in the one-room apartment. "I've been trying to catch up to you all day. I didn't want to take you by surprise, you might have killed me."

That was true, but how would she know that? He held his tongue, waiting for answers to what he'd already asked, rather than pile on more questions.

"You could have shown yourself. I'd have recognized you instantly."

Her mouth managed to flick upward on one side. "I don't exactly blend in. I didn't want to be a target." She sighed and drooped even more. "And to be fully honest, the longer it took me to get to you, the more I wanted to put it off."

Brady frowned. "Why were you trying to get to me in the

first place?"

You know why. He stubbornly ignored the voice in the back of his head, the one telling him there was only one reason for her to be here.

"Sit down." She patted the bed next to her.

He almost refused again, but she'd become so diminished in the few minutes since their fight, he gave in. The mattress bowed and slid them together, thigh to thigh, and an energy he'd never felt before sparked for an instant before it suffocated under inappropriateness.

"Brady, I have bad news."

His throat closed. He wanted to tell her to spit it out, not try to prepare him or cushion it. But there was no way to do that, he knew that from experience. She knew it, too, goddamn her, and instead of holding it forever, as part of him wanted her to, she said it. The words he'd expected since he recognized her, the only reason she would have gone to all this effort to see him in person.

"Chris is dead."

And his world imploded.

Brady didn't remember going to his knees. He just found himself there, some tiny sharp hard thing digging into one of them—probably what brought him out of the dark ball of pain that had engulfed him. Molly remained on the bed but had wrapped herself around him, and his arms were tight around her, a pose that brought back a flicker of memory, of pain that was laughable compared to this. White agony ripped him apart, her words echoing not only in his head, but through his entire body. *Not Chris. Anybody but Chris.*

Molly was talking. Murmuring. Comfort sounds rendered meaningless by her own raw anguish. She'd lost a brother, too, and somehow, that realization was like a balm, taking away the edge, bringing him back to solid ground. He was gripping her so tightly he had to be hurting her, and when he forced his arms to loosen, they cramped. He needed—something. Anything but this static, throbbing mess.

"How?" he rasped, settling back on his heels, unable to rise or move even the short distance back to the bed.

"I don't know. They wouldn't tell me."

His head came up. "What do you mean? Why wouldn't my parents—"

She shook her head. "Not them. The facilitators."

He shook his head. That word made no sense, not coming out of Molly's mouth. The foundation of his world had disintegrated so completely that *nothing* made sense anymore. The edges of his vision closed in, and he reached for it, welcoming the darkness.

· · ·

"Brady." Molly cupped his jaw in both hands, frightened at the glaze that had just come over his expression. He couldn't do this now. No one had been in the hallway when she checked, but they could have heard the scuffle and called the police. They could *not* afford to be detained here. She had to get him pulled together enough to get out of there.

She patted his cheek, but of course it did nothing. "*Brady.*" He didn't move. She needed to shock him somehow. As if he weren't already in shock.

Kiss him, or hit him? She bit her lip. Nope, she couldn't do it. She hauled her hand back and slapped him hard across the cheek. Awareness jolted into him, but instead of reacting violently to the strike, he folded his hand around hers and just held it.

"What happened?" he asked.

Molly took a steadying breath. "Jessica called me three days ago. Someone came to her house to tell her Chris was dead, but wouldn't tell her how. Someone else went to tell your parents."

A metallic *bang* echoed outside the room, probably in the stairwell across the hall. Brady jerked to his feet and pulled

Molly up with him. "We have to get out of here."

"No shit."

"Stay behind me."

She obeyed, pulling her hood back up to shadow her face and tugging her sleeves down over her hands. They made their way out of the tenement and up the street. Once they were a few blocks away, Brady pulled her into the entryway of a boarded-up building.

"Tell me."

She didn't know where to start. She had stayed in touch with the Fitzpatricks over the last three days, making sure they were okay, that Jessica was holding on. Brady's sister-in-law had been hospitalized for monitored sedation the first night, and after that she'd managed to pull herself together enough to function. A little. His parents were desperate to have Brady home, and Molly had promised to get him there as soon as she could. But he was deep, and it had taken a day to get down here, another day to track him down, and all of today to get close enough—and strong enough—to deal with this.

There was so much to say, so much he didn't know, and she wasn't sure how to stick to the Chris-related parts. "I don't know anything. Where it happened, or how, or where he is now. Your parents are with Jessica. She's in bad shape."

"Of course she is," Brady murmured, the words thick with sympathy.

Molly hated the twinge of jealous annoyance that generated. This was not the time, for God's sake. But she'd known all along where Brady's focus would go. He'd need an outlet for his own grief, and Jessica needed him. Molly would be on the outside. Again.

It's not about me. She forced herself to continue. "No one would tell them where you were or how to get in touch with you. Your parents didn't want you to hear the news from a stranger."

He shifted and reached for her hand, his head coming up

so his hazel eyes, now a desolate gray-blue, met hers knowingly. "*You* didn't want that. I can calculate travel times, Moll. You were on your way here as soon as you heard and knew I was out of touch."

She shrugged a little, not sure what to say.

"Thank you." He took a deep breath and wrapped his arms around her. She closed her eyes and clung to him, feeling his body shudder.

After a few seconds he pulled away. "I know there's a lot more to this. You have a lot of questions to answer. But we need to get home."

"Yes. They need you."

"Us. They need us."

She didn't dispute his assertion, but she wasn't part of the family anymore. She was a friend. One who could help them, but only on the fringes. When they got back she'd be shuffling condolence casseroles, making funeral arrangements, ensuring everyone ate and slept and took their medications. She didn't mind that. She *wanted* to do those things, but couldn't help feeling it was inadequate, that they needed, and that she could do, so much more. But that was probably just because of the lack of answers.

"Let's go." He took her arm, started out of the alcove, then stopped again. "Wait. Dammit. I have a meet. I should keep it."

She frowned. "Your parents need you home."

His jaw flexed. "I know. But this is important, and a lot of effort will have been wasted if I don't make this last meet. It won't take long."

She wasn't going to be able to convince him otherwise. "When?"

He glanced at his watch, swiping away the rain that beaded on its face. "An hour."

"Okay. That won't significantly hold us up. I can go gather your stuff and meet you. Airport?"

He thought a second, then shook his head. "No. Here." He

hunched over a small pad he pulled from his jacket's inside pocket, writing down information with a tiny pen. "The first address is my hotel and room number. Everything's in the closet." He hesitated like he was going to tell her something else, but continued, "The second address is where to meet me. I'll have a car there. We'll drive to the next city. It's about two hours away, but we can get more direct flights from there. It'll be faster overall."

"Okay." She took the paper and shoved it into her pocket, though she'd memorized the addresses as he wrote them. "Be careful."

"I will. You, too. This country—"

"I know." She hugged him, then even harder, betraying her worry over his meet. "How long before you're done?"

"The meet itself should be quick. So give me an hour and a half."

"And if you don't show up, take off without you?" It was a lame, half-hearted joke, and he didn't smile...or answer.

Walking away from him felt like ripping out part of her heart. But she focused on her tasks.

His hotel was small but high-end, the concierge eyeing her suspiciously when she entered the front door. She waved the key card Brady had given her, and he nodded, looking appeased. In a place like this, she hated being cornered in an elevator, so she took the stairs up one flight to Brady's floor. His room was right next to the stairwell. Of course. She slipped into the room without anyone seeing her, the entire hotel quiet.

"What a slob!" she muttered. Well, not really, but saying it made her feel better for some reason. She went to the closet first and found a leather duffel and a few clothes hanging from the bar. It took seconds to pack them, along with the pants draped across the unmade bed, the underwear under the desk, and the extra shoes in the corner. Another minute and a half for the toiletries and ditty bag, two minutes to scan and search for any obvious items scattered around the small room.

She had tons of time left. Brady would call to check out of the hotel, so she set the key card on the desk and slung the bag over her shoulder, ready to head out.

Then halted. Nope, this wasn't right.

Of course Brady didn't want to tell her what else needed to be done, but she couldn't leave it *un*done. She dropped the bag and knelt next to the bed, shoving her arms deep between the mattresses. Nothing. She went all the way around the bed without finding what she was looking for. Dammit, her arms were too short. She stood and heaved the mattress up. There it was, in the middle — a small gun case. She couldn't hold up the mattress and reach it with her hand, so she stretched out a foot and slid it closer, then pulled it out and let the mattress fall. The weight of the case told her the weapon was inside. For a second she was furious with him, going to a meet unarmed, but schooled her emotions. He knew what he was doing, far better than she.

She sat at the desk and used the secure satellite phone she'd taken from Brady's DC apartment to make a few calls. Half an hour later, she was at an outdoor café, the case in a tote at her feet, waiting for her contact. He approached, right on time, and the hand-off went smoothly, the only hiccup the troubled grief she saw in his eyes. As her contact passed, hooking the tote she lifted by the straps with her foot, there was a flash when she imagined them hugging, offering condolences to each other. Then he was gone.

But word had spread, and he clearly knew why she was here, turning in the weapon he'd secured for Brady when he entered the country. The grief she knew had been mirrored in her own eyes would be confirmation, and word would spread further still. There was danger in this work, but nevertheless, loss of a SIEGE agent was rare and sent ripples through the whole community, even though most members of the organization wouldn't know which of their own had gone down, nor that Chris had even been one.

It was almost time to meet Brady. Molly finished her coffee, glad the rain had stopped, and stood to orient herself. The meeting location was north, about half a mile, and she decided to walk. She didn't want to arrive too early and linger, calling attention to herself in a city where everything moved, albeit at a different pace than she was used to.

Hefting Brady's duffel and her own smaller bag over her shoulder again, she headed down the street, matching her stride to those around her, weaving through the crowd with purpose but not intent. The sidewalks thinned as she passed an invisible line from "safe" city central to a more hard-knock area. For a moment she worried she'd gone the wrong way. But no, there was a street sign, and she was in the right place. Just a few more buildings, and —

Brady exited an alley about fifty feet in front of her. Glad he was safe, Molly smiled, but instincts she hadn't known she possessed broke her into a run as she registered a movement across the street — a figure with a gun in an upper window. She didn't shout, but Brady took off toward her, as if her running was a signal. A report echoed off the buildings around them. Chips flew from the brick over their heads as they collided, each struggling to push the other to the ground and neither doing more than ducking enough to keep their heads from being blown off.

"Get down, dammit!"

Molly realized she was being an idiot, letting her need to protect her friend override her common sense. He was the one with field experience. She dropped to the ground, huddling as small as she could and covering her head with her arms. *Bang! Bang!* More chips went flying, then Brady was hauling her up and dragging his bag off her shoulder. They sprinted down the street, Brady cursing, Molly panting. Her heart raced with fear or exhilaration or a combination of the two, she didn't know.

They ducked around the corner and Brady skidded to a stop next to an old Jeep. "Get in!"

She jerked open the door, flung herself and her bag inside, and yanked the door closed as Brady peeled out. The street was too narrow to turn around. He floored it across the intersection of the street they'd been on. Molly looked, but everything flashed by too quickly for her to spot the shooter.

"I think we're clear," she said a few blocks later when there was no sign of anyone following them. The adrenaline flash faded, dragging heaviness in its wake, heaviness that dampened any relief or fear she could be feeling.

"Yeah. Seatbelt."

She glanced over. He had his on already. How he'd done that, driving like a maniac and watching for pursuit all at the same time— Okay, she was officially impressed. Her own training had been sufficient to get her down here and find him, to do what she needed to do, but knowing the field agents had so many more skills was totally different from seeing one in action.

She heaved the bags into the back and settled into her own seat, strapping in and bracing herself. For five minutes the darkness she'd been immersed in had been chased away. But now it was back, and she had to face it again. Along with all the questions Brady was definitely about to ask her.

"Did you get what you needed from the meet?" she asked.

"Yeah." Brady's grip tightened on the steering wheel. "It seems pretty unimportant now, but in the big picture, it's vital. Thanks for helping out. You got all my stuff?"

"Yes." She took a deep breath. Might as well dive right in. "I turned in the pistol, too."

"What?" His head whipped around, but they were out of the city now, the road rough and twisty, so he turned back immediately. "You did what?"

"I found your weapon and contacted the supplier to pick it up."

"How do you— Why— Okay, I'm not that stupid." His jaw tightened as he ground his teeth. "You're SIEGE."

"Yes."

"Unbelievable." He rubbed his forehead, elbow braced on the side of the door. "I had no idea. How did I have no idea?"

"You weren't supposed to have any idea."

"You're, what? A conduit? Yeah, you'd have to be, with the shop. Perfect cover. And that's why you've got hand-to-hand training and— Geez, how did you know who my supplier was?"

"I didn't." She twisted in her seat, pulling her legs up and leaning against the door so she could watch him. This would be fun, if only the reason she'd finally been able to tell him was less horrible. "But I knew who to call."

"I can't even believe—" His eyes narrowed and he shot her a look. "You knew I was SIEGE."

"Yes," she said again, this time a bit more warily as they approached sensitive territory.

"But I didn't know you were. How does that work?" He scowled.

"You know how it works. SIEGE keeps us all as insulated as possible. Conduits and suppliers know field agents but not each other. Agents know facilitators but not other agents." Mostly. But how much the SIEGE support people actually interacted was irrelevant. At least, right now it was.

"It can't be coincidence," Brady asserted, eyes mostly on the road. "Did they recruit you because of me?"

"I should be insulted," she said as lightly as possible, nudging him in the arm. "I'm good at what I do." When he angled a look at her, she admitted, "Fine. You're part of the reason. You and—" Her throat went dry, and she stuck to the immediate topic. "And the fact that I was opening a music store. They needed a front in Boston and liked my legitimacy."

"But you're not one of my conduits." He paused. "Are you?"

"You'd know. You'd have given me stuff, or vice versa."

He nodded and seemed appeased that her secret had been passive, not active. He looked as if he was about to ask something else, but suddenly, she couldn't avoid it anymore.

"Brady." Her stomach clenched. "We have to talk about Chris."

"No." His voice went hard.

"You know there's a reason we don't know how he died."

"I don't." Tension and warning laced the words, but Molly didn't—couldn't—heed them.

"The man at Jessica's—"

"Stop, Molly. Now."

"—was a facilitator."

"I'm not hearing this." Cold fury now, and if Molly didn't know him so well she'd be scared. Hell, she *didn't* know him that well anymore, and she *was* scared. But she had to say it anyway. He had to know.

"Christopher was an agent for SIEGE. He died on the job."

Chapter Three

Brady slammed on the brakes. The Jeep skidded on the uneven half-pavement, half-dirt road, its rear end sliding around to the left before he corrected and it came to a stop less than a foot from the ditch.

He barely noticed. He rounded on Molly, the red haze back, this time fueled by fury.

"That's not possible." He felt his lips curl back from his teeth in a snarl, the implications of what she'd just told him crowding into his brain, combining to form a ferocious buzz that drowned out whatever she was saying to him now. The roof and sides of the vehicle bent toward him, squeezing. *Have to get out. Need air.* He shoved out of the car and staggered a few feet down the road, oblivious to the rain that had become a downpour.

"Brady!"

Molly's voice was faint behind him. He halted, pressing his hands to the top of his head as if that could stop the tormenting buzz, like a swarm of hornets. He heard splashes—Molly, running through puddles.

"Brady!" she called again, then her hand caught his upper

arm in a surprisingly tight grip. No, not surprisingly. She'd fought him, and matched him, even though as a conduit she wasn't field trained. He thought about how she'd taken care of the weapon under his mattress, collected his things...hell, how she'd found him and followed him all day, when he was actively trying to lose her. And something in him calmed. Not a panacea, or temporary lid on the cauldron of emotion, but an actual diminishing of the swirl. He could think, and start to sort out how he felt and what he needed to know.

He had a long way to go to understanding, to acceptance, but thank God Molly was here. He took in the dark curls plastered to her head, her blue eyes shining through the rain sluicing down her face. His mouth quirked at the thought — the same thought he'd had hundreds of times over the past twenty-eight years, when she'd bailed him out for doing something stupid, or helped him with schoolwork he'd put off till the last minute, or even talked down some chick he'd led on just a little too long. No matter what was happening in his life, her presence had always been a comfort.

"Where have you been for the last ten years?" he said without thinking, and instantly cursed himself. He *so* did not want to dredge all that up now. "I'm sorry," he said before she got past the hurt, so clear on her face, enough to give him a smartass answer. "I never should have shut you out like I did. I don't deserve to have you here. But damn, I'm glad you are."

"Wonderful." She tilted her head back, a sardonic twist to her mouth, and let the rain fall harder on her face to make her point. "Can we please get back in the car?"

"If we have to." A stupid gesture, meaningless, but he held her door for her as she climbed in, and took the few extra seconds in the rain to round the front of the Jeep. Normally, they'd fire barbs at each other for a few minutes, but when he climbed into the driver's seat and put the vehicle back in gear, the air was far too heavy to allow banter.

"Ask me anything you want," Molly said after they'd driven

for a minute or two. "I'll tell you what I know."

Brady blew out a breath and shoved his hand through his hair, sending droplets of water flying around him. Molly didn't flinch. "I don't even know where to start."

"How about with Chris being recruited by SIEGE?" she suggested. "Remember the consulting job—"

"Yeah." He felt stupid, gullible, that he'd never figured it out. "Right out of school. How did you know?"

"They told me, when they recruited me. Used him as an example when they described what SIEGE does."

Brady remembered his own recruitment. The phone call, the interviews, his excitement at being chosen. Hell. He probably hadn't been hired on his own merits after all, but because of his brother. The interviewers told him they got his résumé off a job site, researched him, and found him to be an ideal candidate for their information brokerage. All lies? Why not? That's what espionage was all about, wasn't it? As unfair as it was, as much as he hated himself for feeling it even for a second, he hated Chris for taking this from him, too. Just as he'd taken so much already.

Stupid, Fitz. It didn't matter how Brady got the job. He was a damned good operator. He'd been awarded two commendations for his role in taking down a couple of terrorist cells and derailing a rising dictator's campaign for power. And the things he'd lost, he'd lost by himself. Chris hadn't done anything to be blamed for.

Brady realized Molly was watching him, waiting patiently for him to get out of his head again. "Sorry."

"It's okay. Anyway, they told me about both of you. Not details, just that you were agents, and that because I knew people in the field, I'd have incentive to do a good job as a conduit."

Brady snorted. "Is that why you agreed? Because they sold you some bill of goods that you'd be helping me and Chris?" But the idea warmed him, until she shook her head.

"No. I agreed because I was dissatisfied." She stopped talking abruptly, and when he looked at her, she was bouncing her knee, her arms folded across her chest. Classic signs that she was holding something back, or about to.

"Dissatisfied with what? Music?"

"No. Well, kind of. Not the music itself, the traveling."

She'd alluded to that several years ago, when she told him she was opening a store because she wanted to stay home. Their conversation had been cursory, though, not the in-depth discussion it would have been a few years earlier. His fault. And suddenly, he regretted the last twelve years more bitterly than he had at any moment during them. An unfamiliar burning seized his heart for a few seconds. His fault. Everything was his fault.

Don't choke now. You need to get home. People need you. Jessica needs you.

The self-lecture didn't help Brady pull himself together, but somehow he managed to refocus, to squeeze out a question about how she'd incorporated SIEGE into her store. He half listened while she talked about having no staff, so she could keep the information and objects safe that were passed through her, not only between SIEGE agents, but from SIEGE to other agencies, and vice versa. She told him about the training she'd insisted on after making a case for someday becoming a target or collateral damage, and needing to be able to take care of herself as well as the items entrusted to her as go-between for the various government and private agencies who passed information through SIEGE.

Slowly, Brady reached equilibrium again, Molly's talk of training enabling him to grab on to it, to compartmentalize everything that hurt, and let the operator take over. *You've been in worse situations*, he tried to tell himself. But of course it wasn't true. More dangerous, maybe. Tenser, without a doubt. But more painful, more personal? Never.

Still, those other situations had taught him how to cope. He had to focus on the here and now, on getting home, one step at a time, one minute at a time. Put everything in a box and close it up tight, to be dealt with…later. Sometime. After he'd finished with everything required of him.

Like getting Molly home. She'd done an admirable job reaching him, but she didn't have the experience he did. It was up to him to get her home safely.

On cue, he sensed the faint, more-felt-than-heard rumble of a powerful vehicle behind them. Nothing visible in the rearview mirror, but they'd just come over a hill. The truck could be right on the other side of it, about to roar up on their tail. It could be a random traveler, or even local bandits. But instinct told him it was whoever had shot at them on the street. Someone had found out about the information he was gathering and wanted to stop him from leaving the country with it. And his mini-meltdown had allowed them to close in. *Fuck.*

"Hang on," he warned Molly. She instantly turned to face forward, putting her feet flat on the floor and wrapping her hands around her seatbelt.

He slowly pressed down on the accelerator to speed up without spinning out or getting stuck. The road was a mess, definitely not suited to a chase. At least, not unless you were the one doing the chasing. He couldn't let their pursuer catch up, or they'd almost certainly be run off the road.

The speedometer crept upward. He glanced constantly from it to the road to the rearview and side mirrors. Still nothing, but he could feel the truck getting closer. Tension mounted almost unbearably, from both him and Molly.

She craned around to check the road behind. "Did you see them?"

"No. But—"

The truck topped the ridge suddenly, a good hundred yards back now. It seemed to hang for a second, then plunged down the slope, half skidding, its engine now an audible roar under the rain hammering the Jeep's roof. Any possibility it had nothing to do with the shooter was immediately quashed as someone poked the barrel of a gun out the passenger side window.

"Get down," Brady ordered, but Molly was already slumping as low as she could without being on the floor. He slammed his foot on the accelerator as they hit a longer patch of asphalt. The vehicle jounced over a pothole, flinging her up like a rag doll, but she didn't utter a sound.

He didn't hear the shot, but caught a spark on the right side mirror out of the corner of his eye. Quickly comparing the values of zigzagging and being a more difficult target versus going straighter but faster, he stayed on track and struggled to come up with a plan.

Another bullet pinged off the back of the Jeep. "How far to the next city?" Molly asked almost conversationally before taking flight again when they splashed down off the pavement into a hole too big to be called a pot.

"Over an hour."

"And we have no weapons," she mused, grabbing the door handle in an effort to control her bouncing. Her curly black hair covered half her face, so Brady wasn't sure what she was thinking.

"Not much we could do even with weapons," he pointed out. "Unless you're also a marksman."

"Nah, never got around to that." She hauled herself back onto the seat because he had gained a little distance and the shooters were being smart, saving bullets. "Any side roads we can take? Any places to hide?"

"Good idea." There was another hill up ahead. If he could get far enough ahead, once they were out of sight he might be able to get them off the road. But only if there was another hill or a bend in the road. Otherwise, their pursuers would know what they'd done, and they'd be sitting ducks.

"Floor it," she told him, bracing herself. "Stop worrying about bouncing me."

"I'm not," he ground out, mashing the accelerator down.

"Does it feel like I've been worrying about that?" Okay, maybe he had been, unconsciously, because the vehicle surged up the hill, catching air when they came up over the top.

"Side road!" she yelled, pointing.

"Barely." But he aimed the Jeep for it, hitting the brakes and skidding again. The rain and slop would hopefully disguise their tire tracks. Molly squeaked when, for a second, the Jeep seemed as if it would tip over, but he hit the gas again and it righted, sliding into a narrow gap between trees in a patch of jungle. It was more like a path than a road, but it was also flatter, less rutted, and the overhanging trees protected it a little from the rain, so he was able to drive faster.

Leaves and branches slapped against the car, catching in the mirrors and windshield wipers. He couldn't hear anything outside their manic cocoon, and was too afraid of clipping a tree to take his eyes off the nose of the Jeep.

"See anything back there?" he asked.

• • •

Molly righted herself and peered over the seat again. She swallowed the blood that seeped out of her bitten tongue and the inside of her cheek, narrowing her eyes against the rain sliding down the flat back window. "I can't tell."

"We need to know."

Without a word she popped the latch on her seatbelt and climbed over into the cargo area. That didn't help much, so she twisted the handle inside the rear window and pushed it up enough to look under it. The pungent combination of wet bark and mold blew in her face, but the truck wasn't visible on the path. She held her breath and tried to listen, but couldn't hear past their vehicle's own crashing progress.

"Anything?" Brady called back.

"No!" A bad feeling welled up. There was a reason the truck was gone, and she was pretty sure it wasn't because they'd lost their pursuers. "Stop, Brady!" She relocked the window and scrambled back into her seat. "Find somewhere to hole up."

"Are you crazy? Where?"

"There!" The road took a sharp turn up ahead, their view blocked not only by the trees but by an outcropping of rock. She had no idea if they'd fit, but urgency built in her chest. "We have to stop. They— I don't know, took another route or something, to cut us off."

"We didn't see another turnoff," Brady said, but not argumentatively. He stopped at the rocky outcrop before the road turned, and backed quickly off the road as far as he could, coming to rest against a sapling. She relaxed. A little. Her side of the Jeep was inches from the rock. A double-trunked tree blocked Brady's door. They were totally trapped if someone stopped on the path. But a couple of branches had fallen back into place in front of them, and she didn't think anyone would notice the few torn leaves unless they were looking hard. They were as hidden as they could be.

They sat, frozen, waiting in total silence. She couldn't even hear Brady breathing. Maybe, like her, he was holding his breath. The engine still droned—Brady had his hand on the key but didn't turn it off, probably wanting to be able to pull away as quickly as possible if they were found. The rain still plunked and pattered, masking any sound from outside, and their visibility was nil. The little bit of outside air she'd let in had filled the car with damp, and their anxiety turned it to steam that had begun fogging the windows.

Minutes ticked past, each one an eternity. She released and re-held her breath three times.

And then the truck that had been behind them surged past from around the bend—in the opposite direction. Molly jumped and gasped, her heart leaping so hard she thought it would lock up. But Brady only tightened his hands on the steering wheel and watched it drive on.

"Good call," he said. "We'd have run right into them."

"Go," she urged him. "Before they realize they went too far

and missed us."

"Hang on." He watched, seemed to be counting. Then he pulled out and turned right, so tight the rock scraped Molly's door with a screech she was sure their pursuers must have heard.

But though she watched, fear building a lump in her throat until she couldn't swallow without a long, slow, burning pain, no one came up behind them.

"What now?" she asked him. "We're going the wrong way."

"I know. Can you get my GPS out of my bag? We can't go back to the main road. I have to find another way."

Retrieving the unit gave her something to do, which eased her throat, then Brady kept her busy looking up coordinates on a map from the glove compartment and navigating him through a maze of back roads through the jungle. It kept them safe, but took four hours instead of the expected two, and by the time they reached the city, they'd missed the last flight of the day and had to get a hotel room until morning.

Molly couldn't say she minded. She let Brady check them into the chain hotel, struggling not to sway where she stood. No one had better attack them here. She was too tired to fight. In fact, she couldn't seem to expand her awareness outside a two-inch perimeter. Her surroundings were a buzzing blur. Or a blurry buzz. Like a Monet painting, or sidewalk chalk. Non-HDTV.

"Come on, Puddle." Brady's hand closed around her arm, his tone amused but weary. She didn't need extra resources to hear that. She could identify Brady *and* his mood in her sleep.

Okay, she'd completely lost it. She hadn't been that unguarded about Brady, even in her own head, for years.

"Don't call me Puddle," she managed, and let him walk her to the elevator. She'd always hated that old nickname, which started the summer she'd first gotten her period and cried every other minute. "What floor are our rooms on?"

"Room."

A spark, a rush, and okay, now she was alert. "Room? Singular?" She slid out of his grasp and leaned against the elevator wall. "You only got one room?"

"Yeah, it's safer." He was watching the numbers above the door. When she didn't say anything, he glanced over. "What?"

"So there was more than one room available."

"I didn't ask. If those guys find us, I don't want you somewhere else." He frowned as the bell pinged. "What's the problem? It's a double. And we've shared a room hundreds of times."

Of course they had, even the same bed back in college, after a couple of parties in his frat house. But that was then. She hadn't even been in the same building with him for a very long time, and never under the pressure of the emotions stewing in them both. Too tired to explain, she just shook her head and stepped out of the elevator.

"Whatever," Brady muttered, aiming for a door at the end of the hall. Molly concentrated on placing one foot in front of the other without staggering, and wondered how drunk she looked to anyone watching. *Was* anyone watching? She pivoted all the way around, and nope, the hall was empty. No visible cameras.

Then she was inside the hotel room. Relief hit hard, and she stumbled the five feet to the nearest bed, falling flat on her face.

Brady hauled her back up. "Not yet, Puddle. You need a shower."

Molly groaned and opened her eyes, startled to find him standing so close. The hard wall of his chest was within leaning distance—oh-so-fucking tempting—and with a slight flick of her eyes, she could see the pulse in his throat, the rough stubble on his jaw, and his perfectly shaped mouth. She could hardly breathe, her heart pounding, her brain short-circuiting with a need she could never, ever give in to.

Especially now.

Strangely, Brady didn't back away. His chest expanded, contracted, as he breathed in time with her. His lips were parted, but she wouldn't look up higher, to see his eyes. She just waited, not allowing herself to hope, though her entire body screamed "Do it!" Didn't matter what "it" was, she'd take it.

And then he stepped back.

"You can go first. You look wasted."

She scrubbed her hands over her face. Fighting grief on every level. "I am. Thanks. Shit. My bag."

"Here." He picked it up off the floor and tossed it onto her bed. She hadn't even noticed him carrying it.

"Thanks. Sorry."

"Hey, no apologies." His voice was soft, admiring. "You were amazing today. I owe you."

"No, that's what family does." It came out without forethought, but she meant it. Unfortunately, the word "family" reminded them both why she'd done what she'd done. Brady's expression went hard, stoic, and the dark well of pain she'd managed to ignore during their adventure overflowed again. "Um…I'll be out as soon as I can."

"Take your time. I've got to call in, get instructions. Let them know…"

Molly couldn't handle the horror in his eyes now, and ducked into the bathroom to escape. She stripped off her still-damp, starting-to-reek clothes, and turned the water on in the shower to heat while she did other necessary things. The moment she stepped under the spray was the purest pleasure she'd ever felt in her entire life. She moaned as the hot water flushed away her tension and fatigue, eased every muscle, caressed and massaged, and oh, she might never leave here. The spray hit tender spots on her back and shoulders that she hadn't noticed, easing the tightness, and when she lathered up the complimentary bar of soap to clear away the layer of grime, she let out a another moan.

But that was one indulgence too much. She burst into

tears, grief and longing digging in, turning pleasure and relief into agony. Chris, whom she'd never see again. Jessica, alone and scared. And Brady, oh, Brady. She dropped the soap and pressed her palms flat against the wall to hold herself up while her body shook, the sobs drowned out by the hiss of the water. She hoped. The last thing Brady needed was to be burdened by her rampaging emotions.

She didn't know how long she cried. The water never went cold. Brady didn't knock on the door or ask if she was okay. So it probably hadn't been that long. But it drained the last of her reserves. She reluctantly turned off the shower and pushed back the curtain. The towels were thin but soft, and she rubbed one over her hair and body, not caring what she looked like. A minute to put on sleep shorts and a tank, and she went out into the main room, not sure what to expect.

Brady stood by the window, peering out through the tiny gap at the side of the curtain. She could see his eyes darting around the city, checking the street below, the windows of whatever building was across from them, the nearby rooftops. He looked alert, focused, but the fist clenched in the drapery told her he was barely holding it together. She suddenly felt guilty, as if she'd betrayed him by hiding her own grief, venting it alone. But then she was glad she had. The release had left her drained, but also neutral, which could be strength. Maybe now she could hold him up without breaking down herself.

She checked the locks on the door—training, not that she expected them to be unsecured—and stowed her things. She stood for a few seconds, watching him, wondering if he'd even noticed she was in the room.

"Brady."

He didn't move, but said evenly, "No sign they tracked us."

"Good." He still didn't move, not a single muscle, and the room almost vibrated with his tension. Molly murmured, "Fitz, come here."

The curtain bunched, and Molly's heart seized as if his fist clutched it rather than the padded polyester fabric. She circled the beds and squeezed up next to him, prying his fingers off the drapery. "It's okay," she whispered. "We're safe here. You can let go."

At first, she thought he would. His face went from stoic to tortured, crumpling like a tin can, and a sharp noise forced itself out of his throat. She leaned into him, offering herself as support, and he clutched her against his chest, burying his face in her neck. His entire body tightened, harder, harder, and Molly held her breath, waiting for the explosion. And also because his arms were banded so tightly across her back she had no room to draw in air.

The explosion didn't come. Instead his muscles slowly loosened, a deliberate progression as he held tightly to his control.

He couldn't go on like that, she knew. Mustn't. He had to give in now, while they were safe, so he didn't cave at the worst moment, later.

"Brady, love," she murmured, raising her head and cupping his face in her hands. "It's okay. Let go."

. . .

I can't.

Brady couldn't form the words. Couldn't explain to Molly that he was afraid if he released the rage and hatred and bone-deep sorrow caged within him, he would never be able to regain control. If he was uncontrolled, he couldn't protect her, or the data he was trying to get home. He stood still, his hands resting on her waist because he couldn't seem to let her go, and she stroked his hair back from his face, murmured to him, comforted him. He wanted to accept it, to sink into her and let her absorb his pain, and he knew she'd let him. But she had her own grief, her own burdens. She didn't need his, too.

Somehow, her body had curved closer, and suddenly, his awareness of her shifted. It wasn't comfort he craved anymore, and his brain clicked off just as a sharp warning flashed across it. He closed his eyes, dropped his head, and for the first time in their three-decade friendship, he kissed his best friend.

Her mouth was soft and warm, and tasted familiar and strange at the same time. She didn't hesitate, just opened to him, wrapped her arms around his neck, pressed her body— Oh, God, she was so soft and curvy and clean and smelled so sweet and she was strength and power and so many things he'd pretended for twelve years he didn't miss, didn't need. He tugged her closer still. She arched, rubbing against his sudden erection, and hunger blazed through him, blinding in its intensity. His hands roamed up and down her back, over her hips, and her surprisingly tight ass. The noises she made in the back of her throat inflamed him even more.

"God, Molly," he gasped, tilting his head back but not seeing the ceiling above him, only a red haze. "I need you. Please—"

"Yes," she said, and pulled his head down to kiss him again, her tongue stroking his, her mouth open, carnal. He slid his hands under her tank top and the feel of her skin was so soft, so hot, he stripped it up over her head, and dropped his hands immediately to her breasts. Her nipples were tight and hard—a sign of her arousal that some minuscule, rational part of his brain catalogued with relief. She wanted this, too. He wasn't pushing himself on her.

She tugged and shoved his shirt off, too, then her hands were rubbing him, all over, her fingers digging in to the muscles of his shoulders, his arms, his back, sending flares of desire every time she clutched at him. Once her nails pricked him, and he gasped, thrusting forward and nearly knocking her over. That fleck of rationality grew slightly larger, nagging at him. He latched on to Molly's neck, breathing in her clean, musky scent, her arousal now noticeable that way, too. He told the rational nag to shut the fuck up, but that only made it fight harder.

"Shit." He squeezed his eyes shut, hard, and set Molly off him an inch or so as he tried to regain a measure of control.

"What?" She was breathless, too, her fingers undoing his fly and dipping—

He grabbed her wrist and ground his teeth. "Whoa. Hold on."

"Brady, come on," she growled. "What's wrong?"

"Is this— Are you— I can't, if—" He couldn't even form a coherent sentence.

But she understood. "Yes, God, yes, fuck me, Brady."

It was exactly the right thing for her to say. He'd heard that word from her a million times, had laughed when she got her mouth washed out with soap for using it. But never had it had this effect on him. His cock pulsed and swelled and she shoved off his jeans and underwear, and then her own shorts and, Jesus, she was naked underneath. She fell backward onto the bed, pulling him on top of her, and for a split second, he almost lost himself and plunged into the hot wetness between her thighs. If he'd moved another inch, let his cock touch that slick heat, it would have been all over. But too many years of care stopped him.

"Condom," he ground out, but couldn't remember where or how to get one. Her breasts were too close, and he bent to lick her nipple, then bite when she arched and cried out. God, she tasted good. He feasted, vaguely aware that her body twisted under him, that she reached for something. There was a thud, something falling, but he didn't care. *Hell, forget condoms*. He moved down her body, kissing and nipping her smooth abdomen, her hipbone, tongue to belly button, inhaling deep, savoring, craving. Another few inches, and there it was. He spread her thighs, lifted them over his shoulders, reveling in her cries as he tongued her. Her clit throbbed, swollen, and she shuddered with every stroke. She was close. He pressed a finger into her—God, she was tight, and she tightened even more, her body tensing, bowing. He lunged upward, needing to be inside her, and let out his own cry when Molly's hand wrapped around him, squeezing. He dimly realized she'd found a condom, was rolling it onto him, the very act almost making him come.

The instant she released him he pushed inside her. She was so wet there was almost no resistance. Her body stroked him, accepted him. He thrust as deep as he could go, his whole body sighing in relief. She wrapped her arms and legs around him, and he slid one arm beneath her back to hold her close while he braced with the other arm, giving himself leverage to pull out, plunge in, and then he went insane with lust and need. He was lost in himself, lost in her, and all he could do was bury his face in her neck and thrust, over and over, until she screamed and closed around him, and he exploded into a million pieces, his yells mingling with her panting moans.

Fucking bliss.

He tried very, very hard to stay in that place, that floating mist of ecstasy, to avoid any hint of reality. Her hands stroked softly up and down his back, and just as he was about to admit to himself he couldn't hide any longer, blackness descended.

Grateful, he let it carry him away.

Chapter Four

Brady fell into unconsciousness so abruptly Molly panicked, fumbling at his neck, trying to lift him enough to find his pulse or check to see if he was breathing. She shoved at his shoulders. His head and arms remained limp, but she felt a slight gust of breath against her cheek. He was alive. She relaxed a little, finding the pulse in his neck. The beat was normal, though still slightly fast from exertion. He was just exhausted, overwhelmed. She stroked her hand through his hair. Poor guy.

That was why he'd had sex with her, of course. She had no illusions about that. But lack of self-deception didn't keep her from holding him close until his weight became too much. She shifted out from under him but stayed near, especially when he curled his arm around her waist. She closed her eyes, trying to succumb to her own exhaustion, but sleep eluded her. Too much swirled through her brain.

Mostly, it was a video of tomorrow morning's conversation. More like Brady's half of it. Because in her mind, it never changed, no matter what she said in her half. He was going to be appalled. He'd apologize over and over. Make a dozen excuses—over and over—that were meant to reassure her but would simply make her feel like shit. She desperately wanted to avoid all that, but had no idea how.

If he knew how she felt, and for how long she'd felt that way, it would be even worse. He'd think he was leading her on, and would hasten to explain that the sex had been cathartic, releasing of emotions he couldn't handle any other way. That he was oh-so-grateful to her for letting herself be used, but it would never happen again.

If she didn't handle it right, he'd send her away. He would think the distance important for both of them, especially if she protested. Brady had that sexist streak that was built into every guy. He'd believe that just because they'd had sex, she would think she was in love with him, and if they stayed away from each other, the feelings would go away.

She snorted softly. What a blow it would be to his ego if she told him the sex hadn't been good enough to inspire the illusion of love. Okay, sure, she'd had a pretty damned good orgasm, and the arousal had been real enough. But the whole time, her brain had kept up a running commentary about how this was all grief with a side helping of adrenaline, and would change nothing between them. Not the way she wished it could.

So the morning would be awkward and uncomfortable in a way their relationship had never been, not even that Christmas when she heard him kiss Jessica in the back hall. She'd already known about his feelings for his now sister-in-law, and he hadn't harbored any guilt for doing what he'd felt he had to do. He'd told Molly that at least it was all out in the open and he never had to wonder or hope.

Of course, after that, he'd distanced himself from his entire family, including her, but still.

Hell. This was going to be much more acutely painful.

Eventually he released her and rolled onto his back, and she pulled on her tank and shorts before trying again to sleep. But as she started to drift off, he jerked, muttering something, and it startled her awake. He flailed and growled in an obvious nightmare. She shifted up on the bed and tried to soothe him back into restful sleep, smoothing his hair off his forehead and putting a hand on his chest, murmuring in his ear, even singing. Nothing worked until she cradled his head against her chest. He rolled toward her, nuzzled, and *then*, of course, subsided into normal sleep again. And she spent at least the next hour trying not to think about his mouth so close to her nipple.

She managed to drift off half an hour before dawn, not really sleeping, but semi-lucid, dreaming about Brady waking her with lovemaking, this time tender and caring and about *them* rather than about…other stuff. But she knew it wasn't real, wasn't going to happen, and when her watch alarm beeped, she'd been waiting for it.

Might as well grab another shower. She needed it after… well, after the thing that didn't happen. That was how she was going to have to handle it. Cut Brady off before he got to say anything at all. He'd get the message. He was smart, and it would be what he really wanted, anyway. She swung her legs out of the bed and tried to sit up.

"O-*ohh*." Cramps rippled up her back and down her legs, even around her sides. The moan of pain reversed to an indrawn hiss. Every muscle in her body was stiff, proving that training and real fighting were *not* the same thing. Layer tension on top of that, plus the…thing that hadn't happened, and she was lucky to stand.

"Holy shit," she breathed, wincing as she rolled her shoulders and hobbled to the bathroom.

This shower was the second best she'd ever experienced. Slowly, her muscles loosened with the warm water and stretching, and after she felt halfway normal, she climbed out and got dressed while she worked at putting on a mask of normalcy and shoving every single emotion into a box. A steel box. With no opening. Just solid steel riveted right around her heart. She sealed it by running through a mental to-do list. Six times.

Then she was ready to face the other side of that bathroom door. She took a steadying breath and opened it.

Brady rose from the bed, closing his cell phone as he did. He didn't make eye contact, but started moving around the bed toward her.

"Shower's free," she announced stupidly, and hurried on in as normal a voice as she could muster—if "normal" meant "uninflected." "Did you check the flight?"

"Yeah, it's on time. We have a couple of hours before we have to be at the airport."

"Okay, good. You have time to get cleaned up. I'll—" She waved a hand vaguely around the room. Neither had left anything unpacked, and Brady had made the bed. Kind of. Pulled up the covers. Crap. She couldn't look at it. *Window*. She'd look for suspicious characters.

She started toward the window as Brady said, "Moll, about last night."

"How did you sleep?" she cut him off, still aiming for the window but unable to get by him.

"Surprisingly great, actually."

His hand came up to her upper arm, his fingers squeezing gently, and Molly fought not to close her eyes, to give into the comfort of touching him. It had been far too long since they'd been this close, in any capacity, and she was on pleasure overload. Or something.

"Good. Better get in the shower. Water's nice and hot." She slid past him and hid her face in the gap between curtain and wall. What a moron she was. *So much for normal.*

"I need to apologize for last night," he said from behind her, obviously still standing in the same place.

Crap. Crap-crap-crap-crap. She scrambled to come up with another topic to head him off. "No, you don't."

"Yes, I do. I was selfish."

No! She could *not* do this! She could *not* have this conversation with him! She blurted, "No, you weren't. Jessica was probably sedated, and I let your parents know we'd call when we got back in the country."

Dead silence. What the hell was she thinking? Bringing up Jessica and his parents and therefore, indirectly, his brother would definitely head off a discussion of sex. But now they were in even more painful territory.

"I just called them, actually." His voice was subdued. "I talked to Jess. She's having a hard time, but said she's managing without the tranquilizers now."

"Good," Molly managed to choke out.

"Mom said to tell you how grateful they are that you came to get me. She's a little confused on why that was necessary, but we'll come up with something."

"*Mm-hmm.*" The soft rasp of his voice, the sorrow behind it, was killing her. *Strap in*, she told herself. *This is just the beginning.*

"So, that wasn't what I meant when I said I was selfish. But I get the picture." She heard the soft swish of fabric. His hand closed over her shoulder for a second, then he moved away. When the bathroom door clicked shut, she let out her breath in a *whoosh* and leaned against the wall. That had been a narrower escape than yesterday's car chase. She focused on the scene outside, one she hadn't paid any attention to, and started cataloging details. Then realized none of them were relevant. She hadn't seen their pursuers yesterday, could barely remember the vehicle they'd been driving, and there were several on the street below that looked like it. So this was pointless. She released the curtain and backed up to double-check the room for anything they'd dropped. Oh, lovely, there was the condom wrapper on the floor between beds, Brady's jeans in a heap next to it. She vaguely remembered hearing a *thump* last night and bent to check. Brady's wallet had fallen out of his pocket; it lay under the jeans. She picked up both and crumpled the condom wrapper into her fist as he emerged from the bathroom in a billow of steam.

She straightened, turned, and froze, every nerve in her body jumping to attention and shouting "*Hell*-o!" Brady stood wrapped in a skimpy towel, water beaded on his sculpted chest and shoulders, dripping off his shaggy hair. She hadn't seen him like this in…ever, actually. Even last night, she hadn't had much chance to look at his body. Part of her told her not to now, that the barrier she was trying to erect wouldn't hold if she did, but the rest of her said the hell with it, she might not ever get this chance again. So she stood and looked her fill. When her upward-stroking gaze reached his face, his mouth was quirked up on one side. She snorted. Male pride.

"What are you doing?" he asked.

"Picking up. These were on the floor." She held out the jeans and wallet, squeezing her fist around the wrapper.

"That's what I needed, thanks. I'll be out in a minute." He took the jeans and went back into the bathroom.

She sighed. The next few days were going to be hell in more ways than one.

. . .

When Molly and Brady finally arrived at the Fitzpatricks' Connecticut home, she was a wreck. Brady had slept more on the plane, which was good for him—he might not get much once they got home. But she couldn't turn off her Brady radar—the sense that told her every move he made, that spiked her tension whenever he woke up and she'd automatically braced herself for him to talk about the previous night again. He hadn't, but she hadn't been able to set it aside, anyway. When she'd managed to close her eyes, her brain insisted on reminding her of all the things she'd never feel again, and prodding the embers of her dying—should be dead—hope. Now that they'd had sex, the faint spark she'd been unable to crush, even after all these years, was growing. So she'd spent much of the flight lecturing herself not to open the steel box, not to let the spark get any bigger. All wasted effort, for two reasons. One, herself didn't listen. And two…

As soon as Brady saw Jessica, Molly knew it was all over.

"Darling, darling girl, thank you!" Donna engulfed Molly in a humongous hug, even before touching her son. "I don't know what we'd have done."

"Don't be silly," Molly said into the shoulder covering her face. "They'd have gotten a message to him eventually." She didn't say who "they" were, knowing Donna would assume it was the company they thought employed Brady.

"But you got him home so much faster." Donna released her, dabbing a tissue at her eyes, a gesture that had clearly become habitual. She looked haggard, her eyes red and puffy, the lines around them and her mouth deeper, dragging the skin of her face lower.

"How are you doing?" Molly asked her, working very hard not to watch Brady on the other side of the foyer embracing his sister-in-law, who was sobbing softly. Even out of the corner of Molly's eye, she could see reverence in his every touch. His feelings for Jessica hadn't changed. In fact, they'd be even worse now.

So much for that spark of hope.

"Oh, you know." Donna led everyone into the living room and settled on the couch, reaching a hand out to Brady, who managed to release Jessica enough to grip it. He settled the two of them next to his mother, and his father sank heavily into the recliner. Molly hesitated, but as they asked Brady about the trip, she decided to escape to the kitchen to get drinks and snacks. She knew neither Donna nor Jessica would have been eating, and maybe they'd be comforted enough by Brady's presence to do so now.

Plus, it gave her an excuse to escape.

She was trying to keep her mind blank while she found a tray and started gathering items. Brady walked in as she pulled a pile of condiments and sandwich fixings from the fridge.

"Jessica says she might be able to manage some soup." He

stood next to the island in the center of the large kitchen. "She can't remember when she last ate."

Molly choked back an irritated reply. Jessica had just lost her husband and had no clue about the subtext of that loss. Brady would be solicitous even if he wasn't in love with her. "Check the pantry wall, there should be some cans in there."

He hesitated, and Molly frowned. Didn't he remember where the pantry was? Hell, maybe not. He hadn't been here in years. But then he gave a little start, as if he'd been lost in his head, and turned to the wall behind him, unerringly opening the door for the canned goods.

Guilt niggled at Molly. She had to tell Brady, before someone else mentioned it. She should have told him long before now, but it had seemed not so much like pouring salt in his wounds—all of them, old and new—but rubbing it in hard with steel wool. But she'd held off as long as she could, and no time was going to be better than now.

"She's a wreck," he said, coming back to the counter and digging in a drawer for a can opener. "And she's confused. She's asking about the guy who came to tell her, and why he was so vague about the details."

"I figured she would eventually. What did they tell her?" Molly had never bothered asking. She was the only one who knew he'd died on the job and that they wouldn't get the truth, so the lie didn't matter. But now she was curious.

"Car accident. You'd think that would be enough, but Jessica's not dumb." He poured the soup into a pan and set it on the burner, lighting the gas and adjusting the flame.

Molly kept her opinions to herself. Okay, so Jessica *wasn't* dumb. And Molly considered her a friend. But she didn't like the way Jess had handled Brady's declaration, way back when, and she was afraid of how she would use him now.

Which brought her back to the news she'd kept to herself. Crap. She hated this.

"Brady." She took a deep breath and said his name again

when he just stared blankly into the soup.

"What?" He blinked up at her.

"I have to tell you something."

Fear flickered across his face before he visibly steeled himself. "What?"

"It's Jessica. I don't think your parents know yet—or they didn't before they got the news about Chris." More fear, and this time not so easily dealt with, so Molly hurried to explain. "She's pregnant. About two months along."

"She's—" Brady stared at her, mouth open in shock, before he turned away and ran his hand down his face. "Oh, man. No wonder... Did Chris know?"

"Yes, but no one else."

"Except you." There was just a hint of accusation in his tone, but he didn't look at her.

She would not feel guilty. It had not been her decision to keep it a secret, or even to know the secret. "Jessica wanted someone with her at the doctor, and Chris was out of town."

"Of course he was." There was more accusation there, but he immediately seemed to regret it. "How far along is she?"

"Two months," Molly repeated gently. "It's a delicate time. I was worried when she first got the news about— Well, she was so hysterical. But being with your parents helps. They probably know now. She would have had to tell them at the hospital."

"Yeah. Mom said something I didn't get, but now—" He moved quickly to pull the pan off the stove as it bubbled up to the top. "I can't even imagine how hard this is for her."

Molly listened silently, assembling sandwiches, while Brady went on about poor Jessica. She was Molly's friend, a raw new widow, facing being a single mother. The weight of all that would be devastating to anyone. Even if Brady had never declared his feelings for Jessica, it would be natural for her to latch onto him right now, and for him to offer whatever she needed from him.

Being jealous of that would make Molly an evil person.

She finished the tray and hefted it to follow Brady, carrying his lone soup bowl, back into the living room.

"Heavens!" Donna jumped up and took the soup bowl from Brady. "Help her! I can't believe you let her carry that heavy thing all by herself."

Brady quickly turned and grabbed the tray. "Sorry. I was a little distracted."

The wry twist of his mouth, the sincerity in his eyes, soothed Molly's disgruntlement. A bit. "It's fine. I would have said something if I couldn't handle it." And maybe she wanted to wallow in her martyrdom, just a little. She stifled a sigh. She really needed to get over herself. How was now any different from twelve years ago, when she'd been in love with her best friend, plotted 24/7 how to get him to notice her, only to have him fall instantly in love with a woman he couldn't have?

You had sex, idiot. That's what's different.

Oh, yeah.

She handed out sandwiches, accepting Rick's thanks and Donna's praise for remembering what everyone liked. She gave Jessica a spoon, since Brady naturally hadn't thought of one, and rolled her eyes at him when he thanked her, all sheepishly charming but hovering over Jessica like a daddy emperor penguin.

"Aren't you eating, dear?" Donna asked Molly, concerned. "You need food more than any of us."

"Of course I am." She hadn't even considered eating, but she supposed it set a bad example not to. Plus, all she'd had since leaving South America was airplane snacks. She reached for the last ham and cheddar, her hand colliding with Brady's. She slapped it automatically.

"You already had one!" she chided. "Take the turkey."

"Yes, ma'am."

Everyone chuckled at the veneer of "old times," and fell silent for a moment while they ate. Then Donna cleared her throat, and Molly knew it was time for a more serious discussion.

• • •

Brady didn't really listen while his mother talked about funeral arrangements and making a list of things that needed to be taken care of, such as insurance. SIEGE would be handling most of that stuff, though she didn't know it. They had a very efficient office staff, which was good for Jessica.

Not that she'd see it that way, he thought grimly. She looked so frail. She couldn't have lost so much weight in the last few days, but he didn't want to touch her for fear of breaking her. She'd balanced her soup bowl on her lap, but her hand trembled as she tried to bring the spoon to her mouth. Broth splashed back into the bowl, a few drops landing on her pants.

In a flash, he was on his knees, taking the bowl gently from her. "Let me help," he murmured.

"Thank you." Her voice was barely above a whisper, and only half as substantial. "It's good." She managed a tremulous smile, and Brady's heart cracked.

"Are you still on…medication?" He hoped they'd given her something safe for the baby. Normally she'd have made sure, but from what Molly had said, Jess might have been too hysterical to mention it. He'd glanced at her belly only once, and she wasn't showing much, despite her thinness.

Jessica swallowed. "No, it was just that one night, and they had me in the hospital so they could keep an eye on the baby." She acted like she thought Brady already knew, had known before now, so she must have told his parents. Or maybe she didn't have the capacity to think that far into the topic. Or maybe Molly had said she would tell him, but had held off without Jessica knowing.

He scowled internally and fed Jess another spoonful. None of that mattered. Just the here and now.

"Did they say the baby's okay?"

"Yes, she's fine."

"A girl." His cracked heart now felt like slivers had

been shoved into it. *Selfish bastard*. "Chris always wanted a daughter." Okay, that was a stupid thing to say. How the hell did he know what Chris wanted? So he'd mentioned it in those demented, rambling, lovesick phone calls he'd made to Brady back in college—that didn't mean he'd still felt that way. But how could he not? As frail as she was, Jessica was still beautiful, now in an almost ethereal way.

A snort that sounded suspiciously like Molly's echoed in the back of his head. But he couldn't help it. He'd always thought about Jessica in ridiculous terms.

"It's too soon to tell, really," Jessica admitted. Talking about the baby seemed to be giving her strength. "I just feel like she's a girl."

"Then she probably is," Brady murmured absentmindedly. He was going to be an uncle. Not the same set of responsibilities being a father would bring, but certainly more now that Chris was gone. Wow. An image flashed into his head, a tiny little girl with wispy blond hair and her father's dark blue eyes. Too many emotions pierced him at once, and he pushed them aside, concentrated on the present, the woman beside him.

After he'd fed Jessica about half the bowl, she sat back against the sofa cushions, her hand over her abdomen. "That's all I can do for now. Thank you, Brady." She reached out to pat his arm. He twisted to put the bowl on the coffee table and regained his seat on the sofa.

"I still feel like I'm underwater." Jessica leaned against his shoulder. "Most of the time, I can't process that he's gone, that I'll never see him again. Then suddenly the pain paralyzes me and I don't know how I'm going to make it." She broke into tears and covered her face. "I'm sorry."

"No, no, don't be sorry." He wrapped his arm around and pulled her to his chest, where she sobbed into his T-shirt. Her hair was soft and fine under his hand.

After a moment he realized his parents and Molly had fallen silent and were watching. His father looked weary, his mother anxiously concerned. Molly wore the implacable mask of a SIEGE agent, but Brady thought he could see pity and compassion behind it. He frowned at her. Which emotion was aimed at whom? He didn't need her pity. And he wasn't going to think about why she thought he deserved it.

After a minute, Jessica's cries faded. She was too weak to sustain them, he thought.

"Come on." He moved to rise and lift her to her feet. "You should lie down."

"I've spent most of the week in bed." But she let him support her down the hall to the back bedroom. "Your parents are so good to let me stay here. I can't face...can't be—" She let out a sob and he hugged her, letting her regain her composure before they walked the last few feet into the bedroom.

The bed was unmade, its mess testifying to her restless sleep—or wakefulness. Brady hurried to straighten and smooth the covers, fluff the pillows, and help her lie down. She curled on her side, facing the edge, one arm protective across her abdomen, the other hand gripping his.

"Don't leave. At least for a few minutes." Tears sparkled in her eyes.

"I'll stay as long as you need me." He gently pulled his hand from hers so he could drape a blanket over her.

She reached for him again and drew in a deep breath. "I keep thinking of silly things," she said, her voice high and tight. "Like how he won't make me potato pancakes on Sunday mornings anymore. The Sundays he's home. He was gone all the time, Brady." She paused to swallow. "I was lucky to get him a full week before he left on another business trip. But when I asked him to cut back the traveling, he said he couldn't. It was too important."

Brady used his own implacable mask to hide the anger burning at her words. He understood what SIEGE meant, how many people had been saved by the intelligence they gathered and distributed. He knew firsthand the holes in a guy that could be filled by that kind of career. But Chris shouldn't have had holes to fill. He had the most amazing woman in the world as his wife. A child on the way. Friends and family. What had been so compelling about his job that he'd refused his wife's wishes?

Chris might have told Jessica he couldn't cut back his travel, but that was a lie. No assignment was mandatory. SIEGE demanded a lot—secrecy, loyalty, a belief in bigger things like patriotism and the greater good. But the company operated on the belief that their people were more likely to fight for those things if they had smaller things to fight for, too. Personal stakes created greater bonds than global ones.

So what the hell had compelled Chris to spend so much time away from the woman he loved?

"Was it always that way?" he asked.

She shook her head. "He's always managed to be here for important things. But he only traveled about half the time. It's been increasing for about a year now."

"Since you decided to get pregnant?" he guessed.

She nodded again, tears streaming down her cheeks. "He said he'd be able to eliminate the travel completely by the time the baby was born, but Brady," she cried, "it's too late. If he had been here, he wouldn't have died."

Brady didn't tell her that people died at home, too, that Chris's insistence on travel hadn't killed him. It was logical, but only partly true. It hadn't been the travel, it had been the mission.

"Please, Brady, hold me." The plea broke his heart again—how many times was this woman going to do that to him?—and he toed off his shoes before climbing onto the bed behind her. It should have felt wrong, as she rolled over and snuggled into him, her sobs subsiding. It shouldn't have felt like welcoming her home, not under these circumstances. But God help him, when she shifted closer, pressing her face to his chest and her knee between his, he wrapped his arm across her back, tucked her head under his chin, and moments later, fell asleep with the woman he loved in his arms. And nothing had ever felt so right.

Chapter Five

Molly struggled through most of the to-do list she was writing for Donna before the other woman noticed that her eyes wouldn't stay open.

"Oh, sweetheart, what am I doing to you?"

Molly pried her eyelids open and frowned at Donna. "What?"

"I shouldn't be so heartless, putting you to work after you spent the last three days traveling, bringing Brady home."

Among other things. "It's okay," she said aloud, to keep herself from mentioning the fighting and the guns and the sex. "I didn't sleep last night, though. I think I'd better go find a ho—"

"If you finish that word, young lady, I will wash your mouth out with soap." Donna surged to her feet, purpose giving her movements a little strength, her cheeks a little color. "You'll stay here with us. I know we're a little crowded, but it's better to be with family right now."

Her voice broke on the last few words, and Molly didn't have the heart to decline. She let Donna lead her up to the third floor, where they'd set up a couple of twin beds under the eaves.

They were draped in red and blue quilts. A small white table between them held two cute lamps, with Brady's old stereo on the lower shelf. Bookcases flanked the doorway, stocked with old picture and chapter books. It was so clearly set up in the anticipation of grandchildren that tears filled Molly's eyes.

"You can use the main bathroom on the second floor." Donna patted her shoulder in sympathy but kept her face turned away, probably to keep herself from breaking down again, too. "You'll share that with Brady. We have our master bath, and Jessica has the little bathroom behind the kitchen. You know, Rick said this house was too big when we bought it." She smiled at Molly and tucked a curl behind her ear. "Now I'm thinking it's just right. You let me know if you need anything, all right?"

"Of course. Thanks, Donna. I'll probably sleep straight through until morning. Then I can get started on some of this." She waved the pad she still held, frowned at it, and dropped it on top of the bookshelf so she could go downstairs for her bag and to use the bathroom.

She realized, after she'd gone all the way through the quiet house and back, that Brady wasn't in the upstairs guest room. Nor was he in the living room or kitchen, where she'd stopped for a glass of water, nor outside near the cars, where she'd gone to retrieve her stuff. He'd never come out of Jessica's room after going to help her lie down.

"It's fine," she muttered, jaw muscles clenching enough to hurt. She yanked on the water spigot in the sink to scrub her hands. "She needs comfort. Brady's like Chris, that has to be comforting." Molly struggled not to let jealousy override compassion and pity. Compassion for Jessica, newly widowed and soon to be a single mom, and for Brady, who'd lost his brother and faced the downside of keeping himself from his family. The pity was for herself, for being so pathetic and mean. And she did feel all that. Really. Except the pity. She'd done nothing to be pitied for.

So she loved the wrong man. Hardly unique.

By the time she'd finished washing up and trudged back up the stairs to the attic, the jealousy had ebbed, leaving only concern. Her friends were both vulnerable, both cared for each other in multiple ways…it was natural they'd turn to each other. But would it last, whatever they were finding down there in that back bedroom? Was Brady destined to be crushed when Jessica couldn't handle the guilt, or decided she didn't love him? Would Brady take over everything for Jessica, letting her wear the title of Fragile Princess indefinitely, so she never built the strength she'd need to raise her child?

"Not my problem."

Molly sank into the surprisingly soft pillow and fell asleep immediately. The first few hours were probably restful. She didn't remember by the time she woke to early morning sunlight filling the room. But in the last however-long, right before she'd awakened, her brain had been working overtime.

The house was still quiet, so she took a brief shower, dressed, and headed out in her car before anyone else emerged. Donna's to-do list would wait. Molly had dreamed all morning about Christopher's accident, of the little bit that had been told to the family. It nagged at her. She didn't know why, because nothing in itself stood out as odd. Chris may or may not have had an accident, or been killed by someone else, or gotten caught up in something that had nothing to do with him. It could be anything, and SIEGE was going to reveal nothing to family members who had no clue about Chris's secret life.

They probably wouldn't reveal it to her, either, but she had to try. In the years she'd been a conduit she'd made some quiet, solid connections. She'd never made an error with anything that passed through her hands, had been constantly available, insisted on training beyond what they usually gave to staff at her level, and therefore gained a lot of respect. Add that she'd never demanded anything of SIEGE, only gave to the organization, and they kind of owed her.

That was one way to look at it, anyway.

She pulled into a Starbucks and, after buying coffees doctored to everyone's individual tastes and all the croissants in the case, she got back into her car and called headquarters. Wherever that was.

"Dixson." Her handler's mellow, smooth voice came across as cautious. Molly smirked. He knew why she was calling.

"Byrnes. Protocol ten."

"Standard."

Molly keyed in a code on her cell phone designed to scramble her signal so no one could intercept and hear what she and Dixson said to each other. He was doing the same on his end, and once she heard the triple-click that told her it was engaged, she relaxed.

"Checking in," she told him, though that was the least important reason for her call. "I retrieved Brady Fitzpatrick. We're in Connecticut now. I don't know when I can reopen the shop—"

"Don't worry, Byrnes, you're on bereavement leave. We're using other conduits while you're away. A local is checking on your shop periodically while you're gone. Just pass-bys," he assured her when her protectiveness spiked. He knew her well, and she had to smile.

"Thanks, Dix. That makes things easier."

"How are you holding up?"

Molly let her head drop back against the headrest and stared up the visor while she fought the tears and raw throat that welled at his sincere concern. No one had asked her that. No one. They'd assumed they knew how she felt, been aware of her fatigue, and shared their grief with her, but it was different to have someone actually *ask*.

She swallowed a few times, then croaked, "I'm doing okay. You know. It's...hard," she finished lamely. Of course it was hard. She cleared her throat. "What do you need from me?"

"Well, we hate to ask you to work…"

"Sure you do." It was easier to talk now. She sat up and checked her surroundings. "You want me to handle the exchange of the intel Brady brought back."

"Actually, that's exactly what we want you to do." He sounded proud. "Are you okay with that?"

"Of course. But I'd like to do it differently." She braced, hoping he'd go for this. "I want to bring it in myself."

To his credit, Dixson didn't hesitate. "Why?"

"Because I need to talk to someone about Christopher."

Dixson sighed. "That's not a good idea, Molly."

The need to know more, the sense that something wasn't right, grew more powerful. "Why not?"

"You're not family."

She made a deprecating noise. "I know more than the family does already. Come on, Dixson." Her heart began to pound. "Let me come in. Let me talk to someone, get more than the vague, meaningless official statement. Something. This isn't the usual casualty," she pointed out, striving to balance logic and emotion. "His brother and I both belong to SIEGE."

She bit back more argument and left it there for Dixson to roll around. He took four breaths before heaving a sigh. "All right. I'll text you the address in New York. But don't expect a lot of answers," he cautioned. "It's not up to me, what you get told."

"No problem," she said lightly, adrenaline gushing through her system and making her want to jump and yell. She curbed the urge for at least the semblance of calm. "Thanks, Dix."

"Don't   thank   me."   He   grumbled   something uncomplimentary and hung up.

Molly grinned at the phone, but it faded under the returning weight of grief and obligation. Getting a meeting guaranteed her nothing, but her expectations weren't high. She just wanted an opportunity.

Her phone beeped. She checked the text and found a time — four o'clock that afternoon, surprisingly soon — and an address in New Rochelle, New York, only about half an hour away from the Fitzpatricks. She'd thought he meant New York City, but it probably made more sense to house the headquarters of a non-government spy agency off the beaten path.

It was nearly eight, and the others were probably up and moving around by now. She started the car and headed back to the house, her body growing heavier with every mile. Oh, well. At least Donna's to-do list would keep her busy and make her feel useful.

. . .

Brady woke with a start, adrenaline drenching his system when he didn't immediately know where he was. The light in the small room was dim. Blue wallpaper with tiny white flowers, one window with dark-blue drapes pulled closed, blocking out the sunlight. Someone in bed with him…

His first thought was *Molly,* but his second called him an idiot. The woman he could barely see, her back to him, a blanket draped over her, was blond. Jessica. Of course. He stifled a yawn with his right wrist while checking his left for the time. Eight twenty-seven. Had to be morning, since there was some light filtering past the edges of the curtains. They'd slept all night, and judging by her position, Jessica hadn't moved at all. Hadn't —

He lurched upward and swung over to check her pulse and breathing. Both were normal, thank God. Unlike his. He eased off the bed and hurried out of the room before his racehorse panting woke her. His thundering heart had calmed by the time he reached the kitchen. A good thing, since Molly stood there unloading croissants from a white bag onto a plate. Five Starbucks go-cups stood lined up along the counter.

"You're awesome," he assured her, checking the marks on the cups to find his grande café Americano. "How do you remember this stuff after — " Wincing, he sipped to keep his big mouth occupied.

"After so much time?" she finished for him. "It's easy when you're so fucking predictable."

"I am not!" he defended automatically, but had to concede when she looked pointedly at the cup. "Okay, about some things I am." He shifted uncomfortably when her eyes flicked for a nanosecond toward the back bedroom.

"How's Jessica?" She plopped a croissant on a paper towel, grabbed her cup, and sat down at the table in the breakfast nook.

He snagged his own pastry and joined her, part of him acknowledging how good this felt. Natural. "She seems to have slept well. Other than that...I don't know. She's..." He shrugged, but Molly nodded.

"What's the plan for today?" He couldn't stand more sitting around and wallowing.

"Your mother gave us a list. She's a little bugged about how long it's taking to get his body back here, so we have to check on that. Jessica needs to go home, go through the mail, pack a new bag. She needs to refill her prenatal vitamins, too—she's only got one left." She rattled off half a dozen other things, without even stopping to think about it.

"I can take Jess over to the house, get her prescription." He tore a piece off his croissant and put it in his mouth, chewing slowly, waiting. He could barely stand the weight of Molly's reaction, but when he finally dared to lift his eyes to hers, she wasn't looking at him.

"Fine. I'll make phone calls. Your parents started the funeral arrangements—Jessica hasn't been able to handle it. But I think your mother would have wanted to do it, anyway, so it works out. I'll drop the intel you brought back at a nearby conduit." She shrugged. "And we need to write an obituary."

Guilt filled him. She was taking over, doing his job. He knew she was doing it because she loved them, and she alone had the strength to pull them through, but she was *his* friend, and he hadn't been a very good one in return for a long time.

Then, to top it off…

"Moll."

She froze, narrowing her eyes at him. "What?"

"We have to talk about the other night."

"No, we don't." He'd never heard her voice so hard. She drained her cup and stood. "It didn't happen, Brady." Her bright blue eyes flashed at him, daring him to push. "I know what it was. We don't need to break it down into its parts."

He couldn't help but snicker at the word "parts." Molly shook her head and laughed. "You are such a *guy*."

"I know." He stood and reached for her, but she grabbed her paper towel, wrapped it around her cup as she moved away from him, and dropped everything in the trashcan by the back door.

"You go take care of Jess. I'll get started on these phone calls." Then she was out of the room. And he'd let her go.

It wasn't right. He needed to apologize, to explain what had happened, but what good would it do if she already knew? And she knew. She'd always known. So maybe it was better to honor her wishes and pretend it hadn't happened.

Okay, then. Moving on. He took care of his own trash and prepared a croissant for Jessica, carrying it and her coffee back to her room. And despite the reason for it, despite how difficult going to their house was going to be, he couldn't help but feel some small anticipation about spending the day with Jessica.

• • •

Molly pulled up to the gate barring the entrance to the parking lot at SIEGE HQ—or Global Information Exchange, their cover company and the name on the big sign out front—and waved her generic-looking ID badge in front of the scanner. At the beep and flash of the display, she pressed her left thumb to the print scanner. *Welcome, Agent Byrnes* flashed briefly before the gate lifted and she pulled into the normal-looking parking lot. Did every SIEGE location have her data, or was it only programmed in here today because she was expected?

The five-story office building in front of her looked totally nondescript, though she bet it had bulletproof glass and a security system so advanced it wasn't available on the open market. She parked and walked to the front doors, kind of surprised not to see anyone else around. Wouldn't some people be ending their workdays now? The parking lot was more than three quarters full. Maybe they used a typical seven-to-three, three-to-eleven, eleven-to-seven shift schedule. That would explain why there was no turnover right now. And of course they had to have support staff here around the clock.

She found herself absurdly excited as she approached the main entry and a huge black guy in an impeccable suit opened the door for her. She lifted her badge, he matched it to her face and nodded, and as she passed through into the lobby, she felt like a real spy.

Oh, sure, she'd been in SIEGE for several years. But her training facility fronted as a dojo—physical training in the main building, conduit training in a secret back room. She'd never been in any other company building. How deep underground did this structure go? *Alias* reruns flashed in her head.

She approached the reception desk, where a very young-looking man dressed as a regular security guard sat behind a bank of monitors.

"Sign in, please. Name?"

"Molly Byrnes." When she finished signing the electronic pad, he pointed to a scanner like the ones health clubs had for key-tag membership cards. She waved her ID badge in front of it and he nodded, checking something on his computer.

"Fourth floor." He tipped his chin toward the elevators. Molly swallowed her disappointment and decided that asking up or down would make her look like a dork.

Once she was on the elevator, she dropped her geek self. Time to be professional. She started thinking about what she'd say when she got upstairs. She didn't know who she was meeting with—if they'd give her a PR person tasked with appeasing her with glib-speak and sending her on her way, or someone who actually had answers, even if they didn't want to give them to her.

The elevator dinged, the doors opened, and a smiling fortyish woman with a dark ponytail that matched her suit and her eyeglass frames greeted her.

"Please come with me, Ms. Byrnes." The woman turned without waiting for a response.

Molly gave a mental shrug and followed, looking around at nothing interesting as they went down a basic, light-gray walled, gray-carpeted hallway lined with closed doors sporting numbers or vague department descriptions rather than occupants' names. The woman led her into a small conference room containing a narrow cherry conference table and gray fabric chairs on wheels. They matched the carpet but were comfortable, Molly found when she sat.

"Coffee?" the woman who had not introduced herself offered, gesturing to a cart in the back of the room.

"No, thank you."

"Okay, then." She sat and folded her hands on the table, a practiced smile on her face, the room's light angling off her glasses so Molly couldn't see her eyes clearly.

Okay, PR flack it was.

"How can we help you today, Ms. Byrnes?" the woman asked, as if she were an attorney representing a hospital that had cut out the wrong organ.

Molly dove in. "I want to know more about Christopher Fitzpatrick's death."

The woman's expression didn't flicker. "Under what aegis?"

Molly pressed her lips together to keep from gaping. Dixson had sent her to *this*? Never mind about that thank-you basket.

"Under the aegis of being a very close friend of the family, who happens to also be a SIEGE...member." She'd almost said agent, but that would have been a bad move. Ms. Flack might not have the status to know Molly's role in SIEGE, but if she did, she'd think Molly had pretensions to something grander, when she was just using the word that had flashed on the gate scanner. And if Flack *didn't* have the status to know Molly's role, then telling her she was a conduit was also foolish. Not because Flack couldn't be trusted, but because it made Molly look careless.

"I'm sorry, Ms. Byrnes, we have no further information to share on the matter of Mr. Fitzpatrick's demise. It was a regrettable situation and we understand the family's grief…"

Blah, blah, blah.

It was what she'd expected, but frustration bubbled up, anyway. "Look, lose the plastic robot stuff, okay? I'm one of you. I *know* there's more to Chris's death, I *know* you can't give me details. I just want to know *something* more than the pat lie you've given his widow."

The change in the woman was instantaneous. "I told them this wouldn't work." She pulled off her glasses and tossed them on the table, dropping back against the chair so hard it rocked and rolled, and rubbed her eyes. "I don't know why they bothered."

Finally, something real. "Can I have your name, please?" So Molly could stop mentally calling her Flack. Sooner or later it would escape her mouth.

"Aldus. Ramona Aldus."

"And you're a facilitator," Molly guessed, since a PR flack would never break the mask.

"Yes. I'm in charge of family communications during Agent Fitzpatrick's settlement." She crossed her legs, her hands laid loosely across her lap, her eyes visible without the glasses and their glare.

Molly relaxed. "Settlement?"

"Yes. You know what a SIEGE member is entitled to. It's in your contract."

Molly supposed it was, but she hadn't given much thought

to it. Not since she signed up, and not much even then, because she wasn't going to be in the field. She considered the path she wanted her questions to take. She didn't want to play games with Aldus, who now seemed ready at least to talk openly about Chris's death, if not to share much. But there was always a smooth, natural way to lead from subtopic to subtopic.

"How long will the settlement take? All the details?"

"Well, first we must concentrate on disposition of the remains. That's always the family's first concern," Aldus said.

Molly smiled a little. "Yeah, it's at the top of my to-do list. When can we have his body?"

Aldus's curved lips held a hint of sympathy. "Tomorrow. I'll give you the location for transfer before you leave. You can have the funeral home handle pickup."

Molly didn't think so, but she kept that to herself. "And is there paperwork they'll need to complete?"

"I'm afraid Mrs. Fitzpatrick—Agent Fitzpatrick's wife, not mother—will have some life insurance forms to sign in order to receive the benefits. Everything else we can handle internally."

"Will the family be able to have an open casket?" Molly knew what this answer would be, and Aldus looked appropriately mournful.

"I'm sorry, no. The damage was too extensive."

"From the car that hit him."

Aldus didn't respond, which most would take as tacit agreement, but added to the puzzle Molly was trying to piece together. Great, now she had a vague idea that she *had* a puzzle, and one piece to put into it.

"Where was Chris when he died? I mean, why is it taking so long to get his body? It was almost a week ago." Her professional demeanor cracked on the last two words, which came out wavery. She swallowed hard and kept her gaze focused on Aldus, who pretended not to notice.

"I'm sorry, we can't divulge his location, as it was mission related."

That confirmed one assumption, at least. "But he *was* out of the country. That's why it's taking so long to get his body back here."

"I'm sure the family is anxious for closure," was all the facilitator said.

Molly plugged away at her for another fifteen minutes, but couldn't get anything else from the woman. Finally, Aldus leaned over the table, her expression earnest and open. "Molly, I know in our business it's easy to see nefarious conspiracy everywhere, but trust me, there was nothing odd about Christopher's death." Her bright red fingernails clicked on the polished surface, punctuating every other word. "He was out on a job, there was an accident, and he was killed. It's awful, and I'm sorry, but that's all it is."

A knot eased at Ramona's words, floating up to swell Molly's throat, but it was the familiar burn of tears, not the conviction that something was off and that she had to find out what it was. She didn't want to croak, so merely nodded her thanks.

As Ramona escorted her to the elevator, Molly should have felt better. Nothing the woman had said or didn't say had fed Molly's sense of dissatisfaction. In fact, her sincerity had soothed it, if not banished it completely. There was nothing more Molly could do, anyway, which gave her permission to let it go.

She hesitated in the lobby, still deserted save for the baby-faced desk guard and the guy at the door. Dammit, she'd forgotten to hand over Brady's intel. She crossed to the desk and smiled at Baby-Face when he looked up expectantly but obviously poised for action. No one was going to take this guy by surprise.

Thing was, anyone here could receive the packet she carried. But she didn't want just anyone, and had to proceed carefully. After rapidly discarding a few opening phrases, she decided to pretend she knew what she was doing. "I was wondering" or "Is it possible" set up a "no" answer right off the bat. "I'd like to see Conrad Dixson if he's available," she said.

Baby-Face studied her for a few seconds, then said, "I'll check. If you could stand over there, please?" He chin-pointed to a pillar several feet away, out of hearing range if he spoke softly.

Molly nodded and stepped away, pleased with herself, but a little annoyed at Dix. She hadn't even known if he was in this building. He could be anywhere, since a handler did his or her job remotely—at least, in Molly's experience. She'd never met the man in person. But since he *was* here, why hadn't he met with her himself?

Her phone rang. She flinched and checked the guard, who ignored her. *Phew*. She hadn't thought to look for a sign about cell phones. She pulled it from her pocket and checked the display. *Hmph*. She flipped it open. "Yeah."

"What are you doing?" Dix sounded exasperated, but not angry or anything else negative.

"I have Brady's intel." She clenched her jaw, waiting for his response.

"Just give it to the desk guy, he'll send it up."

"I wanted to meet you. We never have. Is there a policy against it?"

He cleared his throat. "Not specifically, no."

"Are you busy right now?"

"I'm always busy, but I could spare a few minutes."

His tone was grudging, and it took Molly a moment to think of why. "I promise I won't mention Christopher."

"Then come on up to the eighth floor. I'll meet—"

"Me at the elevator. Thank you, Dix. I'll be right up." She disconnected and waited for a signal from Baby-Face, who had probably been on hold while Dix talked to her. He nodded, and she went back to the elevator, excitement rising with the car. Dix was a friend. A good guy. Someone who had her back, who knew pretty much everything about her, and didn't judge. How many people had one of those in their lives? She wondered what he looked like. She'd always pictured him kind of short, with a linebacker build and dark hair. But people rarely looked how they sounded.

The elevator dinged and the doors slid open. Molly smoothed her palms down her jeans and stepped out, her head swiveling. No one was in the foyer, but a man strode quickly down the corridor from her left. Tall, blond, quarterback instead of linebacker. Big hands, bright smile, and sparkling eyes. *Yum.*

Blinking at her reaction, Molly couldn't help but smile back as the man reached her, one of those big hands held out to shake, the other already reaching to brace her shoulder.

"Molly Byrnes. Awesome."

She laughed. "Conrad Dixson. Finally."

He looked a little sheepish. "Yeah, sorry. Come on down to my office." He motioned with his head, and they walked together past more ambiguously marked office doors.

"So no cubicle farms here at Global Information Exchange, huh?"

"Nope. Too much secrecy." He grinned. "This is the handler floor. About a third of the SIEGE handlers work here, and the individual offices keep us from overhearing each other, being distracted, and so on. Come on in, have a seat." He settled next to her on a comfortable sofa at one side of the small office. Its cushions were plush and oddly lumpy—not uncomfortable, but an indication that Dix often slept in his office. The office was sparse for a place he had to spend most of his time. No personal photos or mementos, only one picture on the wall—a generic print of the Eiffel Tower at sunset—and a dusty potted plant on top of the filing cabinet behind his basic-black desk. There were no chairs in front of the desk. A low, small coffee table in front of the sofa and a large bookshelf next to the hall door were the only other pieces of furniture.

Molly turned to him. "So now I can picture you here when I talk to you."

"If you want to." Dix grimaced and stretched out an arm across the back of the sofa so that his light brown suit coat fell open. He had a coffee stain below the pocket of his white dress shirt. He smiled again, and Molly was charmed.

"Before I forget." *Again*. She felt her face flush and looked down as she pulled the file envelope from her satchel. "The South America intel." She handed it to Dix, who stretched to toss it onto his desk.

"Thanks. Good to have that final."

"So." Molly settled sideways against the back of the sofa. "How come we haven't met before? More to the point," she added, feeling like directness was going to have to be her default mode if she was going to handle all the secrets she had to keep around the Fitzpatricks. "Why did you arrange for me to meet with Aldus instead of you?"

All traces of pleasure slipped from his expression. "I thought it best, considering why you were here. And I have to admit…" The sheepish look was back. "I didn't want to meet you."

Molly tried to hide how much that hurt her feelings. "Why not?" Other questions crowded behind that one, about changing handlers, and if she'd done a bad job, or if he just didn't like her. But she held them off, waiting for that first answer, hoping it was something innocuous so she could end the ache that had sprung up.

"I— It's— Damn." He shook his head when Molly chuckled. "Man, you mess me up." He gestured between them. "This is why. When I'm on the phone with you, I can hold on to my suave manliness. In person—" He winced.

She burst out laughing, hurt forgotten. "What are you talking about? Are you shy?"

"Not usually." He stopped smiling ruefully, and her laughter faded into an *uh-oh*. "But then, I don't usually have a crush on my conduits."

"Oh. Um." Talk about emotional whiplash. Heat rushed up

her body, and she knew her face had turned fuchsia.

"Yeah, see?" He ran his hand down his face, turning away from her to stare across the room. "I've had a crush on you since the first day we talked. It's completely inappropriate, but I figured as long as we didn't meet, it didn't matter. That's why I didn't want to be the one to talk to you today."

His cheek muscle twitched. Molly wondered if that was a tell, if there was more he wasn't saying, but she was too caught up in his revelation. She couldn't remember the last time a guy had shown interest in her—at least, not the gross kind. How was she supposed to handle this?

How did she *want* to handle it?

"Then why didn't you say no when I called up? Or you could have kept it to yourself when I insisted on seeing you—which I would have, and I'm pretty hard to resist when I get pushy."

Her attempt to ease the tension that suddenly filled the room only pierced it a little.

Dix glanced at her, then away and down. "I thought it better to get it out in the open. And maybe…to see…"

Her heart rate picked up and she curled her fingers into her palm, her nails scratching against her jeans, the sound betraying her nervous elation. She didn't know what to say. As always, Brady's face, laughing, filled the back of her mind.

When she didn't respond, he leaned forward to brace his elbows on his knees and clasp his hands in the air between them. But he didn't speak again, not to push her, and not to erase what he'd said. He was giving her time to process, even though it looked like the wait was killing him.

Her first reaction was to pull away. To say something carefully regretful that would preserve their working relationship and not hurt his feelings but put a definite stop to his overture.

Then something in her rebelled at her usual response to male attention. She'd never consciously "saved" herself for

Brady, but part of her belonged to him and always would, which always got in the way, eventually if not immediately.

But everything was different now, especially with regard to Jessica. So Molly had to start looking at her future differently. Like at all.

And Dixson had several items in the "pro" column. His looks, to start. She didn't know him all that well as a person, but as a handler, he was excellent. She knew him to be smart, quick thinking, serious about his work and his people, but with a great sense of humor, one that was compatible with hers.

The only real reason *not* to date him was their job connection. No way was she going to jeopardize her career over a guy. Not when she'd found where she belonged after so many years of lonely drifting.

But maybe the job didn't have to get in the way. She had no idea what the rules were.

"What happens if I say I'm glad you did?" she asked.

He looked over his shoulder, then straightened. "What do you mean?"

"I mean, what if I said I haven't had my own crush, but new possibilities have recently opened my eyes?" His expression, which had fallen on the word "crush," brightened again with the rest of her sentence. She laughed. "I can see why you're not a field agent."

He gave the rueful smile again. "Yeah, I failed the poker test. Now you know the depth of my humiliation."

It was said as if he intended it to be a joke, but she caught an undercurrent she couldn't identify. "Why would that be humiliating? You just have a different kind of skill set."

"Oh, it's not, really." He waved it off, but not believably. "Only if you're a legacy."

She cocked her head. Legacy? Did that mean his father had been a field agent? How many family ties did SIEGE mine, anyway? She opened her mouth to ask who'd recruited him and then hesitated, realizing it was the kind of question that could be grounds for reprimand or discipline. As a conduit, she wasn't allowed to ask her contacts anything so direct. SIEGE was built on the understanding that information had power, and protected itself accordingly.

"Never mind," Dix said. He flashed a hopeful grin. "So you're saying you'd be interested? In me? In going out with me, I mean? On a date? Or whatever?"

"Maybe." She shifted to support her head on her hand. "Are you allowed to do that?"

"No." He shook his head. "You'd need to be reassigned."

Her heart sank, dragging down the bubble of lightness. Having Dix as a handler was part of the reason she loved her job so much. But if things developed between them *outside* that job, she wouldn't need it quite so much.

"So, dating within the organization isn't disallowed, as long as you don't work directly together?"

"Right." His eyebrows puckered. "Actually, I'd have to check on that. I never really paid attention."

Molly's phone rang again. She checked her watch. It was after five, and Donna wanted to have dinner at five-thirty. She was probably calling to get Molly's ETA. "I'm sorry, I should get this." She stood and pulled the phone from her pocket to silence the ringtone.

"No problem." Dix rose to stand in front of her. "So…"

"So check out the rulebook and let me know what you find out." She smiled at him, making it open and inviting. "And if you need to give me a new handler, make sure it's someone as good as you."

He walked her to the door. "Giving me the impossible tasks right off the bat, huh? Setting the tone?"

"Something like that," she responded with a wink. She thumbed the phone to activate it as she strode toward the elevators. No voice mail message, not yet, but before she'd gotten halfway down the length of the hall, the ringing started over, same number. She sighed. "Hello?"

"Molly, dear, good. I was just wondering where you were. Dinner should be ready soon." Molly let Donna ramble on as she descended to the lobby again, nodded good-bye to Baby-Face and Giant Door Holder Guy, and got into her car.

"Brady and Jessica still aren't home, and there's no answer at Jessica's. I called her cell phone but it's here in the living room. And Brady's not answering his, which you know is so unusual, at least when he's home. Here. You know. So where are you?"

"I had a business thing to take care of," Molly told her, starting the engine. "I'm about half an hour away. Is there anything you need me to pick up?"

"No, no, we're all set, but did you get the paperwork from the bank? Jessica is so worried about access to bank and credit card accounts, and of course the death certificate hasn't arrived yet, and—"

"Yes, I got the paperwork. Listen, I don't want to drive while I'm on the phone. I'll be back soon. You can all go ahead and start without me." After they got through Donna's protests, Molly got her off the phone and drove out of the parking lot after having her ID badge scanned again.

She wasn't looking forward to a long drive—longer because she was smack in the middle of rush hour—thinking about possible reasons Brady and Jessica weren't answering their phones.

She'd just have to think about dating Dixson instead. And with that, the drive didn't seem so horrible after all.

Chapter Six

Jessica was driving Brady batshit nuts.

He never thought he'd say that, would never have imagined it possible. But seven hours in her sole presence wasn't the dream he'd conjured up during college and on too many dark nights during too many lonely missions.

After getting her out of bed, coaxing her to eat, and prodding her through showering and getting ready to go to her and Christopher's house, they'd driven over in silence. Her long, quiet sleep hadn't been as restful as it should have been. She still had shadows under her eyes, was slow to respond to anything he said, slow to move, slow to think. It was like she was 90 percent underwater and unaware of it. Brady vowed to be patient, but she'd immediately and repeatedly tried his resolve.

First was the prescription she asked him to refill while she went through the mail that had accumulated. He'd gotten all the way to the pharmacy before he looked at it and realized it was birth control pills. She didn't answer the phone, so he drove all the way back to get the right prescription, for prenatal vitamins.

Once he got back from that trip, he found her sitting like a zombie at the kitchen table, bills and junk and sympathy cards all jumbled together in front of her. He helped her sort everything out and went online to pay bills, because she still had access to the joint bank account despite her fear that they could cut her off at any moment.

"They don't even know Chris is dead," Brady told her unthinkingly. Jessica burst into tears, and it took half an hour to calm her down enough to resume doing what needed to be done.

"Are you hungry?" He pushed himself wearily to his feet, hands flat on the table, thinking she should have some lunch, at least for the baby's sake.

"Not really," she'd murmured, reordering the stack of cards so the smallest ones were on the top of the pile. "I guess I could handle a little something."

"How about a sandwich?" He opened the fridge and was hit in the face with a massive stench wave. "*Hawgh.*" He gagged. Pressed his fist to his mouth. Gagged again. *Shut the door, genius.* He'd slammed it and stood frozen until his gorge stopped trying to erupt like a volcano. "Maybe not a sandwich."

Jessica hadn't reacted to the smell or to Brady's reaction to it. "There are crackers and peanut butter in the cupboard," she told him, pointing listlessly.

"Sound good to you?" He'd reached to open the cupboard. Man, he was going to have to clean out that refrigerator. *Ugh.* Some of that stuff had to be older than last week. Why the hell would it smell so bad so quickly? Last month was more like it.

"Not good, but manageable. Something. Protein. Good for the baby," she murmured.

"Okay. I'll make you some, and you take it to the bedroom to eat while you pack more clothes to take to my parents' house."

Once he had her settled in the bedroom, he'd braced himself and gone back to the fridge. Stood and stared at it.

Went searching for a surgical mask, and found a bandana in the garage that he hoped Chris hadn't worn running or something. It smelled faintly of motor oil. Better than rotten—

Eggs. Hard-boiled and ancient, tucked in the back of the fridge. Also fruit, soft and moldy, so squishy he dug under the sink for rubber gloves before cleaning out *that* drawer. The last inch or so of milk in the jug had spoiled, too, and someone hadn't put the top on correctly, so that odor joined the mix.

Brady had been glad Jessica was in the bedroom and couldn't hear him cursing with every new find. He got rid of anything that had spoiled or would spoil, hauling the garbage out to the curb. Who cared if trash day wasn't until next week? Then he'd scrubbed down the glass shelves with baking soda and rinsed out the produce drawers. It had taken him hours.

It was now after five. His mother was going to have a hissy explosion if they didn't get back in time for dinner. Stretching against the kink in his back, he went to Jessica's room to see if she was done packing. He found her sitting on the side of the bed, surrounded by clothes and an empty suitcase. He stifled a sigh. How the hell hard was it to throw a couple pairs of jeans and a few shirts into a bag?

Okay, pretty damned hard, he supposed, if you were a one-week widow, pregnant, and helpless. But she wasn't even trying to help herself, and that frustrated him. He took a deep breath before circling the bed and kneeling in front of her.

"Jess, honey." He took her hands and tried not to ask what was wrong. What wasn't? "You haven't packed anything."

She blinked at him, gray-hazel eyes swimming, then swept her gaze around the room. "What time is it?" She sniffed and pulled a hand away to touch the back of it to her nose.

"Nearly five-thirty."

"Oh, your mother is going to have a fit." She stood and started tossing items into the suitcase. Brady realized she did have a system in the mess. Kind of. Pants in one pile, shirts, undergarments… He turned away, but was heartened that she hadn't been haphazardly tossing stuff around.

"I know. I can't believe she hasn't called." He pulled out his phone almost out of habit, and frowned, thumbing the power button. "Crap. Dead battery. Still, she'd call the house phone."

"No, I unplugged it." Jessica shoved a pile of extras into an open dresser drawer and shoved it closed with her hip. "I couldn't handle…while you were gone to the pharmacy, it rang three times. Two were friends, and that was hard enough, but the third one asked for Christopher. I don't even know who he was, I just hung up, but it was—" She broke down again.

Brady shoved his phone back in his jeans and wrapped his arms around her. "I know, sweetheart. I know. I'm sorry." He held her and rocked, warmth surging through him when she wrapped her arms around his waist and pressed her face to his chest. He kept assuring her it would be okay until she stopped crying.

She leaned back, her arm still around his waist, so he didn't let go of her. "Oh, Brady, I'm sorry. I'm such a mess. What you must think of me."

"I think you're struggling through a very difficult time." He brushed her hair back, his fingertips grazing her cheek and neck. She shivered and closed her eyes. Brady went still. He recognized that reaction.

"Brady," she whispered, tilting her face back, her lips parting.

He flashed back to that stupid Christmas, when he'd kissed her and told her he loved her, and she almost admitted she loved him, too, but loved his brother more. It was just a flash, though, a quick superimposition of her young, happy face over her current ravaged one. She didn't so much look older now as haggard, with the circles and no makeup and lines deepening across her forehead and around her eyes and mouth. They didn't detract from her beauty, not for him, and he zeroed in on her lush, pink mouth. A shudder went through him, a burst of need and pent-up desire, and he bent his head, his eyelids dropping—

And then that lush mouth trembled.

What the fuck are you doing?

He straightened, disappointment slapping at shock. He couldn't believe he'd almost kissed her. His brother's frigging widow. *The woman you love.* No. Right now, she was Christopher's widow. He couldn't let her be anything else.

Not yet…

• • •

"This is becoming a habit." Brady scraped his fingers through his hair and yawned as he trudged to the kitchen island, where Molly had once again supplied breakfast.

"It's easy. And necessary." She flicked her paper cup but didn't look up from where she sat in the breakfast nook, fully dressed in jeans and a hoodie over a snug white tank top, a cream-cheesed bagel and more Starbucks surrounded by papers and files spread over the small table.

Brady sliced an onion bagel and popped it in the toaster. "What are you looking at?"

She sighed. "Just paperwork."

"For the bank and stuff?" He grabbed the fridge handle and hesitated, holding his breath before opening the door, snagging the cream cheese tub, and slamming it closed.

Molly finally looked up. "What's wrong with you?"

"I've been traumatized." He told her about the refrigerator.

"It couldn't have been that bad," she dismissed, almost with irritation.

"I am not exaggerating." He yanked his bagel from the toaster and shook his burned fingers. "There was some old rice in the back, I swear it had been festering for over a month. It smelled like—" He cringed. "I don't know, like a toilet that had been festering for a month."

Molly laughed. "Oh, come on."

He held up the cream-cheese knife and evoked their

childhood oath. "I swear on the Black Knob of Gillencrest," he said. "It was that bad."

Molly's brow puckered. "After only a week?"

He shrugged. "There were a lot of leftovers. Looked like she hadn't thrown anything out in a while." He sorted through the go-cups to find his and carried it and his plate to the table. "She was adjusting to the pregnancy, maybe she didn't have the energy or something."

"Maybe." Molly shifted some papers, some of which had "Global Information Exchange" at the top.

"What are those?" He pulled a paper out and read it himself. It was a release for life insurance. The reality of Chris's death hit him in the gut, harder than it had since Molly first told him. He stared at the paper, not seeing it, not thinking, just enduring an overwhelming wave of pain. His vision closed in until all he could see was black words on white paper. Then fingers slid the paper from his grasp and covered his hand. Warmth seeped from the contact, giving him the strength to shove back the grief until he could focus on Molly's sympathetic face.

"Thanks."

She smiled and patted his hand before taking a big bite of her bagel. "So, besides the Fridge of Doom," she said around the bite, "how did it go at the house yesterday?"

Brady blew out a breath. "You wouldn't even believe it."

"Of course I would. You're the only one who thinks Princess Jessica is perfect."

"*Shh!*" he scolded. He leaned sideways to make sure she wasn't coming down the hall. "That's not nice." Molly raised an eyebrow. "Okay, fine, if I thought she was perfect, yesterday showed me she's only human. But we need to cut her slack under the circumstances."

"Sure."

Brady searched for sarcasm, but decided she'd meant it. "Anyway, she's so out of it she sent me to the drugstore to refill her birth control prescription."

Molly laughed, then frowned. "She hasn't still been taking them, has she?"

"How the hell should I know?" He chewed and swallowed. "I figured she gave me the wrong package. She wanted her prenatal vitamins."

"Yeah, Donna said she was out." Chin in her hand, Molly tapped her fingers against the tabletop. "That seems to have happened fast."

Exasperated, Brady stared at her. "What are you trying to say?"

"I don't know." She also twisted to look down the hall, her mouth pursed thoughtfully. "It's just odd."

The shape of Molly's mouth, too much like a pucker, and the word "odd" triggered Brady's brain the way things do, making it jump to the completely unrelated topic of sex. Specifically, sex with Molly. Which he suddenly remembered in hot, desperate detail. His whole body heated.

Fuck. He'd managed to avoid thinking about it all week. When she'd deflected his attempts to talk about it, he'd honored her wishes. So why did the memories have to pop up now?

Along with other things.

"Molly."

She turned back to him, her eyes bright and hard. "What?"

He faltered, taken aback. "I…uh…how's the store? I mean, as a store, not as a front."

After studying him for several long, uncomfortable seconds, she apparently decided to take the question at face value. "It's good. Lots of colleges around, the symphony, you know. I have a broad customer base."

"Do you miss the travel?"

"Some. Mostly not. I never got to really see the places I visited." She lifted a shoulder. "It burns you out, that kind of travel. As you probably know."

"Yeah, but I see more than the inside of performance halls. I have to get to know whatever city I'm in. You could, too, if you became a field agent. Ever consider it?" As soon as the words left his mouth, he regretted them. He didn't want her to be a field agent. Granted, working for SIEGE wasn't as dangerous as working for other alphabet agencies—Chris's death and their adventure in South America notwithstanding. But it was still more dangerous than being a conduit.

Thankfully, Molly shook her head. "I like having my own city, my own home, steady work."

"A chance to have a family?"

Damn. Where the hell had *that* come from? He sat back, afraid of her reaction. She didn't disappoint.

"Why, because I'm a woman? I should stay home and sustain the population while the menfolk do all the traveling?"

Brady opened his mouth to defend himself, then caught the humor in her eyes and chuckled. He shook his head. "You had me going."

"Well, you should think before you speak." She started sorting the papers. "No, a chance to have a family was never part of the equation." Her sharp movements almost dared him to ask why, but he was a smart man. Or he'd learned from his mistakes. Or he just didn't want to know the answer.

"Thanks for helping out with everything," he said, and her shoulders visibly relaxed.

"No problem." She scribbled on a few sticky notes and slapped them onto the various piles she'd created. "Have Jessica sign these." She pointed to the first pile. "We should get them in the mail today so she receives the settlement check quickly. This stuff is for your mom." Her hand rested on the second pile. "Mostly answers to questions she had, and stuff I've done that was on her list."

"Why can't you tell them yourself?" he asked. Jessica's door opened at the back of the house, and he caught a glimpse of her ducking into the bathroom. His heart started to pound at the idea of seeing her.

"I have to go." Molly drained her coffee and gathered up

her trash. "The last pile is stuff that still needs to be done. You and your parents can talk about who's going to do what. I'll be back in—"

"Where are you going?" he interrupted. "It's only eight o'clock." He narrowed his eyes when she stood, not looking at him. "Molly."

"I have some arrangements to take care of. Some stuff to pick up." She carried her detritus to the bin by the back door and almost made her escape to the porch. Brady caught her arm as she pushed through the screen door.

"Where are you going that you don't want me to know?" She kept her head down, and he worked through the possible— Oh. *Hell.* "You're getting his body, aren't you?" The excitement at Jessica's imminent appearance was instantly gone, replaced by a pressure in his chest. He didn't give Molly a chance to answer, knowing he was right. "Why? Let the funeral home do it."

"I can't." She looked up at him now, finally, anguished but honest. "I have to do it myself, Brady. I just...have to."

He understood. But there wasn't a chance in hell she was going alone. He started to follow her and got as far as the top step of the back porch before he registered his bare feet, and from there, the running shorts and ripped T-shirt he'd dragged on when he got up this morning.

"Wait for me," he ordered.

"Brady, no."

He ignored her protest and turned her to face him, patting the pockets of her hoodie, then her jeans.

"What are you doing?" She jerked away and he grabbed her around the waist with one arm, digging for the lump that had to be her keys.

"You're *not* leaving without me."

She drew in a sharp breath and he froze, suddenly registering their position. He'd dragged her to his body. Her left breast was squashed against his chest, her left leg between his, the fingers of his right hand only inches from…well, they were buried deep in her pocket. Instead of releasing her, his arm around her back tightened, bringing her even closer and pushing out her breath. Her long black eyelashes swished upward, exposing a plea he couldn't interpret. Did she want him to let her go…or kiss her?

Kiss her.

He didn't analyze the whisper, or consider what it meant. It sounded like a reasonable suggestion. He actually bent his head before a different, louder voice inside him yelled *Are you fucking crazy?* He jerked upright and let go of her, pulling the keys free as he did and pretending for all he was worth that the keys had been his goal all along.

"I'll be right back. Stay here on pain of death." Then he escaped inside the house, striving to regain his breath and his freaking sanity.

• • •

Holy. Fucking. God.

Molly sank onto the top step of the porch and dropped her forehead to her knees. *What the hell was* that?

Brady had almost kissed her. This time in full control of himself. No, maybe not. He was trying to stop her from going to get his brother's body without him, and that had to have dredged up more pain and turmoil. Maybe it was a knee-jerk comfort response. Like programming. But God, she could still feel his hand in her pocket, inches from—

"*Guh.*" She straightened and rubbed her hands on her jeans. Then there'd been his lean, hard body full length on hers, which definitely remembered what he'd felt like naked and wanted to feel it again.

Think of something else.

She'd seen the look on his face when Jessica came out of the bedroom. Molly had immediately needed to escape, to avoid watching him fawning over Princess Jess again, to keep her crushing pity at bay. She hurt terribly for Jessica, for her loss and everything she must face all on her own, but at the same time, Molly had no patience for the other woman's weakness and dependence. This wasn't how Molly would have predicted her friend would react to tragedy.

Ten years ago, Jessica had graduated from interior design school and launched right into her own business, ignoring anyone who told her it couldn't work, that she didn't have the experience to make a success of it. She had succeeded, joining two dozen local organizations, building relationships, doing a couple of pro bono jobs to create references and referrals. Molly never knew if she eventually grew tired of the business or if it just petered out, but about three years ago Jessica had shut it down and become a housewife. Maybe she and Chris had been having problems trying to have kids; Jess had never confided that deeply in Molly. Their conversations became all about Chris and his "work," and dinner with his family, and a little bit about Jessica missing her own family, who lived too far away to visit often. Then she'd gotten pregnant, and it seemed everything was perfect again—at least as far as what Jessica wanted.

Now Molly knew Jess had lost herself, had tied her identity too closely to Christopher, and with his loss, was truly floundering. Molly would be a better friend if she helped Jessica find her way again…but that would mean getting in Brady's way. At the rate he was going, he was just going to slip right into Christopher's place and rescue the damsel in distress.

Let him. It's what he wants. What he'd always wanted, since that stupid day at the train station.

Who was she to decide it was wrong for either of them?

Before she could answer her own question, Brady emerged from the house, now wearing jeans and a long-sleeved T-shirt and carrying her keys.

"Ready?" he asked.

"You don't have to go," she told him. "The casket will be latched. It's not like an identification or anything, and I have the power of attorney your parents drew up." It gave her authority to handle all the stuff that Jessica was unable to, and Donna and Rick shouldn't have to.

"He's my brother," Brady gritted out, not looking down. Molly stood, and regretted it when he continued, "You're not even family."

If the words had been borne on the edge of a blade, they couldn't have sliced deeper.

She couldn't move, staring at him as he went down the steps, oblivious to her pain.

But then he said, "You shouldn't be shouldering our burdens. Not alone." He was halfway down the sidewalk when he realized she wasn't there. He turned. "You loved him, too, Molly. I know this isn't any easier for you than it is for us."

That wasn't the balm it should have been. "It is," she said softly, still battling the hurt. She took a deep breath. "Not easy, but not as hard. I loved him, yes, and he was like a brother to me, even if he wasn't my brother."

Brady winced, as if suddenly realizing how he'd sounded. "I didn't—"

"It's not the same. I know that, and that's why I wanted to do this for you. I wanted to spare you." She blinked and refocused on practicalities and conspiracies. Going alone wasn't just about sparing him. The facilitator had alleviated her vague uneasiness yesterday, but a tiny spark still lingered. She had to put it to rest, and hoped to do that today. It would be a lot harder to accomplish if Brady was with her.

"Oh, Moll." He came back to the porch and up a step, wrapping his arms around her in a hug. She rested her chin on his shoulder, inhaling deeply as she hugged him back. He smelled of deodorant and shaving gel, the same ones he'd used since college, even though he hadn't had time to shower yet today and certainly hadn't shaved.

"I love you, Moll. You're still my best friend, even after all I've done."

"I love you, too, Brady," she whispered. And just wished he meant it the same way she did.

. . .

"Have you talked to your parents lately?" Brady asked after they'd been on the road a few minutes.

Molly grimaced. "I don't really want to talk about my parents."

"And I don't want to talk about anything related to Chris or his death or my family or—"

She managed a laugh. "Okay. Yes. I talked to them right before I left for South America."

"Shall I explain what 'anything related' means?" He gave her a mock glare.

"Sorry. Anyway, I call them regularly. It's a duty."

"And?"

"And Dad is on disability, has been for five years. He's a total cliché. Lazing around the house while Mom works her ass off, or so she says, at the dry cleaner. All they do is complain about each other." She didn't bother trying to keep the bitterness from her voice. Brady knew the score. Had always known.

"And ask for money?"

"And ask for money. Of course."

"Do you give it to them?"

"Sometimes." She looked out the side window, not wanting his judgment. "Christmas, birthdays, Mother's Day, and Father's Day. Never just money."

"You don't owe them anything," Brady said gently enough that she turned back.

"I do. Not much," she acknowledged. "But they did enable me to get through college."

"You got through college on your own," he corrected firmly. "Hard work and top grades. Scholarships."

"And financial aid because they were such losers."

He laughed and shook his head. "Well, they did spawn one

hell of a kid. I don't know how you turned out so great."

"I do." She waited until he looked at her, one eyebrow lifted. "It was you."

He turned back to traffic, looking uncomfortable. "My parents, you mean."

"All of you. If all of you hadn't given me an escape, showed me what a real family could be like, that it was possible to be a different kind of person, I'd never have become who I am."

She thought about that as they drove on, Brady now intently following the GPS instructions. In truth, the Fitzpatricks' influence was as deep and pervasive as her parents'. They'd lived as neighbors the entire time she was growing up, and early on, the mothers had been friends. Or at least friendly acquaintances, with their kids only a few months apart in age and play dates so easy. Her own mother probably had been decent when Molly was an infant and toddler. She didn't remember, but pictures showed her smiling and doting, only looking hard and cynical and tired of life as the years wore on.

Molly only really remembered the fighting, though. That her parents were still together was her life's greatest mystery. She couldn't blame either of them more than the other; they just clashed, repeatedly and unstoppably. Maybe they loved each other, maybe it was habit or codependence. Who knew? The bottom line was that the older she'd grown, the more time Molly had spent at the Fitzes'. And the more they became her true family, no matter what Brady said.

And then she chose the same college Brady went to. It had a great music program, but if he'd gone somewhere else, Molly wasn't sure she wouldn't have followed him anyway. And though she had other friendships, spent years away from Brady and his family, toured the world and had her own career that had nothing to do with them, she'd still wound up in a new career inexorably tied to Brady's and Chris's.

True, they'd never come through her shop, never used her as a conduit, hadn't known—until now—that she was one. But she never would have been SIEGE without them.

Being SIEGE meant having a greater purpose, doing things that served the world at large, not just herself or culture or the arts or the soul, depending which perspective you took on the musical world. But it had also kept her connected to Brady, when their relationship had been stretched to the barest of threads.

Was that bad? Wrong? Would a psychologist label her choices unhealthy?

Brady cursed. "GPS should stand for 'Great Piece of Shit.' " He stabbed at a button. "This can't be right."

Molly brushed his hand aside. "I'll do it." She navigated menus back to the main route. "Take the next right, and the building is on the left."

"Fantastic." He blew out a breath. "You're awesome."

She sat back, smiling. *Screw psychology*.

The building where they were to pick up the body was a hangar near a private airstrip, which further confirmed Molly's belief that Chris had been out of the country when he was killed. She didn't know why that mattered so much. Most fieldwork was done outside of the US, after all.

Brady parked and shut off the car, but sat staring at the ugly building. Molly could imagine what he was thinking—that it was an ignominious place for his brother to be resting. That he didn't want to face the proof, the irrefutable evidence that would make it all real. That no brother, especially a younger one, should have to deal with something like this.

"I'll go," she started to say, but he spoke at the same time.

"We can't put a casket in this car."

He said it matter of factly, but with a hint of surprise that made Molly want to roll her eyes.

"I know that." She held back the "dipshit."

"Then—"

"The funeral home is meeting us here," she admitted. She'd hoped he wouldn't ask, at least not this soon. She didn't want to start up the "Then why are we here?" discussion again. But Brady just nodded, still staring at the sheet-metal structure in front of them, his hand on the keys but unmoving. Molly waited patiently, letting him work up to it. For her part, she was itching to get in there…but just as willing to put it off forever.

They sat for a few minutes, the only sound their breathing. Molly went into a kind of Zen state, her brain powered down, her senses full of the scent of the man next to her, the size of him filling her car. Not in a sexual way, just full awareness of his presence. She let herself connect with him while they sat there.

A plane buzzed into view, coming in for a landing on a strip beyond the fence enclosing the hangar, and Brady drew in a deep, sharp breath. "Okay, let's go."

She started to get out of the car and halted, one foot on the ground, when Brady grabbed her hand. He didn't say anything, only squeezed and let go before shoving open his own door.

They walked together to the glass entry on the side of the building, Brady's stride strong and fast, as if he was now determined to get it over with. She hurried to keep up, the pulse in her throat beating an urgent rhythm.

A man in a dark suit that fit his ramrod spine perfectly met them inside the door, which opened onto a large storage area. The walls were corrugated metal, the floor concrete, the room full of parts and equipment and boxes and pallets.

"How may I help you?" the man asked with an air of already knowing, but not comfortable with that knowledge.

"I'm Brady Fitzpatrick, here to pick up my brother's…" His voice trailed off. Molly slid her hand into his and he gripped it hard.

"I…see. I'm very sorry, sir, if we'd known you'd be coming personally, we wouldn't have— We'd have— We thought the funeral home was making the transfer."

"They are." Molly stepped forward. "We're overseeing. Can you show us where the casket is being held?" The word somehow didn't seem as morbid as "coffin."

"Of course. If— Again, I'm sorry. These aren't exactly the accommodations—"

"It's fine," Brady interrupted, his voice tense but not accusatory. Molly knew it wouldn't have mattered if they'd arranged a plush room or a special "mourners" entry. Prettying up the atmosphere didn't change anything.

They followed the facilitator—because that was what he had to be—around the end of an aisle of metal shelving and down a corridor between a baggage truck and more shelves. At the end, a simple oak casket sat on an expandable wheeled cart next to a cargo access door. Brady's step faltered, and Molly stopped next to him, propping him up a little with her shoulder.

The casket was basic rectangular with a rounded top and carved edges, iron handles on the side. The wood on either side of a half-folded flag draped across the middle gleamed in the diffuse light from high windows. Several feet of open space surrounded it. For respect? Or ease of movement? Whatever the intent, the result was loneliness, abandonment.

Molly's throat swelled and her eyes stung. Pain stabbed her left hand where Brady's grip had tightened even more.

"There is some paperwork to be signed," the facilitator murmured.

This was her chance. "You go ahead," she told Brady. "I'll stay with him." He hesitated. *Go, go, go.* She waited with a façade of patience for him to nod and follow the other guy toward what looked like an office on the other side of the hangar. Perfect.

As soon as they were halfway across the building, Molly hurried to the coffin. She laid her hands on the lid and closed her eyes, taking a deep breath and focusing her awareness. But there was no sense of connection, or grief, or finality. There wasn't anything but smooth wood and the faint hint of pine furniture polish.

Hurry. Her eyes popped open. Right. They'd be back any moment, and the funeral home would be here in a few minutes, too. She checked for hinges, found them, and hurried around to the other side of the oak box. They'd said he couldn't be viewed, they couldn't have an open casket, so she braced herself and took a deep breath before tentatively trying to lift the lid. Of course, it was locked down. There was no visible latch, so she felt along the edge for a release. Her left hand came up against a small metal rectangle, but it had no button or lever. Crap. She so didn't want Brady to catch her at this.

Crouching to see the mechanism, she cursed under her breath. There was a small hole in the side. Not a regular lock for a specific key, though it might as well have been. It needed a hex key. She had a multi-tool on her keychain, but Brady still had it with him. She straightened and looked around. Maybe there was something here. She dashed over to the closest shelves that looked like they held tools and parts. Her throat caught when she tried to swallow. She dug through a pile of things she didn't recognize, looking for a hex key or something similar, opening a couple of boxes and finding a ratchet set and regular screwdrivers, but no hexes.

"Come on," she muttered, peering through the open shelves to see if Brady and the facilitator were coming back yet. Coast was still clear, at least as far as she could see in the crowded space. What the hell would she say if they caught her? The wheel was bent. No, that would be too obvious. Her zipper was stuck. Ridiculous. There was nothing she *could* say to explain her behavior.

"So just get on with it and don't get caught. Dammit!" she growled to herself.

Maybe she could do this at the funeral ho— Wait. *There.* A dirty blue vinyl sleeve, back in the corner. She stretched to reach it, her fingertips scrabbling for a hold before they caught on the edge and pulled the holder close enough. *Yes!* She grabbed the whole thing and dashed back to the casket. Still no sign of Brady or the other guy, or anyone else, for that matter— but she had to keep alert. A countdown ran in her head, making her fingers want to fumble the keys. She squinted at the hole and chose a key that looked like it would fit, sliding it carefully into the hole so it didn't scratch the finish. Too big. She tried the next one down. Still too big. Dammit! She bit her lip to keep her breathing from getting too fast and loud, and chose the next one down. *Ahh*, just right. She twisted, and the latch released.

Molly shot upright and shoved the lid up, more concerned with getting the task done than with what the task actually *was*. So when she looked down into the white satin-lined interior, she wasn't thinking about what she expected to see.

But it certainly wasn't empty space.

Chapter Seven

Brady stood in the cluttered, fuel-smelling office, fighting to keep control. The papers he had to sign for the transfer contained so many clinical, final words they were like nails being hammered into his chest. How many times was he going to be hit with the finality of his brother's death before it was really final? Almost worse than that, whenever the nails drove into him, all he wanted was Molly.

He breathed through his mouth, staring to try to keep his eyeballs dry as he scribbled his signature and initials in the designated places. The facilitator stepped forward to take the papers and nudged a tissue box that sat on the corner of the desk. Brady just swiped under his eyes with the back of his hand before striding angrily back to where the coffin stood waiting.

Molly was several paces away from it, near a stack of shelves. Brady frowned at her flushed face and tousled curls. What had she been doing? She met him at the casket, her chest heaving as if she'd been running. He met her bright eyes for a split second before she turned away, and he instantly knew she was hiding something. With the facilitator hovering behind them he couldn't question her, and just then the overhead door rolled up and the funeral home's hearse backed up to it.

A few minutes later, the home's staff had loaded the coffin, signed their paperwork, and driven off. Brady and Molly followed the hearse out of the parking lot, the burn finally easing when he turned the car in the opposite direction.

He drove for a full block before saying a word. "What's going on? And don't play dumb."

Her typical response sounded staged, prepared. "I never play dumb."

He had to give her that. "So?"

She didn't answer. He rolled up to a traffic light and glanced at her. She was frowning intently out the windshield, but not seeing what was in front of her. He knew that look. His heart skittered before resuming its normal beat. The light changed and he drove on, deciding that whatever she needed to tell him should wait until he wasn't driving.

Half a mile from his parents' house, he turned off into a small park. The lot was mostly empty, only one minivan belonging to the young mother and two toddlers playing on the playground in front of them. The smaller of the two was trying to climb up a short plastic slide. The older brother reached the top, turned around, and slid down, a shit-eating grin on his face, but their mother snatched up the little one before feet came in contact. Their laughter penetrated the car. Brady rubbed the heel of his hand over his breastbone, the ache intensifying.

"Tell me," he said.

"Oh, Brady," Molly whispered, still not looking at him. "I wish…"

"What?" Tension locked around him. "You wish what?"

She shook her head, as if the wish was either too obvious or too impossible.

"Molly, for God's sake, just tell me. You're killing me here."

She finally turned, and Brady stopped breathing at the look in her eyes. They blazed, the brilliant blue so full of… hope? Anger? Determination? He realized she'd been so quiet not from despondence or sorrow, but from intent. She was practically exploding with whatever she didn't want to tell him.

Drawing in a huge breath, she said, "I opened the coffin."

Horror ripped through him. "Fuck." He leaned his elbow on the car door and rubbed his hand across his upper lip. "Why the hell did you do that?" He struggled to focus, to keep at bay the images her words generated. Jagged red lines across his brother's cold, white face, criss-crossed with black stitching. Gaping wounds, cold and hard.

"I had to," she said, her voice stronger. She turned toward him and drew one leg up on the seat, the other braced flat on the floor. "I've had this feeling all along. I didn't know what it was, couldn't pinpoint anything that made me, I don't know, suspicious." She shoved the jumble of shiny black curls back on her head. They *sproing*ed around her fingers, but the sleekness in front opened up her face in a way he hadn't seen in a long time. He briefly wondered what else she'd been hiding since coming to get him in South America, then dismissed that as a stupid, obvious question.

"And what did you find?" he asked in a low voice, expecting her to describe bullet holes or knife wounds.

"Nothing."

He went blank. "What?"

"Nothing."

"Nothing to support your suspicions," he clarified. Something in the back of his brain was roaring approval, but he didn't know why.

"No, I mean nothing. Brady." She twisted further and grabbed his hands. Hers shook until she tightened them so hard it hurt. "Brady, there was nothing. In the casket. It was empty."

The roar grew, but his conscious brain wasn't as quick as his subconscious. "What are you talking about?"

"The coffin was empty," she repeated with emphasis. "Your brother wasn't there. Chris wasn't there. Brady, he might not be dead."

• • •

Molly sat on a bench at the edge of the playground, hunching against the brisk breeze that had chased away the woman and kids half an hour ago. She hadn't taken a jacket when they left the house, and debated calling to Brady to get him back in the car. How much time did he need, up there at the top of the climber?

Probably as much time as she'd let him have. She sighed and pushed to her feet, folding her arms across her chest as she crossed the wood chips to the little ladder. Her average-sized feet barely fit on the toddler-sized steps, so she reached up to the crossbar at the top and hauled herself to the platform. There was no room for her on top of the covered slide, which Brady straddled, staring out across the nearby soccer fields.

"Brady." She'd been doing that a lot lately, saying his name as entry into his thoughts.

"I've been going through the list." He swung one leg over to sit sideways, not quite facing her, and still staring outward, but at least talking again.

"Me, too." She leaned on the rail next to the slide opening. "Ways I could be wrong, ways a mistake was made, reasons it could be true."

"What do you know that I don't?" He'd put on his agent tone.

She started at the beginning. "The coffin was latched and not easily opened, but not locked. The satin inside looked untouched, but I didn't really have time to—"

"Did you look at all of it?"

"I…" She didn't know what he meant.

"Did you see the entire space? Maybe he— Maybe the remains—" He swallowed audibly.

"No," she hastened, getting it. "I mean, yes, I looked all the way down, and no, there was absolutely nothing in there."

"So why didn't the funeral home question it?"

Molly had been watching them load the casket into the hearse for exactly that reason. "It was heavy. They struggled. I'm thinking they put something in the base of it—blocks, or lead, or something—so it would feel the way it should carrying a 180-pound man."

Brady nodded and leaned forward, bracing his hands on the plastic next to him. "They won't open it, because they were told all the preparations were taken care of. They're only supposed to handle the ceremony and burial."

"Right. So ideally, everyone just accepts that he's in there, we proceed with the funeral, and move on with our lives."

That took care of one list. Acutely aware of time passing, of Rick and Donna and Jessica at home waiting for them to come back and assure them they had Chris safe and sound— Oh, God, that was a poor choice of words. Molly straightened to ease the dull ache in her chest and resolutely moved on.

"Mistakes. It's the wrong coffin."

Brady shook his head. "There was a code stamped on the paper and the end of the coffin. Non-removable. And I saw the facilitator compare the numbers before they moved it out."

Something new crowded into Molly, something she'd been working hard to keep at bay ever since she saw that wide, satiny blankness. "Okay then, right coffin, but Chris is in the wrong one."

"SIEGE doesn't make mistakes like that."

She shrugged even though Brady couldn't see. "We're human. We all make mistakes."

Brady sat frozen for a few seconds, then nodded. "All right, then. Before we go any further, we have to figure out if it's a mistake." He finally looked her way. "Suggestions?"

"We should ask. Talk to D—my handler. Or your handler," she added, not really sure how Brady's setup worked. "Since I've been dealing with all the arrangements, though, and already talked to them about—" Shit. He didn't know about that.

His eyes narrowed. "About what?"

She sighed. "I went over yesterday, to drop off the intel you'd gotten and try to get answers about the accident."

"Went over? To New Rochelle?"

She nodded, wondering if only conduits weren't told the location of headquarters.

He frowned more. "And?"

"And they blew me off. But it's a channel of communication."

"Okay. We'll arrange a meet." He launched himself off the slide and landed on the tanbark ten feet below, then grinned up at her. "Coming?"

She stared at him, locked into place by the brilliance of his smile, the lightness in his eyes, the suddenly strong, square set of his shoulders. His legs planted wide, hands on hips, he looked like the old Brady, and the steel box inside her creaked, the pressure of the swelling emotions inside it almost overwhelming her. Brady's smile widened, a clear challenge.

Molly grinned down at him. "Yep." She grabbed the rail, bounced, and swung her legs up to the top of the rail, just touching down as a boost to go over, and landed lightly next to Brady. "Let's go."

Neither one brought up the reason they suddenly felt so light—that Chris might actually still be alive.

Molly dialed Dix's number before they even reached the car. For the first time in the years she'd been with SIEGE, he didn't answer.

"You've reached the desk of Conrad Dixson. Please leave a message and I'll return the call asap." Typical business speak, but his voice was somber, tense. Molly had no way of knowing, of course, when he'd recorded the message. It could have been luck that she'd never gotten his voicemail before. But it still shredded the bubble of happiness she'd had around her for, oh, thirty seconds.

"Dix, Molly. Call me, please. As soon as you can."

Brady seemed to sink into himself again. "He didn't answer?"

"No."

He opened her car door and circled around to the driver's side. She hesitated, then decided to keep letting him drive, even though it was her car.

"Handlers never not answer the phone," Brady said grimly, starting the car and backing out quickly. "It always goes to someone else if they're not available." He accelerated out onto the street so fast Molly was glad there was no one about, though at this time on a Friday, it was almost eerie.

"What do you think it means?" she asked.

"No idea. Let's get home, check on the others, and go down there."

"I can handle that."

They drove to the funeral home first, to confirm arrival of the coffin and final arrangements for the funeral on Sunday. Brady's words and actions had an edge of energy, as if what he was doing wasn't relevant to anything, only an irritating inconvenience. Molly felt it, too, but tried to caution herself against the hope feeding that edge. They'd stopped listing possibilities, but they still existed.

And just because Chris's body was missing didn't mean he wasn't dead.

• • •

When Brady and Molly got home, his mother and Jessica met them at the door. "How did it go? Everything go smoothly? What did the funeral home say? Can we do the—the funeral as scheduled?" His mother's questions battered at Brady, dragging him back into heavy reality.

"Yes, Mom. Everything's fine." His voice reflected the weight he was feeling, but she didn't seem to notice as she hugged him, sagging in relief that turned to grief as she started to sob.

Brady looked at Jessica, unprepared for the devastation on her face, as if she'd gotten the news of Chris's death for the first time. Seeing his mother's pain made him ache with sorrow and regret, but Jessica's was a switchblade in his gut. The urge to tell her about the empty coffin surged, but only for a moment. Knowing that would make it a lot worse for her if it was only a mix-up.

He didn't believe it was, though. As soon as his mother released him he reached for Jess. She dove into his arms, shaking but not sobbing, her eyes dry. Brady wrapped his arms tighter, squeezed his eyes closed, tried not to let anyone see the furious hope behind them.

There were so many reasons *not* to be hopeful. Chris wouldn't do this to them. SIEGE didn't need to hide agents by faking their deaths.

But instincts honed in his job told Brady that was exactly what they'd done. *Why? Why put us through this?*

Molly's hand brushed his back as she passed, a casual, comforting touch. But it jolted through him, fusing with the hope he was struggling to keep at bay. He raised his head. Their eyes met, the acknowledgment in hers grounding him. They'd get to the truth.

Eventually.

• • •

Brady's patience didn't last long. The day ground on with no word from Molly's handler. He wanted to drive down to New Rochelle immediately. She wanted to wait, to give her handler a chance to call back. His mother had turned clingy, and Brady hadn't been able to come up with an excuse for them to leave.

And to top it off, Molly kept making suggestions of things he could do with Jessica, until finally, he cornered her taking out the trash.

"Leave me alone about Jess," he said through gritted teeth.

Molly raised an eyebrow. "That's what I'm trying to do."

"Not *with* Jess, *about* Jess." He glared at her exaggerated innocence. "I mean it. I don't know what you're trying to do, but—"

"I'm trying to help a grieving friend," she interrupted. "She needs you. And from all appearances since we got back, you need her."

Brady bristled at the disapproval permeating her prim tone of voice. "Hey, she just lost her husband. Or thinks she did. I'm—" He grabbed the hand Molly put up in his face and jerked it down. "I've only been trying to comfort her. She's fragile. She is," he couldn't help insisting when she *hmph*ed. "But she's my brother's widow. I'm not making moves. That's disgusting." Morally speaking, anyway. He couldn't say the idea hadn't crossed his mind. "Plus, if—" He couldn't voice it, couldn't risk someone overhearing him say, "If Chris is alive." But Molly understood. She gave a short nod and turned away, which for some reason stoked the frustration and anger he had been tamping down all day. He grabbed her arm.

She whirled back, his emotions mirrored in her expression. "I get it!" she burst out, but then stopped, her eyes locking on his. Her body practically vibrated with tension.

God, her eyes are blue. His forehead crinkled, and whatever he'd been about to say faded from his mind. His tension changed. It stopped being painful and started being...needy. The air held a slight chill, but heat shimmered between them. He had the odd sensation of being on the verge of the most exciting thing he'd ever experienced.

And then those blue eyes shimmered, wavered, and he realized they'd filled with tears.

"Molly."

"Don't," she whispered, and they spilled over.

Appalled, he pulled her into a hug. "No, Moll, don't. It's okay. I'm sorry. I'm so sorry." He wasn't certain what he was apologizing for, but it was the only thing he could do. Molly crying was far worse than Jessica crying. Jessica was made for tears. He'd probably seen Molly cry three times in their entire lives. And never because of him.

She shook with sobs she wouldn't release, and he squeezed her harder, rubbing his hand over her back in a motion he hoped was soothing. Regret and helplessness swirled through him. What could he do? What did she need? He had no idea.

Seconds ticked by as he held her and she grew tenser in his arms, not burrowing into his comfort nor pulling away. He sensed her fists were clenched at her sides, and slid one hand down her arm to check. As soon as it wrapped around hers she released her grip, and his fingers automatically entwined with hers. He struggled to understand what had caused this—if it was Jessica or Christopher, or just him and what they'd done in South America. Maybe he should ignore her moratorium on the subject. Maybe they really had to talk about it. Apprehension prickled up his spine, and suddenly he had no idea what he'd say. The lines he'd prepared the other day no longer seemed to fit.

He curled his hand so hers was inside it, and she finally relaxed, easing against his chest and turning her face slightly into him. He was about to open his mouth, to say who-the-hell-knew-what, when he spotted his mother inside the screen door, watching them. Her expression was uncharacteristically implacable, and that unnerved him more than anything. Instead of speaking, he moved his hands to Molly's shoulders and eased her back. She swiped a hand under one eye, saw his mother standing there, and smiled up at him.

"Thanks, Brady. I need to go check the…" She trailed off and trotted up the steps. His mother opened the door for her and said something Brady couldn't hear. Molly shook her head and disappeared inside, but his mother came out and glared down at him, arms folded across her chest.

"What?" Brady spread his own arms, feeling like he was ten again and didn't know which thing she'd caught him at.

She sighed and dropped her arms. "Come here." She sat heavily on the top step, patting the spot next to her.

"It's chilly out here, Mom. We should go inside." But he

obeyed when she shook her head. "You okay?"

She shrugged. "Everything's set up for tomorrow. I'll be better after that." But Brady knew better, and her tone said she did, too.

"I wish…" He didn't know how to finish the sentence. He wished it had been him? As if that would be easier on her.

But she had a different interpretation. "I wish you hadn't stayed away so long, too."

Brady took a deep breath. "Mom—"

"I understand why you did," she interrupted. "I hated every minute of it, but I understood. We can't help how we feel about people."

He blew out a breath and didn't bother asking how she knew. She probably hadn't needed to be told, but Molly would have explained. She'd seen him that day. The day hope had shattered. He didn't know how much she'd overheard, but it didn't matter. She'd known enough from the beginning, from the moment he'd met Jessica and crashed in a lovesick heap at her feet. She would have explained to his parents, so their hearts didn't break at his absence.

"It was selfish," he admitted. "I didn't think about how it would hurt you and Dad. I just knew how much it hurt me."

"Oh, Brady." She shook her head slowly. "You're not the only one with regrets. We let you do it. I think if we'd dragged you back instead of giving you space, you'd have gotten over her more easily. You'd have been able to see what was in front of you. And we'd all be so much happier."

He wasn't sure what she was getting at. "Seen what? Chris and Jess?" Just saying their names made his throat burn. "That's what hurt so much."

"No." She didn't say "you moron," but her look of disgust did. "Watching them would have made you pine more for what you couldn't have. I mean seeing what you *could* have. Instead of twelve years of wallowing in misery, you could have been happy. We all could have."

Brady bristled. He hadn't pined *or* wallowed. That was the whole point of staying away, even if it stretched out longer than he'd ever expected. But he knew that wasn't what she was getting at. He didn't want her to spell it out. Already, his insides were writhing. So he angled the topic a little.

"You're right." He glanced over his shoulder to make sure Jessica wasn't anywhere around, and lowered his voice. "If I'd spent more time with her, I wouldn't have put her on such a high pedestal. I'd have seen her flaws and maybe gotten over her faster."

His mother raised an eyebrow. "Faster?"

He shrugged, unwilling to admit anything. "Circumstances are pretty extreme right now."

She chuckled. "Oh, hon. They are. But they don't need to be."

Brady frowned. "What do you mean?"

"Some people are high maintenance. Chris—" Her voice cracked, and she swallowed. "Chris was taking more— He was traveling for work more and more, and there was good reason. Whenever he was away, she came over here." Now she glanced around. "She drove me near insane with her inability to entertain herself."

Brady managed a chuckle around the knee-jerk reaction to defend her. "She had a business."

"That she ran poorly and abandoned." She rocked back a little and shook her head. "I love her. She's been like a daughter to me. But that doesn't mean I think she's perfect. And hon," She turned to look at him, her gaze as piercing as it had been when he was fourteen and hating not only that she thought she knew what was best for him, but that she really did know. "Jessica isn't right for you. Especially now."

"She needs—"

"—to figure out on her own what she needs."

He blew out another breath. "Like you're letting me do?"

She patted his knee. "I'm your mother. I stood by and let

you try to figure out what you needed for far too long. Now I'm just going to tell you."

"You don't need to, Mom. I know what you're going to say."

She *hrumph*ed. "You do not."

"You're going to say Molly—"

"Hell, no." She rocked to her feet, using his leg to brace herself. "I'm going to tell you to leave her alone. You're much too late, sweetie." She waited for that to sink in, and though he didn't respond, she nodded and went into the house.

Brady draped his forearms over his knees and stared out across the back yard, watching the yellowed maple leaves swaying in the afternoon breeze. His thoughts drifted, touching on memories. The kick to his gut when he'd met Jessica and thought it was love. The heartsickness he'd lived with until he told her—and was shot down with just enough hope to feed the disease. He'd barely seen her since, so those moments had become frozen. Touchstones. But in reality she wasn't what he'd wanted her to be, and he knew mere habit ruled his emotions now. Habit that was already breaking.

When he and Molly had been in high school and college, best friends with no benefits, his friends had needled him about his "wife." She'd been a constant, her personality and approach to life so complementary to his own, it was no wonder everyone expected them to get together. But he'd known her his whole life. His feelings hadn't exactly been brotherly, but he'd never felt "that way" about her. Until this week. Until the worst thing that had ever happened to him knocked him out of his bubble, and he'd taken action without thought.

That night down in South America, when he'd lost himself in his best friend…how was that different, emotionally speaking, than the way he'd lost himself in a fantasy over Jess?

His mother had warned him off Molly, yes, but he had a sneaking feeling she was using reverse psychology. Everyone thought men wanted what they couldn't have. Well, he wasn't going to fall for that. It didn't matter if his mother thought he belonged with Molly, that he would be happy with her. He wasn't rushing into anything.

It took two, anyway, and Molly had made it very clear their night together hadn't meant anything deeper than comfort.

A familiar, sweet scent accompanied the squeak of the back door opening again. Brady buried an automatic craving, almost as disgusted with himself as his mother had been, but not for the same reasons.

"Dixson called," Molly said from behind him. "He wants to meet us."

Brady stood without turning, afraid his training had abandoned him and everything he'd been thinking about would show on his face. "Now?"

"Now."

"Then let's go."

Chapter Eight

Molly and Brady met Dix outside the Starbucks in the food court at the mall two towns over. Dix hadn't stayed on the phone long, and that, coupled with the odd meeting site, iced the pit of her stomach. She spotted him almost immediately, smack in the center of the half-full crowd of tables and chairs, a soda cup in one hand, the remains of a meal from the Chinese restaurant shoved to one side of the table.

Brady caught her arm as she zeroed in on Dix, both visually and physically. When she frowned up at him, he motioned toward the row of food counters. Molly nodded. They'd look more natural if they got something to eat before joining Dix. But the logic of the action didn't give her patience.

"Stop bouncing," Brady muttered as they moved forward in line at the sub shop. "You look like you have to go to the bathroom."

"Then that's what I'll do. Get me a side salad and bottle of water, please." She dashed off to the ladies' room without waiting for a response. Thank God he'd given her something to do, even if he'd meant to insult her into obedience. She tried not to rush, but Brady was still several people from the counter when she emerged from the restroom. After a moment of hesitation, she walked over to Dix and sat down.

"Hey," she said.

"Hey." He didn't shift position much and just gave her a casual nod.

"What's going on?"

"Nothin'. What are you up to?"

Molly glanced around, expecting to see someone walking by, but there was a good twenty-foot cushion of space around them. Probably why he'd picked the spot. But why here in the first place?

"Knock it off, Dix. What's really going on?"

Dix's expression stayed neutral, but he tilted his head a fraction, toward Brady. "Don't you want to wait for him?"

She kind of had to, at least about Christopher. But that wasn't the only thing she had to talk to Dix about, and she wasn't sure she wanted Brady to hear the rest, anyway.

"Why didn't you answer your phone?" she asked.

Dix's eyelids flickered. For someone whose emotions were transparent enough to keep him out of the field, he was hiding them well now. "I'm on leave."

"What?" She fell back in her seat in surprise. That wasn't what she'd expected to hear. "Why?"

This time, the answer was projected clearly on his face. He looked away, hunching forward and grabbing his soda.

Her heart sank. "Because of me." He didn't move, and she sighed in frustration. "Dix, talk to me."

His turn to sigh, and he hunched even further. He looked so dejected and kicked-puppyish, it made her want to get up and walk away to spare him telling her whatever embarrassed him so much.

Finally, he shook his head and met her eyes. "I asked them to reassign me. Of course, they asked why. I told them the truth."

She wasn't going to assume what that meant. "That you wanted to date me?"

He nodded and sucked on his straw. "Did *not* go over well. They suspended me."

Anger sparked through her, growing in layers as each reason to be angry occurred to her. "That's insane. You followed policy and protocol, right?" He nodded. "You did nothing improper before then. And they left me without a handler."

"You're on leave, too, basically. You shouldn't need a handler. Not until after Christopher's funeral."

Brady dropped his tray on the table and glared at both of them. "Thanks for waiting for me."

"We haven't talked about anything yet," Molly bit out, annoyed that she couldn't ask Dix if he'd changed his mind about her. Not in front of Brady. "He's been suspended."

Brady raised his eyebrows as he sorted out the food and drinks on the tray, handing Molly her salad without looking away from Dix. "What'd you do?"

Dix mumbled something and turned back to Molly. "Something's odd about all of this," he told her, glancing slightly at Brady to include him without meeting his gaze.

Brady frowned. "We know. That's why we're here."

"He means his suspension," Molly said. "He doesn't know why we're here."

"It has something to do with your brother, I know that." Dix straightened and slid his cup away. "When they asked me why Molly'd come in, I said to hand over your intel. When they asked why I needed to be involved, I said she had questions about your brother, and that's when everything shut down. When they froze me out." He looked at Molly. "So what is going on?"

She hesitated. She trusted Dix, wanted to tell him the truth, but it was Brady's decision, as Chris's brother. Brady nodded, and she turned back to her handler. "Chris's casket is empty."

Dix's mouth fell open and he leaned away. "Whoa."

"Yeah. Our reaction, too."

"How do you know this?"

"Um." She examined her salad, stabbing at the lettuce with her plastic fork. "I looked."

"You broke into a coffin?" There was a hint of amusement in his voice, but it overlaid something more jarring. She couldn't put her finger on what it was, and when he spoke again, it was gone. "You must be pretty fired up," he said to Brady.

"Yeah. They just keep giving us the accident line. I don't know what this means. But there's something strange going on, that's for damned sure."

Dix looked at Molly again, puzzled. "Why did you look in the coffin, anyway? What did you think you'd find? Or not find…?"

"It never occurred to me that he wasn't dead until I saw the emptiness." Hope welled again. God, reality was going to be hard to face if Chris really was dead. "I just had a bad feeling. There wasn't anything in particular. Things just felt…off."

He drew his soda cup toward him again and picked at the edge of the lid. "You were obviously right. After you talked to Ramona, administration holed up for two hours in the soundproof conference room. I didn't really think much about it at the time, but add that to all the rest—"

"And you get a cover-up," Brady said grimly. "I didn't want to believe it."

"I don't, either. I've worked for SIEGE for ten years and have never seen anything like this." The jarring undertone was back, like an unrosined bow scratching somewhere in an otherwise perfectly tuned strings section.

"Well, I'm not so surprised." Molly shrugged when both men turned to her. "Come on, we're in the spy business. I know we don't do wet work and stuff, but even the way we get information has to get us in trouble sometimes."

"Yeah, maybe. But I haven't heard of anything like this, either." Brady unwrapped his sub but didn't pick it up. "I guess that's one reason they keep us so compartmentalized." He eyed Dix again. "So why did they suspend you?"

Dix shifted in his chair, hooking his elbow over the back of it. "I asked for reassignment."

Brady narrowed his gaze at him, then aimed it at Molly. "For any particular reason?"

Crap. She became extraordinarily interested in her salad.

She shouldn't care if Brady knew she was interested in dating Dix. And honestly, she didn't care. A small part of her felt he deserved it. Well, maybe not so small. But she felt a lot stranger at the possibility that Dix might sense she'd had feelings for Brady.

Past tense, Moll? Uh-huh, right. She could feel the weight of Dix's gaze on her and stuck a cherry tomato in her mouth.

He finally said, "I didn't want to be Molly's handler anymore."

Brady didn't say anything, and she sneaked a peek. He was scowling, but looked like he was trying not to. Brotherly protectiveness? Professional disapproval? Or something else?

"Has she done something to make you not want to work with her?"

Dix gave a little snort. "Just be herself."

The tension around them changed. Molly could sense Dix relaxing and Brady tensing even more. *Get over yourself*, she thought, and stopped hiding in her food.

"Dix, we need to get into SIEGE."

He winced. "Yeah, I thought you'd say that. But I'm suspended, remember?"

"We don't need you to get us in." Brady's voice had gone colder, sending a shiver up Molly's spine. "We just need some direction once we're inside."

Dix looked incredulous. "You don't need me to get you in? How the hell do you think you'll do it without help?"

"We'll worry about that part. I've got it covered." Cold and now hard, too. He'd figured it out.

Molly tried not to feel thrilled that Brady didn't like Dix's interest in her. That *wasn't* why she wanted to go out with Dix.

She wanted to go out with a guy who liked *her,* wanted to be with her, didn't just use her for his—

No. Unfair. Brady hadn't taken anything from her that she hadn't wanted to give. But it was about time she expanded her focus.

"Please, Dix." She laid her hand over his and tried to show promise in her eyes, because she was damned if she was going to set up a date in front of Brady. "Tell us where we can look. Where we're likely to find anything. We promise it won't lead back to you." She hoped she could keep that promise, especially since Brady didn't look all that interested in agreeing to it.

Dix took a deep breath. "All right. Here's what I can tell you."

• • •

"Angle it down this way."

Molly gritted her teeth and shifted the flashlight she was holding. She *hated* being the lovely assistant, standing and following and holding. But Brady was the one with all the skills. He'd gone into the building before regular office hours were over, pretended to check out, and hid inside until most of the staff had left. Then he let Molly in—probably disabled an alarm or two, but she didn't ask—and found the offices they had to search. His lock-picking skills got them inside and into the cabinets in seconds each time. And then she held the flashlight while he dug through the contents. So annoying.

So far, everything had gone smoothly. They'd been up here for only about ten minutes and had searched every office Dix directed them to, avoiding or disabling the fairly routine security measures he'd warned them about. A few minutes ago, she'd expressed disappointment that they hadn't encountered more high-tech deterrents.

"The more high-tech the visible security," Brady had said, "the more you're telegraphing how important the protected space and items are."

"So there's *in*visible high-tech security?" she'd asked, wondering if the elevator they were in was notifying someone right now of their presence, shooting their images over to another office or the director's smartphone or something. "Stuff Dix didn't mention?"

"Yep. He probably doesn't know about it."

"But we're not avoiding or disabling those things."

"Not possible." Brady turned to her. "Besides, I don't care if they know I was here."

The coldness in his voice had chilled her, so she'd stopped asking questions. Now, fifteen minutes later, the likelihood of getting caught was making her antsy again.

"We need to go," she urged him as he dug his picks harder into a hidden cabinet's lock.

"Not yet." He inhaled, held it, and let it out slowly, then plied the picks more delicately. "This file cabinet was behind a panel, and this lock is damned tough. If it's anywhere, it's here."

"It" being God knew what.

"All right. But hurry," she couldn't help adding. She glanced over her shoulder. The hallway stayed dark through the crack they'd left in the office door to avoid getting locked in. Dix had named four administrators who were likely to have the kind of information they sought. This was, of course, the fourth office. None of the first three had yielded squat, and Molly worried that they kept everything on the computer. "Squat" included any other kind of major paper file, not just information on Christopher. They either had a central repository Dix wasn't aware of, or they didn't keep paper at all.

She and Brady definitely didn't have time to try to hack the computers.

A *click* drew her attention back to him. He hissed with victory, and the cabinet door swung open to reveal four file boxes, neatly labeled "ACTIVE PERSONNEL" with an alphabetical range. They both reached for the Fs at the same time. Molly clenched her fist and backed off. Brady flipped through folders and grabbed one. She saw "FITZPATRICK, C" in the beam from her flashlight, then Brady shoved the file inside his jacket and locked everything back up.

"Let's go."

She followed as they ran silently through the building. Moments later, they were in her car, driving normally down the street.

Normally, except for her pounding heart. "I can't believe no one showed up. That was way too easy." Her fingers traced the edge of the fat file she held, but she didn't open it. Brady was driving, which surprised her. She'd have thought he'd want her to drive so he could look through the file.

"I did some things to prevent it," he told her. "Here." He steered abruptly into a gas station and pulled up next to the trash can at the end of a bank of pumps. "Toss the gloves."

Molly rolled down her window and tossed the grocery bag full of wadded-up paper napkins—some of which were wadded around the latex gloves they'd worn—into the can. They were far enough away from the building that no one would search for them here. Even if they did, fingerprints inside the gloves would only prove they'd worn them, not where they'd done so.

"What kinds of things?" she asked as they pulled back out on the street and headed home in the mid-fall dusk. It seemed like it should be midnight, but it was only just before seven.

"Better you don't know, in case we do get caught. You can claim I dragged you along and you don't know anything."

She hated that idea as much as she hated being the lovely assistant, but didn't say so. Her feelings weren't relevant to anything. "Did you see the labels on those boxes?" she asked.

He nodded once, sharply.

Her voice quivered a little, from trying so damned hard to keep the elation out of it. "That's a good sign." Though Chris's file being in with other active personnel didn't have to mean he was alive and still on a mission.

"They could just be slow to remove it," Brady said, echoing

her thoughts.

"I know, but—"

"My hopes are high enough already, Moll. Let's wait until we read it. Okay?"

She sighed. "Yeah, okay. We need a cover story for your mother," she reminded him.

"Yeah. I got nothin'. Any ideas?"

"Of course." She nodded. "There's a superstore up here. We need supplies." Her cover story would keep her up all night, but it would serve a dual purpose—provide a reason she and Brady were gone, and do something nice for the Fitzpatricks. Brady stayed in the car while she shopped. She almost argued, because she didn't want him reading the file without her. She should be there when he saw the truth, whatever it was. He'd need her if the information confirmed Chris's death. And okay, she was eager to know what the file said, and it wasn't fair of him to see it first. Sure, Chris was his brother, but he wouldn't even have the file if Molly hadn't followed her gut.

She pushed the cart faster down the main aisle, toward the crafts section. But what if her gut was wrong? Well, it couldn't be *wrong*, the coffin was empty. *Something* was going on. But what if that something was just covering what Chris had been doing? What if it didn't mean he was alive? She'd worked hard to keep that hope from building, but she'd sensed Brady's mood getting lighter and lighter after their meeting with Dix, and even while they searched the offices. He was going to be crushed if his hopes weren't borne out.

And if they were? If Chris *was* alive? That opened up a hundred other possibilities for heartbreak.

She grimaced and grabbed foam board, markers, glue, and a beginner's scrapbooking kit, then headed for the counter, dragging her thoughts back to Brady and what he was discovering, sitting alone out in her car.

• • •

Brady ignored the file on the passenger seat. Or tried to. The diffuse light from the parking lot's metal halide lamps filtered into the car and made the manila folder glow a little. Enough to call to him. He snatched it and shoved it between the bucket seat and the gearshift. He wasn't looking at it here, in the darkness and out in an open parking lot, when he only had time to skim. They had to get home. He'd probably have to wait until everyone was in bed before he'd have enough privacy to read the file. Plus, it didn't feel right even to glance inside without Molly.

Molly. Dammit.

When they'd met with Dixson, it was obvious the guy was interested in her. Two weeks ago, Brady would have been glad. She was so solitary. But she had a big heart and deserved someone who loved her as much as she would love him back.

There were a few times in college Brady wondered if she felt that way about him, even a little, but she never really acted like it. No jealousy of his girlfriends or hookups or anything. If she was ever going to display feelings, surely it would have been when he went nuts for Jessica. But all she'd ever been was protective.

Then that night in South America had happened. It was all a blur to him—heat and need and raw pain. She hadn't turned clingy or suddenly had expectations, or any of the things women usually did after sex. She hadn't acted like their friendship had changed a bit. And mostly, Brady didn't feel it had. He was glad she was here with them. With him. His family couldn't have coped with this tragedy without her, and since he'd been gone so long, he couldn't have taken over arrangements and stuff nearly as smoothly as she had. So he was grateful.

But gratitude didn't explain the rage that had roared through him when Dixson had looked at her like she was pastry. It didn't explain the awareness that seemed to vibrate between them every time they were alone and standing close to each other. Residual body sense…or something else?

When his mother had warned him off her earlier today, he'd thought it would be easy to heed the warning. Friendships shouldn't be messed with, especially the kind they had. Even though he hadn't seen her much in the last ten years, their relationship was obviously intact. Though maybe fragile now, because of the sex.

His body heated, a wave of lust rushing through him when he thought of sex with Molly. He closed his eyes and remembered her under him, opening to him, crying out and biting him. Dixson suddenly became part of the image. Dixson fucking Molly, Molly crying *his* name.

Brady's hands clenched and his jaw popped from grinding his teeth too hard. *No way. Not in this lifetime.*

The car's back door opened and he jerked alert. Molly tossed a bag and something gigantic and white in the back seat, then climbed in the front.

"What's it say?" she asked.

Brady blinked at her, struggling to get some control. Her scent filled the car, getting his body's attention. "Huh?"

She tapped the file with her fingernails. "The file. What's it say?"

"Oh." He twisted forward and cranked the ignition, hoping the movement hid his confusion. "Nothing. I mean, I don't know. I didn't look."

Molly pulled her seatbelt on and looked relieved. "Thanks for waiting."

"No biggie. What'd you get?"

"Stuff for making a tribute board." As he pulled out of the lot, she elaborated. "When we get home—I mean, to your parents' house—distract your mother while I run the supplies upstairs. But it's okay to be obvious about it. I need to get my hands on photo albums. I want her to know what I'm doing—what *we're* doing, actually, because then you can hole away with me and look at the file while I make the board. For the funeral tomorrow," she added, when he shot her a "WTF are you talking about?" look. "If she thinks we're doing this as a surprise, she'll leave us alone. And we should do it anyway. People will expect it."

Brady shook his head in awe. "You're a genius." And she was. The plan was perfect.

Except for one thing.

He'd be holing up with Molly in her bedroom all night long.

Chapter Nine

Molly escaped upstairs with her supplies, but left the door open so she could hear into the second-floor hall below, where Donna had stopped her son.

"What are you doing with those?" Donna asked.

Brady answered, "I felt like flipping through them. You know."

After a beat, his mother said, "I know. I'm not sure you should be alone, though."

"I'm fine, Mom. Running around a lot. I just want…"

Molly could tell by the way he let his voice trail off that he wanted her to fill in the blank.

"Okay, hon."

She must have hesitated, because Brady said, "What?"

"I'm a little worried about you. You've been so focused on Jessica, and everything else."

Molly pictured Brady quirking his lips in a rueful smile.

"I'm fine, Mom. There's plenty of time to grieve, too."

"I know. It's not that, really. It's more like…you haven't yet accepted that he's dead."

Uh-oh. Brady was good at hiding things, but this was his

mother. *Nobody* was good at hiding things from their mother.

Brady drew in a noisy enough breath that Molly heard it all the way upstairs. "I probably haven't," he cleverly admitted. "Because it would mean admitting all my guilt and stuff. Speaking of which, where's Dad? *Ow!*"

Donna must have smacked him. Molly smiled.

"He's out in the shop, of course. How cliché can you get?"

They moved on to mundane things, and Molly retreated to organize her supplies. A few minutes later, Brady appeared in the doorway.

"We good?"

She nodded from her cross-legged position on one of the beds. "You get the photo albums?"

He dropped them on the bed in front of her, bouncing her neatly arranged tools out of place. She scowled at him, but he wasn't looking. He'd sat on the edge of the other bed, clutching Chris's file.

"You want help with that?" he asked with obvious reluctance.

Molly pulled the albums closer and flipped the top one open. "No, we'd get lost in 'Remember this?' and it'd take all night. I'll work on the tribute board, you read the file to me. Softly, so your mom doesn't hear us," she added, and he grimaced.

"Yeah, that's all we'd need."

Molly raised an eyebrow. "Why?"

Brady finally looked at her. "What?"

"Why is that all we'd need? What's she gonna say?"

He opened his mouth, looked at the albums, and shrugged. "Nothing, I guess. Let's get to work." He shifted to lean against the wall, his legs stretched out over the edge of the bed, and flipped open the file folder with exaggerated casualness.

Molly sat unmoving for a few seconds, thought briefly about efficiency and timing, then dropped the three photos she'd selected so far and launched herself across the room to land next to him. "Okay, I changed my mind. I can't stand it."

Brady flashed a grin at her, an unguarded, happy expression she hadn't seen in so many years. It took her breath away, and since he was inches from her, she had to fight the urge to kiss him, a reward for his happiness.

"What about the tribute crap?" he teased her. "You said you'd work on that."

Molly pinched his bicep, then leaned into his side and looked down at the file. "You'll help me after we look at this."

"Okay." His shoulder slid against hers as he took a preparatory breath. She wrapped her arm around his and threaded their fingers. He grabbed on, holding tight as he slowly turned over the file's cover.

Attached to the left side was a basic personnel sheet and Chris's photo. Her heart caught at the steady, open smile on his face. She scanned the page, noting data they could both recite by heart. Just the basics, nothing revelatory.

The top page on the right side was blue and blank. A cover page, to keep passersby from catching a glimpse of anything sensitive. Brady flipped it back and tucked it under. The next page was a mission sheet, according to the boldface label at the top. Boxes listed the agents involved, handlers, suppliers, carriers. A mission goal had its own box, then parameters, locations, logistics and, on the back—upside down so they didn't have to remove the page or turn the file to read it—details of the mission.

Molly's pounding heart slowed before she'd read more than the date at the top. January, this year.

"So, they must have different files for each year," she guessed. Her fingers tingled as Brady loosened his grip slightly. "Odd that it's in chronological order going forward, instead of in reverse order."

He shrugged, reading the details of the old mission.

"Do you want to skip ahead?" she asked, running her thumb over the edges of the papers. Her nail caught on something harder at the bottom. "If there's anything in here that's going to tell us something, it'll likely be in the back."

"Probably. But no, let's read straight through. Missions sometimes connect, and whatever's going on could go this far back. We'll have a fuller picture if we read it all."

"Okay." She let go of his hand so he could use both to turn pages. "Let's do it, then."

For the better part of two hours, they read. It only took three mission summaries for Molly to suffer a surge of guilt.

"I'm not supposed to be seeing this stuff," she said. "I mean, neither are you, but at least you've been on missions. I'm not supposed to know any of this. Where you guys go, who you deal with, how decisions are made…"

Brady turned his head. "You can be trusted with anything you see or hear. Don't worry about it."

His words warmed her, but didn't ease her discomfort. "The directors probably wouldn't feel that way."

"They won't know."

She knew that wasn't true. Even if by some miracle their break-in at HQ wasn't discovered, if they acted on any information they found, SIEGE would know. And if they found nothing worth acting on, unless they somehow returned the file without anyone ever knowing it was gone, the directors would know she'd seen it. They'd never believe Brady didn't share it with her.

But feeling bad about it was pointless. What was she going to do, stop? Not let Brady tell her what he found out? Hardly.

So she sucked it up, and they read on. Most of the summaries followed a predictable pattern that, she came to realize, meant the mission had gone like clockwork. Information gathering was pretty boring, at least when reduced to its basic details. She couldn't tell what kind of info was gathered in each mission. Some of the wording no doubt indicated what Chris was collecting, but she wasn't knowledgeable enough to decipher it. Brady probably was, but if he decided something was important, he'd tell her.

She fought a yawn and read on.

• • •

After two hours and three months of mission summaries, Brady needed a break. He went downstairs to get them drinks. Molly, thank God, stayed upstairs to work on the photos. He needed a break from her as much as from the files. Being so near her for so long was driving him nuts.

His socks whispered against the floorboards in the second-floor hallway. He heard murmuring behind his parents' door and checked his watch. Ten-thirty. Not that late, but tomorrow was going to be a hellacious day. The stairs creaked as he descended, the ground floor holding an empty stillness. There was a small light on in the living room, plus the one over the stove in the kitchen, but when he peered down the back hall, he couldn't see light through the crack under Jessica's door.

Good. He wasn't up to supporting her right now. He decided to make Molly a cup of tea and swished the kettle to check the water level before turning on the burner. She'd asked for juice, but heating the water gave him a few minutes alone.

God. He leaned against the island and pinched the bridge of his nose, squeezing his burning eyes. His head swam, but not from the tedium of report-speak or the lack of helpful information in those reports. It swam from soaking in the heat of Molly's body, pressed against his side from shoulder to ankle, her breast brushing his forearm every time she shifted to see the file at a different angle.

He'd tried holding it closer to her, having her hold it, and reading to her, but she was still always too close. Without being close enough. Her natural scent had strengthened as their bodies warmed so that he couldn't inhale a clean breath—and didn't really want to. Over the last two hours, she'd licked her lips six times, and each time it called his attention to her mouth. He had never paid any attention to it before. Even in South

America, he'd been in such a haze of pain and need, he barely remembered kissing her.

Now, just the word was enough to make him harden. Not a full-blown woody, but more than passing interest.

He didn't know what it meant. Proximity? Basic, unfulfilled need? Confusion because of everything that was happening? He couldn't figure it out until this stuff with Chris was settled. And that meant ignoring whatever pull Molly had on him.

The water in the kettle made that surging noise as it heated, pulling his thoughts back out of the attic. He folded his arms and focused. Chris's missions had come across straightforward enough. There was a short string of them in early spring that was connected, but after that, he'd been all over the place. And already in May, he'd increased the number and length of the missions he took on. A week, instead of two or three days.

Brady's mother had always updated him on family stuff, too, and from what he could remember, Chris traveled a lot before that, but was never gone very long. So what had changed? The baby? No, that was too early. But maybe if they were planning for one… It still made no sense. He'd think Chris would try to stay home more. It wasn't like they got paid by the mission. Okay, some generated extra hazard pay, but not the ones Chris had loaded up on last spring.

The kettle began to whistle, and Brady grabbed it before it screamed, pouring water over some icky-smelling herbal teabag.

"Who's that for?"

He jumped. Water splashed onto his left hand and he cursed, shaking it off. He glared at his father. "Molly. She's making this"—he waved his hand up and down—"thing. Photo thing. Tribute. For tomorrow." He finished pouring, set the kettle down, and grabbed a paper towel to wipe up the mess. The stinging in his hand, he ignored.

"That's nice of you, to bring her tea. She likes it with honey." His father leaned casually on the doorjamb, hands in his pockets.

Brady glowered. "I know how she likes it." He snatched the honey pot from its spot on the counter. "You have something to say." It wasn't a question. He recognized his father's body language.

Amusement flashed over his father's face. "Right to the point? No small talk, random conversation, crap like that?"

"Yeah, 'cause we're so good at that," Brady muttered. "You always have something to say."

His father nodded, then pushed away from the wall. "Come sit for a minute." But he didn't walk to the breakfast nook. As Brady did as he'd been told, Rick got two mugs out of the cupboard, inserted coffee pods in the fancy coffee maker, and hit the button to brew. He didn't say anything until the coffee was done.

When he set one mug in front of Brady and sat across from him, Brady said—sullenly, but he didn't care—"I was going to have soda."

His father ignored that. "How are you holding up, son?"

Brady shrugged and wrapped a hand around the hot mug. "How do you expect?"

"I expect you're probably struggling with a lot of stuff."

He grimaced impatiently. "I had this conversation with Mom already."

"I doubt it." His father drank, implacable. "Your brother died before you could reconcile with him, his widow is nearly incapacitated and playing on all your old feelings, the family is relying on you to take care of everything, you're falling for your best friend, and you don't know where Chris's body is."

As his father talked, Brady endured a needle to the heart, a pang of old longing, a rush of resentment that had him opening his mouth to protest, then a bigger rush of shock that left it hanging open. He didn't know what the hell to say first. Not even first—at all. His mind had gone horrifyingly blank. This was not how he'd been trained to deal with surprises.

"I'm not falling in love," came out of his mouth. He snapped it shut before it could say anything else stupid.

His father chuckled and drank more coffee. Brady mirrored him, because what the heck else was he going to do? *Stay silent. Wait for the other person to fill it. Don't respond to accusations—that gives them credence.* He recited the frigging training manual to himself, but his father just sat there, drinking coffee, waiting.

Oddly, Brady calmed instead of panicked. He sat back and watched his father watching him. As he did, an awful suspicion began worming its way into his head.

Rick chuckled again. "You're good. Even with that slip. So you want to talk about Molly first, huh?"

"I don't want to talk about anything, but you seem to. So what's on your mind, Dad?" He clenched his jaw and told himself to shut the hell up.

"Whatever's on yours. Something's got you all tangled up." His father's dark eyes held warm sympathy.

Brady swallowed and shook his head a little. His mother thought he'd done enough damage with Molly, shutting her out along with everyone else. He knew that would be well within her capacity to forgive—if he hadn't used her so heinously when he first heard about Chris. Yeah, she'd blown it off, and he had no doubt she'd understood, but the more time he spent with her, and the more he thought about what they'd done and why, the more he regretted it. What if they'd done it without the haze of grief and agony? What if he'd made love to her, instead of trying to lose himself in her?

He wasn't so sure he deserved forgiveness.

"So where've you been hiding yourself all week?" he asked his father, who gave a knowing look at his deliberate change of subject.

"I've been around. You know your mother. The more of us feeding her flitting, the worse it gets. I just stay out of her way."

"Mom doesn't flit."

His father snorted. "You haven't been paying attention. Then again, you haven't been here to notice much the last couple of days."

He said it with enough care that Brady knew he wasn't making idle conversation. Not that his father ever made idle conversation. There was a purpose to every action and every word.

His suspicion sharpened. "I've been helping Molly with the list Mom heaped on her."

"*Hmm.* What did we need in New Rochelle?"

Brady's heart started to pound, his suspicion growing by the second. "New Rochelle?"

His father darted him a sardonic look, but when he dropped it, the grief and fatigue he'd been hiding all week was revealed. "I know what's in New Rochelle, son. I know what you and Molly were probably doing there. And I'd like to know what you found out."

• • •

Brady stood outside the door to Molly's bedroom and nudged it open a couple of inches before going in. As he'd expected, she was cross-legged on the first bed again, sorting through pictures and grumbling to herself. She obviously didn't see him standing there.

"Doesn't take half an hour to pour juice." She glowered at a picture of Chris and Jess at their wedding before tossing it onto the growing stack on the floor. "Jessica probably stopped him."

Brady couldn't stop a surge of pleasure. She was jealous! The jumbled mess in his heart that he'd been trying to untangle smoothed out a little. If she had feelings for him beyond friendship…

Now is not the time, he told himself, thinking of where he'd left things with his father. The older man had only revealed enough for Brady to know he'd been a part of SIEGE at one time. He'd pressed Brady for all the information he and Molly had gathered so far and then backed off, leaving this mission to his son.

He'd left it with just enough urgency that Brady knew he had to get to the bottom of Chris's death, fake or real, before he could do anything to resolve his own issues.

"Not Jess. My dad." Molly's head jerked up and he gave her a wry look. "Not very alert, are you?"

She unfolded her legs and moved back over to the other bed, settling into her original position. "You sneak like a thief, that's all," she accused. "What took so long?"

"I told you. Dad." Brady joined her on the bed and swapped her tea for the file. "He finally came out of hiding, and I couldn't very well cut him short when he wanted to talk."

"Is he okay?" The question was sincere, not tossed off because it was expected, and Brady loved her for it. She could have pushed them to dive back into the file.

"As okay as any of us. He suspects something."

"What, we haven't covered our tracks well enough?" She smiled, and Brady's gaze caught on her smooth, pink lips. Again. They were close enough to lean over and—

He cleared his throat. "Yeah, apparently not." He dragged his gaze across the room to the pile of photos next to her bed. "He wanted to know where we got off to all the time, you and me, and told me to make up my mind before I made a mistake."

Molly's arm tensed against his. She seemed to realize he could feel it and moved away a little. "Make up your mind? About what?"

Brady shook his head. He didn't want to go there, but couldn't seem to keep himself from inching in that direction. Part of him wanted to lay it all out for her. Molly had always helped him see things more clearly. But he eyed the thick file they were only halfway through, and the pile of photos awaiting Molly's artistry, and knew it would have to wait.

"Nothing. Let's get through this and see what's going on."

After another hour and a half of reading, Molly reluctantly moved to the other bed to work on the tribute board. Brady's entire body relaxed when she did, and he hoped she didn't notice. Sitting on the floor, he leaned against the bed next to her and read the mission statements, pausing as they got near the end.

"You notice something about these?" he asked her.

"Yeah, they're not so clockwork." She snipped at the edges of some frilly-looking border paper. "I can't interpret the spy-code, but it looks like he encountered trouble during each of the last three."

"Yeah." Brady let his eyes unfocus and imagined the cases. "Communication problems, so meets didn't go as planned, and at least twice the source backed out. He had to recover the info himself." As opposed to receiving it from someone willing to hand it over.

"And what was that about an extraction?"

Brady smiled and opened his eyes. "You're picking up the lingo."

"Yeah, well, after this many reports, I should." Some scraps of colored paper fell to the floor next to him. He wasn't looking, but he still knew that she'd set down the scissors and started glue-sticking stuff onto the board. The air moved when she did. Warmed when those movements brought her arm closer to his head. Caused the faintest of electric traces across his skin.

"Hey." Molly nudged him with her elbow. "You there?"

"Barely." Brady pinched the inside corners of his eyes, pretending he'd been distracted by blurred vision rather than her presence. It wasn't even like a lust thing. He was just super-aware of her, in a way he never had been before.

"Right. The extraction. He was supposed to get a pickup from a remote exchange and the driver never showed. He had to steal a vehicle."

Molly shifted to unfold her legs. One dangled over the side of the bed next to him. It was smooth and glossy, her soft yoga pants or whatever they were riding up to her knee. She must have shaved recently. Without thinking about it, Brady raised his hand to run his palm over her calf. Yep, smooth. A few seconds later he registered how stiff the muscle was under his hand, and that Molly wasn't breathing.

Crap.

He dropped his hand and cleared his throat. "So, uh, how's the—thing—coming?"

"I'm almost done." Her voice was low, almost husky, and desire trickled through him. "How many more missions?"

"Just this packet at the back." Brady set the file on the floor and leaned forward to straighten the fasteners and remove all the pages on top of the plastic sleeve on the bottom. The move pulled him away from Molly, but she drew her leg back up on the bed anyway. He heard rustling and a scrape, and the bed creaked. When he peered over his shoulder, he saw she'd leaned the finished board against the wall and climbed off the foot of the bed. Avoiding him, obviously.

He sat up and turned to study the board. She'd made a timeline of Chris's life, pictures of him as a baby, then a child, then older, mostly with his family, some with friends. The usual milestones were there, like graduation and his wedding and the day his Little League team won a tournament. Each image thickened Brady's throat until the lump burned and made his eyes water. He could feel Molly watching him and tried not to blink.

"What do you think?" she asked, her voice still not normal.

"It's...uh...it's perfect." He had to swipe his sleeve across his eyes. "You did a great job." His own voice came out squeezed. The lump didn't diminish, even when he swallowed. He focused on the decorations she'd glued on the board. The background was some kind of navy blue plaid or something, and silver and black wavy borders framed each picture. She'd somehow gotten hold of objects that had been important to Chris, and attached those between photos.

"How did you get these?" Brady fingered a track ribbon and pointed to the boutonniere from the wedding.

"Your mom was looking through a box of memorabilia the other day. I told her I'd put it away for her and brought it up here instead."

"So you planned this board all along."

She shrugged. "If I had time."

Brady's eyes filled again as he gazed at her, overwhelmed with gratitude. "Molly, you're—" His throat closed, and he couldn't get another word out.

Immediately, she came around the foot of the bed and put her arms around him. "I'm sorry, Brady," she whispered, clearly trying to comfort him. But grief wasn't what he was feeling now. Gratitude wasn't even the right word. It went deeper than that. He tightened his arms around her back, absorbing the hug, and tilted his head down to inhale her. As soon as skin met skin, heat flared. It was only his cheek to her temple, but the softness reminded him of her calf under his hand, and suddenly he was aware of the press of her breasts, the rest of her body, soft but strong and, at the moment, relaxed fully against him.

He lowered his head more to angle his face into her neck. He slid his hands up her back to her shoulders, tugging her closer. She sighed when his mouth met her neck.

"Molly," he murmured, aching. "I need—" He didn't know how to say it, wasn't even sure what he felt.

She pulled back enough to cup his face in her hands. Her touch was gentle, sweet, and he closed his eyes, turning in to one palm.

"Brady." She waited for him to open his eyes. "Whatever you need, I'll give you."

But her voice cracked, and as steady as her gaze was, he saw the pain beneath it. She thought he needed comfort, just like the first time he'd lost himself in her, trying to bury his agony.

She was wrong. He wouldn't use her again, nor let her think

that was what he was doing. He released her, but kept his hands on her hips so she wouldn't move away. "Molly, I don't want—"

"Okay!" She cut him off and pulled away, avoiding his eyes and bending to pick up the plastic sleeve of papers.

"No, listen. I mean—"

But she'd already lifted the flap and pulled out the pages, her eyes going wide and her mouth dropping open slightly. "Oh, my God."

"What is it?" he asked.

She slid the pages out further and turned them to face him, horror haunting her expression. Icy cold doused whatever frustration and need had been burning in him when he saw the red letters stamped across the page.

CANCELED.

Chapter Ten

Molly had never felt a change in atmosphere as sudden and terrifying as the one just now. The dim light in the attic bedroom was no longer cozy, but sinister. Hope had winked out of existence, the block letters spelling out the possibility, not that Chris was alive, but that he'd been murdered.

Brady's legs had given out and he'd dropped onto the side of her bed. The disorientation of going from "about to be kissed" to "unspeakably shocked" left her dizzy. But she had to overcome it. Had to, once again, be strong.

And to start thinking logically. She stared at the pages in front of her. They weren't the usual mission report. "Brady, wait." She flipped through the half-dozen sheets of paper, skimming, catching phrases and sections on each. "This isn't a completed mission."

"No." He sounded empty, distant. "He didn't complete it."

"No, I mean, this isn't a final report. Wouldn't a final report be in here by now? What if—" She swallowed. "What if 'canceled' means the mission? Not Chris?"

Brady stared blankly up at her. Then understanding slid into his expression. His eyes focused again, heating up. He stood. "Maybe. I never had a canceled mission."

"So you wouldn't know what the report would look like."

"No." A tiny spark of hope flared in his expression.

"Okay." She inhaled deeply and took his hand. "Come here. Sit. Let's look at this." As she backed to the other bed, drawing him with her, his hand tightened on hers until her bones shifted. They sat, and she set the file aside to concentrate on the special sleeve she'd taken the papers from. It was opaque and green. The white label on the front had no words, only the notation "#476-1B" in stark black type.

"Do you know what this means?" She showed Brady. He took it from her, flipped to the blank other side, then back again. "No. It's not a mission number. Those are all six digits."

"Right. Data's not designated this way, either. That's by date and an agency code." She felt him look at her and shrugged. "I never figured out which agencies were which codes."

"I'm sure SIEGE would be happy to hear that."

"*Pfft*. I can't be the only conduit paying attention." She didn't pick up the papers right away. Brady's tone was clearer, and he looked less shell-shocked. She wanted to give him a little more time before they started reading and all the blood drained out of his head again. "So what do you think the number refers to?" she asked him, but he shook his head.

"No idea." He held out his hand for the papers. She reluctantly handed them to him, and they started reading together. The top of the first page was similar to the mission reports, with basic parameters in a code she couldn't decipher. But Brady knew enough to make reasonable guesses. He pointed to the space on the form for location.

"This is strange."

"So far, everything is."

"He went to Canada."

She shrugged. "So? Don't you guys go everywhere?"

"Yeah, but we spend a lot more time in unstable countries." He studied the papers, his brows dipping. "*I've* never gone to

Canada."

"Maybe he was meeting someone who'd fled one of those unstable countries?"

"Maybe. That would have a low-risk expectation."

She didn't remark on the obvious, that if this was Christopher's last mission, it had been anything but low risk. True accidents could happen anywhere, of course, but his missing body alone told them that wasn't the case here.

"When did he go? Does it say?" She hated that she couldn't figure out the coded language. It was English, and some of it she'd figured out over the fifty-plus reports they'd read, but not enough to decipher this one.

"The date of departure is three days before his reported death."

"So this has to be where he was when he died. Took them a long time to send his body down from Canada," she mused.

"His non-body," Brady corrected, but absently. He frowned harder at the last page. "If I'm reading this right, they determined he'd become a threat to the organization and decided to terminate him."

Iciness radiated from Molly's core. "In which sense of the word?" she nearly whispered.

Brady slid the papers back into their sleeve, his movements stiff. "I can't tell. They didn't fire him, because the facilitators are acting like he was a highly regarded member of the company."

"But they could have planned to do it after this mission, and he died first." She took the sleeve and slid it over the fasteners in the file, adding all the pages on top of it. She wasn't sure why. Were they going to return everything? Brady took the file from her and shoved it under the mattress, shrugging when she raised her eyebrows. Not the best hiding place…but she supposed that depended on who they were hiding it from.

"If they meant terminate permanently," Brady said in a low, hard voice, "then they might have carried it out."

"We have to investigate." She knelt on the floor and took

Brady's hand. "We need to find out what really happened. And where he is. What I don't get is, if they killed him, why was the coffin empty?"

Brady nodded, but the nascent hope was gone, replaced again by bleakness. "I'll go to Canada."

"*We'll* go to Canada." She squeezed his hand. "But first, we have a funeral to get through."

· · ·

Brady stayed in Molly's room overnight. They slept on separate beds, a few feet from each other. Molly felt a little like they were back in college, when they'd been studying late or just hanging out, and crashed in the same room. Or the holidays, when she'd stayed here and shared Brady's room, but 100 percent platonically. Looking back, she had to wonder why Rick and Donna had allowed it so easily. Why they'd believed there was no possibility of anything inappropriate.

Molly couldn't get to sleep right away, as exhausted as she was. She could tell when Brady finally relaxed and dozed off, though he slept silently. She wondered if SIEGE and other spy agencies required surgery for deviated septa, or didn't hire agents with sleep apnea. Her mind wandered while her body slowly relaxed, her breathing coming into rhythm with Brady's. Other things would hamper being a spy. Like flatulence. That would attract attention from the people around you. One of the musicians she toured with always sneezed at least seven times. That drew attention, too. Did these kinds of things come up during recruitment? Would someone be fired or pulled out of the field if the condition came to light? A handler or facilitator could sneeze. But she got the impression that facilitators had a lot of field experience and only moved up when they reached a certain age…or stage of life.

Her eyes popped open and she was suddenly wide awake. What if *that* had been what was going on? If facilitators had to log a certain amount of time in the field before being considered for promotion out of the field, maybe Chris was increasing his mission time lately because he wanted to come inside. He didn't know about the baby back in the spring, but they had been planning by then.

Maybe. But even if she was right, it didn't connect to or jibe with the last mission in Canada. Could that have been training instead? She almost pulled out the file to check, but she wouldn't have been able to decipher it any better now than she could before. Brady probably didn't know that code, either, so she didn't give in to the urge to wake him.

But tomorrow, they should definitely talk to Dix.

• • •

A limo picked up the family at nine the next morning. Everyone was subdued, and not just in manner. They all wore dark colors—Jessica and Brady in severe black suits, Brady's mother a midnight blue dress, his father a charcoal suit. Molly wore the black, black-tiered skirt she'd been wearing when Jessica called her with the news, and paired it with a light gray sweater that did nothing to relieve the somberness. All of them, Molly noticed, were pale, even ashen. All thoughts of missions and hope and cancellation took a back seat to raw grief.

Molly had wanted to drive her own car, but Jessica had clung to her and insisted they all go together. Her entire body was trembling, the movements so fine Molly wouldn't have known if the widow hadn't been holding onto her. The skin of Jess's face was taut across her jaw and cheekbones. She'd lost weight this week, and only tension seemed to hold her together.

After an endless ride that regardless ended much too soon, the limo turned into the parking lot of the funeral home. They were slightly early, so the family could be in place in a receiving line before others arrived. As the Fitzpatricks gathered at the front of the viewing room, Molly spoke with the funeral director. He confirmed the program, explained a small problem with the flowers and how he'd adjusted for it, and said nothing to indicate, by words or demeanor, that he knew the casket didn't contain a body.

His assistant got an easel for Molly to set the tribute board on, and Donna broke down as soon as she saw it. Jessica only stared at it vacantly for a moment before turning away. Molly felt a pang of hurt feelings, but then she wondered what the action had meant. Was Jessica simply numb after so many days of pain? Or did it truly mean nothing to her?

When the first group of people appeared at the doorway, pausing to sign the register, the director lined up the Fitzpatricks near the casket and tribute board. Molly started to fade to the back of the room, but Donna caught her, putting a death grip on her hand.

"Oh, no, you're up here with us, dear."

"It's family only," Molly murmured and tried to pull away, but Donna's glare made her relent.

"You are as much family as any of us, and more than some," she hissed, and Molly had to bite her lips to keep from smiling as she let Donna drag her into the line.

She supposed the normal order would be widow first, then the parents, then brother, then the de facto sibling. But Jessica was still so weak, she ended up bracketed by Brady and Molly, with Donna and Rick starting the line. Molly tried to get Jess a chair, but she refused it, stiffening her spine and insisting she had to be strong for the baby's sake.

"The baby needs you to take care of yourself," Molly murmured as the first mourners approached. "If you pass out or crumple, how is that good for the baby?"

"I won't." Jess lifted her chin and accepted the hand of a Fitzpatrick cousin, the first of many.

Molly had to give Jessica credit. The more people offered their condolences, the more stable she seemed, as if drawing energy from their concern and sympathy. And the people kept coming. The viewing was scheduled for an hour, but after an hour and a half, family and friends were still lined up to speak to the immediate family and offer silent words casket-side. Molly stepped away to ask the director if it was a problem, but he assured her there was plenty of time between events and they could allow the line to run its course.

She was surprised at how many of the people she knew. There were Fitzpatrick cousins, Donna's parents and siblings and their families, even friends of Chris's who'd come long distances, after they or their parents had read the obituary in the old hometown newspaper. None seemed surprised or disapproving that she was in the receiving line. They offered her condolences in the same tone, and hugs of the same strength, as they'd offered each Fitzpatrick.

As Jessica seemed stronger, though, Brady seemed to flag. His expression grew more stoic, more drawn, with each hug and shaken hand. A couple of people even mentioned—very awkwardly—the distance between the brothers over the last decade. He said less and less to each person, and by the end, Molly was afraid he was the one who was going to collapse.

When the director sat them in the front row and the pastor of the Fitzpatricks' church approached the podium, Brady abruptly stood and escaped through the side door. Donna caught Molly's eye and jerked her head in that direction. Without worrying about impropriety, Molly followed him out.

He sat on an old-fashioned love seat in the anteroom outside the rest rooms, leaning forward, his head braced in his hands. She sat next to him and rubbed his back, not saying anything.

After a moment, the tension in his shoulders started to loosen. He didn't move, but he did talk. "I should never have agreed to give the eulogy." It came out muffled by his hands held over his face.

"Why not?" Molly asked, but she knew the answer.

"I don't have a right. You heard people." He straightened, rubbed his face, and dropped back against the love seat. "I disappeared for too long. I wasn't a brother to him. I punished him for something he had nothing to do with."

"Bullshit."

Brady stared at her, semi-astonished. "What?"

"I call bullshit. When did you see him last?"

He frowned. "I don't know. August, maybe? We were in DC at the same time."

"And how many times did you talk to him since then?"

"I don't know," he repeated more impatiently. "A few."

"So you didn't disappear. You were in touch, maybe even more than many families are." She rested her hand on his knee. "You can't let people who know nothing make you feel this way. Their opinions don't matter. Not about this."

He folded his hand around hers. His skin was hot and dry, and she had a split second of longing to be able to touch him like this all the time. Then he blew out a breath and stood, tugging her up and folding her into a hug.

"Thanks, Moll. You always make everything right." He kissed her forehead and went through the doorway just as the pastor introduced him for the eulogy.

Not everything. She stood out of sight and watched him stride to the podium. The longing flared again, stronger and longer than a moment ago. She had suppressed it forever, but dammit, she was tired of doing that. She wanted to comfort Brady as more than just his best friend. More than the person who shored him up and sent him on his way. His mother did that. Molly wanted to be the one he came back to.

"Christopher Fitzpatrick was an extraordinary human being," Brady started, and Molly focused on his words instead of his presence. "Everyone says that, at a funeral. And of course, it's always true, even if the guy was a bastard." Brady smiled wanly, which allowed those gathered to chuckle. His body, which he'd been holding stiffly, slowly returned to familiar, fluid lines as he shifted his feet in his shiny dress shoes. His weight settled equally on both feet, his back straight but relaxed. His hands, though, clutched the sides of the podium, and his jaw twitched as he looked down, as if at notes. But there were none. He was doing this all from memory, unrehearsed.

"But Christopher truly was extraordinary. Most of you could list what made my brother special." He nodded at a group sitting halfway back on his left. "His high school baseball team rode his glove to three championships." Then at someone in the center section. "His teachers praised his work ethic and dedication to good grades." Brady smiled, and the softness that entered his eyes told Molly he was looking at Jessica. "And his wife—well, Jessica married him because he was sweet, and doting, and loved his family. *Then* she found out about all the stuff that made him normal." More laughter, and Molly swallowed hard, her throat already burning with tears.

"But Chris was never more extraordinary than he was as my brother."

She realized Brady hadn't mentioned Chris's job. Come to think of it, no one had come through the receiving line who'd said they had worked with Chris. Wouldn't SIEGE have sent people? If not those who'd actually worked with him, like his handler or supervisor, at least some facilitators or even a conduit or two to fake it. With all the time Chris had spent at work, it looked very odd that no one had come to pay tribute.

Brady was telling a story about the baseball team, when as a prank Chris had sabotaged Brady's glove during tryouts. While he spoke, Molly tried to figure out a way to search the crowd without being noticed. She couldn't move across the doorway, and that would only allow her to see half the seats, anyway. Behind the casket, the walls were angled in three parts, instead of one flat wall, presumably to frame the display. The far wall had a small, high window with a heavy velvet drape on the other side of it.

As Brady transitioned to a more heartwarming story about Chris helping him with a bully, Molly headed down the hall. It got darker the further she walked, obviously meant to discourage guests from going that way. The hall had rooms off it to the left, but Molly ignored them and continued to the end, where the shadows were deep enough to make her squint. The wall in front of her had a heavy, floor-length drape hiding a window to the outside. She pulled the drape away, letting in a flare of daylight that allowed her to see better. She spotted a door to her right that hopefully led to the room with that little window overlooking the casket. She gingerly tested the handle. It turned easily and silently, so she opened the door and slipped inside. The room had no lights, no unbarred windows, and she couldn't see a thing. But she could hear Brady's voice on the other side of the wall, muffled though amplified by the microphone.

She stood still, letting her eyes adjust to the dimness. Slowly, shapes became detectable. A sofa, a small desk. And a glow of light seeping around a curtain on the wall. She went to it and carefully ran her fingers down the soft, old fabric, feeling for a center seam. She didn't find one. She'd have to peek in from the side.

She tweaked the drape enough to see half the gathered people, a sea of black and navy and gray. Jessica's head was bowed, her shoulders shaking, and Donna and Rick each had an arm around her. Most of the faces were pointed toward Brady. Molly studied the ones she didn't know. Some she recognized after scrutiny, usually as old friends, looking a decade older than when she last saw them. Others she remembered from the receiving line and dismissed as not being coworkers.

In the very back of the room, in the last two rows, sat half a dozen strangers with ramrod spines and stoic faces. Their expressions and manner of dress, and the way they held themselves were familiar, though. They might be facilitators or administration from SIEGE. She studied their faces. She might have seen that one guy in the lobby when she was in New Rochelle. She hadn't paid much attention to anyone walking through. With a tiny gasp, she recognized the supplier who'd retrieved Brady's pistol in South America. And there, on the end, was Ramona Aldus, the facilitator who'd assured her everything was aboveboard, with the exception of Chris being dead. She looked different. Instead of the elegant ponytail, her hair had been scraped back into a tight bun that altered her features slightly. The glasses were bigger, less stylish. She raised a hand to scratch her cheek, and Molly saw that her nails were still bright red.

She moved to the right side of the curtain, careful not to brush against it and make it wiggle. The left side of the gathered crowd was much like the right, only without the rod-spined group.

Brady finished his eulogy and stepped around the podium, his back blocking Molly's view. She needed to get back out there. But as Brady crossed to his seat and cleared her range of vision, her gaze landed on a figure out in the reception area. The figure was lurking, obviously to see without being seen, and just as clearly trying to disguise himself, with a hood up and sunglasses on, hands shoved deep in coat pockets.

Molly dropped the curtain and dashed toward the door. A stupid move, given the complete lack of light. Her toe caught and she flew forward, landing hard on her stomach, her hands scraping across a rough carpet. She lay for two precious seconds, lungs empty, and hoped no one had heard the fall. She managed to scramble to her feet and get to the door without hitting anything else. Then a mad dash up the empty hallway, her feet thumping against wooden floorboards under worn Persian rugs. She flashed past the doorway to the main room too fast to see anyone's reaction, but seconds later, footfalls came up behind her. She had no doubt whose they were.

Her hand caught the molding to swing her around the archway into the lobby. The hooded guy was nowhere in sight. She kept going, turning the front door handle as she shoved through and stumbled out onto the front walkway.

He was gone.

"Dammit!"

"What the hell?" Brady landed next to her, his tie askew, and looked up and down the street. "Who were you chasing?"

"I don't know." *Damn*. She was too out of breath for that short of a dash. Maybe because of getting the wind knocked out of her when she tripped. Or maybe because she'd gone a week without running or working out. She shoved her hands against the stitch in her side and sucked in a bigger breath.

"Why were you chasing someone in the first place? And where were you? You missed the eulogy."

"No, I heard it. You did a good job." She scanned up and down the street again and crouched a little to see into the driver's side of a passing car. Little old lady. Not the lurker. She quickly explained what she'd seen, finishing as Rick came striding out and joined them.

"What in blazes is going on? I would have expected you two to act like that fifteen years ago, but not now. Not here." He scowled fiercely at Molly, then at Brady, before his expression cleared. "All right, that's done. Tell your mother I ripped you a new one," he said to Brady. "And now, tell *me* what's really going on." He waited while Molly and Brady exchanged a silent look, but not long enough for the look to be interpreted.

"Was Christopher murdered?" Rick asked tightly.

Molly jolted. Her heart slammed twice before settling into a faster-than-normal rhythm.

Before she could recover, Brady answered honestly. "We don't know. Something's wrong, but we haven't gotten any answers yet."

Rick kept his gaze steady on his son. "But you've been trying to find out."

"Of course."

"And it has something to do with SIEGE."

The shock she'd felt a moment ago was static electricity compared to the lightning bolt created by Rick's statement. But then an overwhelming sense of, "Oh, yeah. Of course" dissipated it. Chris, Brady, why not Rick, too? In fact, Dix had mentioned being a legacy. Maybe SIEGE was all about family ties.

Brady hadn't batted an eyelash. She'd already seen that his spy skills weren't strong enough to hide personal shock. After a few seconds, it became clear Brady wasn't going to call his father on the revelation. How long had he known?

She remembered that he'd been trapped by his father the night before. His mood had been strange when he brought her tea. He must have found out just last night. Why hadn't he told her?

Molly turned to Rick and demanded, "How do you know about SIEGE?"

Rick's face was expressionless, but his eyes twinkled. "How do *you* know about SIEGE?"

She felt a smirk tug at the corner of her mouth. "I don't."

"Exactly." Rick sobered and waved a hand. "We'll discuss this later. But now tell me why you ran out of there like bats out of hell."

She hesitated, but he was right. This was much too public a place to demand to know if *he* had been a frigging spy, too. Maybe still was. "I saw someone," she stated evenly. "Lurking back here in the foyer. It looked suspicious."

"Could you tell who it was?" Brady asked. "Was it—" He couldn't finish the question. Molly didn't know if it was emotion or discretion he swallowed back, but she knew he was asking if it could have been Chris.

"No. Too short, too squirrely. I don't know, maybe it was just some kid looking for drugs or something." As unlikely as that seemed. Father and son seemed to agree, both shaking their heads.

"Too coincidental," Brady said.

"Coincidences happen," she countered. "But it was still odd. Especially the way he left. He didn't know anyone had spotted him."

"He probably heard your feet pounding down the hall."

Rick scowled at her. "Must be a conduit," he grumbled, but before Molly could respond in affront, Donna hurried outside to them. Her face was white, her mouth pinched, the lines in her forehead etched deeper than they'd been even this week.

"What the *hell* are you all doing?" She didn't wait for an answer. "Get your asses in there." Her laser-strong gaze zeroed in on her son. "This is the hardest day of my life, and you, young man, are not making it any easier." She whipped around and stormed back through the door.

"Crap." Brady closed his eyes and swiped a hand over his face. "Why didn't she just punch me in the damn gut?"

Molly rubbed his back. He wrapped his arm around her shoulders, and they followed his father back into the building.

Once they got inside, though, Rick pulled her away from Brady and led her over to a corner of the wide lobby. "Did you see the person leave? The one you were chasing."

She shook her head. "I saw him up here, but by the time I got down the hall, he was gone."

"So he could still be in the building."

She grimaced, feeling stupid. "Yeah. Or he could have been and gone out another exit by now. Or—" She slipped past a few people who were coming out of the viewing room and stepped to one side of the door, where she could see the entire room and both exits. With people milling around, those who were going to the cemetery standing in groups, those who weren't inching toward the exit, it would have been easy for the hooded person to blend in unseen. But there was no sign of him.

Molly's cell phone buzzed in the pocket of her skirt, just as she caught a glimpse of movement behind the casket. She ignored the phone and started moving in that direction. The prevailing flow of foot traffic was against her. She tried to avoid sharp cuts or obvious dodges, which meant staying close to the wall and making slow progress. Through a gap between black suits, she could see a shape like a pointed hood jutting above the far side of the casket, at about the spot where the latch was.

Her phone buzzed again. A natural need to answer warred with the urgency of catching the Hoodie and finding out what he had to do with Christopher. The phone only stopped buzzing for a few seconds before it started up again. But she was so close now…

With a lunge, she came around the side of the casket and caught the arm of the person kneeling there, startling him so much he fell back onto one elbow. The hood slid off bright blond hair, the sunglasses knocked askew and no longer hiding eyes. It was a girl. A very *young* girl.

"Who are you?" Molly demanded, more confused than anything else.

The girl scrambled to her feet, but Brady appeared on the other side of the coffin, blocking her exit. She spun wildly, searching for a way past them both, but she was trapped.

"Please! Let me go! I wasn't hurting anything, I promise." The girl, who looked about fourteen, half-hid behind a flower display, as though she didn't want anyone in the departing crowd to see her.

"Who are you?" Molly asked her again, keeping her voice low. She doubted the girl had any connection to Chris's death, but she'd been acting so suspiciously it demanded an explanation.

"I can't tell you." The girl's voice had gone high and scratchy. "Please, just let me go."

"What's your name? Your first name," Brady amended, moving closer to her. When his body blocked her from a view of the room, she seemed to relax a little.

What the hell was going on?

"Shae," the girl offered, possibly thinking if she cooperated a little, they'd let her go more quickly. She glanced around nervously.

"Do you know the man this funeral is for?"

Shae looked up into Brady's face for the first time. Her fair complexion went completely white, and Molly eased to her side, worried she was about to pass out.

"I...um... No. I mean, yes. I mean— No, I don't know anyone here."

Well, that clarified things. Molly's phone buzzed again. Frustrated, she pulled it out and checked the display. Dixson. *Crap*.

"Hello?"

"What the hell, Byrnes, I've been calling you nonstop. Where the hell are you?"

Sudden cold anger made her tone arctic. "I'm at Christopher's funeral."

Silence. Then a soft curse. "I'm sorry, I forgot the time." His remorse, however, was fleeting. "You and Brady need to meet me at Westchester County Airport right now."

"Airport?" Molly looked around. The Fitzpatricks were talking to the driver of the car that had taken them to the funeral. They were almost ready to go to the cemetery. Jessica sat forlornly in a chair next to them, dabbing at her eyes and nose with a handkerchief. "Why?"

"I have information, and you and Brady have to leave immediately to act on it."

Adrenaline surged, tearing her in two directions. "Dix, we have the burial."

Brady turned at the sound of her handler's name. Shae took advantage of his distraction and darted around him.

"Wait!" Molly called out. Half the heads in the room turned toward her. As Shae started to run past the tribute board she faltered, then halted, and whirled to face Molly, her expression distraught.

For half a second, everything froze. The young girl's face was right next to a photo of Brady and Chris as preteens, in their baseball uniforms, arms around each other. Even though Chris was beaming and Shae's eyes were wide with fear, the resemblance was uncanny. Unmistakable.

A gasp behind Molly told her Brady had seen it, too.

"Jesus," Molly whispered, then said to the girl, "Go. Get out of here."

Shae spun and dashed down the center aisle and out the door, no one making a move to stop her. She pulled up her hood as she went, and no one reacted as if they'd seen what Molly and Brady had.

"*Byrnes!*" Dix must have been calling her name repeatedly.

"What?" It came out sharply enough to draw Brady's attention from Shae.

Brady's niece.

Chris's daughter.

"I don't give a shit what you tell them."

Molly gaped at the phone. She'd never heard Dix curse before. "What the hell is wrong with you?"

He didn't apologize or explain. "You and Fitzpatrick get here *now*. Meet me at departures. This may be your last chance to find out what really happened to Christopher."

Chapter Eleven

The small terminal at Westchester County Airport was full of hectic bustle, full of commuters and families, all with somewhere to go. But Brady hardly noticed.

He stood next to Molly outside the security gate, waiting for her handler, lost in numbness. He had no idea what she'd told his parents about missing the burial and couldn't summon any kind of emotion about it. Maybe he wouldn't have been able to, anyway, without Chris's body actually being in the casket. But this shock had been one too many.

Christopher was dead. Or not. Possibly murdered. His body was missing. The woman Brady had pined over for twelve years turned out to be an annoying princess. He was falling hard for his best friend. His father was, or had been, a friggin' spy.

And Chris had a goddamn daughter.

Brady's only anchor in this quicksand of chaos was Molly's hand in his. He hadn't let go of her except to let her drive, and he couldn't imagine being without her. Which was strange, given how little he'd seen her over the last twelve years, and yet it felt more right than anything else in his life ever had.

Molly shifted with impatience, and he unconsciously

tightened his grip so she wouldn't let go. She squeezed his hand and stilled, but continued to glower up and down the crowded terminal.

"He said we had to get here *now*, so where the hell is he?" she muttered.

"Getting your tickets." Dix strode up and handed her two ticket sleeves.

She flipped one open to check it, and Brady saw their destination. "Vancouver?"

"Corporate purchase, but you'll need ID at security, of course. I hope you have your passports."

"Always," they said at the same time.

Dix eyed their clasped hands and frowned. His stance widened and his chest puffed out a little. Brady twisted his hand so his fingers intertwined with Molly's. She shot him a surprised look at the possessive move, but he didn't care. Dix may have an interest in Molly, but she was *his*.

"What's going on?" Molly asked as she tucked the tickets into her jacket pocket.

Dix's jaw tightened before he spoke. "I found information on that encoded mission you were asking about."

At that, Brady automatically scanned the area. No one stood within earshot, but they all kept their voices low. "What kind of information?"

"Your brother wasn't on a standard mission. There was no client agency we were collecting information for."

Brady went cold. "What does that mean?" The logical answer was wet work, but SIEGE didn't do wet work. That had been a major selling point twelve years ago, when they'd recruited him.

"It could mean a lot of things." Dix moved closer. Closer to Molly than to Brady, who curbed the urge to tug her into his side. This wasn't the time or place for that battle.

"What do *you* think it means?" Molly asked Dix. She looked up at him, and Dix looked down at her, and when his expression softened, anger burned through the cold in Brady's veins.

He clenched a fist, the rational corner of his brain telling him to cool it. Molly must have noticed his tension, because she stroked her thumb across his knuckles—though she didn't move away from Dix. In fact…was she actually batting her lashes?

It's called blinking, moron. He let the stroking thumb calm him enough to focus on what Dix was saying.

"I think it's an internal matter. I don't know who assigned the case or what Chris was investigating. But it looks like they thought someone in SIEGE was—is—dirty." His jaw tightened, his eyes icy. He clearly didn't like that idea. But any organization could be corrupted, because any person could be corrupted given the right circumstances and incentives.

"So what are we going to look for?" she asked.

"You're meeting a guy—the rendezvous details are in there." Dix nodded at the slender folders he'd handed her. "He's leaving the country tomorrow for an indefinite length of time. Miss him, and it's over."

"What is he supposed to tell us?"

Dix shrugged. "SIEGE has an office in Vancouver. I think Chris was up there to investigate someone high up in the administration."

"How do you know all this?" Brady asked. Molly shot him a scowl at his hard voice, but he didn't care. He didn't have any reason to trust Dixson. Hell, it could be Dixson Chris had been investigating.

"I promised not to divulge my source," Dix said. Standard bullshit. So it didn't mean anything, but it didn't make Brady happy, either.

"What's this guy going to tell us?" Molly asked.

"I don't know. Hopefully enough for you to figure out what happened to Chris. But—"

"But we can't trust him," Brady said. "Right?"

"Hell, no. Be fully prepared for anything." Dix glanced at his watch. "You've got to go. They'll be boarding soon."

"Thanks, Dix." Molly let go of Brady and hugged her handler. Hugged. Her *handler*.

Disgusted, Brady stalked off to the security line, getting his passport and boarding pass ready. Molly joined him too many minutes later, but didn't say anything until they were through security. Afterward, neither of them said much beyond, "We'll buy clothes there," and "That way to our gate."

Fine with him. He had to get his jealousy under control. Molly would eat him alive if he showed it—more than he already had.

The gate area was crowded, with every seat taken. People already stood in line for boarding, some sitting on the floor or leaning against the glass, watching the baggage and maintenance people do their jobs. Way too many people to allow conversation. So they didn't talk until they were in the air, in their seats at the very rear of the plane.

• • •

When the seat belt sign pinged off, Molly sighed and eased her seat back, allowing herself to relax for the first time all day. It had already been a long one, and it was only midafternoon. They had a very long flight ahead of them, too. She'd be able to sleep a little, but not until Brady unloaded. He'd been piling it up all day. Which topic would he hit first?

"What did you tell my parents?" he asked, finally breaking the silence.

She grimaced apologetically. "I said you couldn't handle going to the cemetery."

Brady groaned, and she felt a twinge of guilt for laying the blame at his door.

"I bet that went over well," he murmured.

"Jessica went a little hysterical, said she couldn't get through it without you. Your mother cried and said it wasn't like you, but then she told Jessica to find a backbone, she had to be strong for her baby, and Christopher wouldn't want her to be so needy. It worked, a little." She glanced at him. "Your father knew I was lying, and he stood up for you. Still..." She breathed against the heavy weight on her chest. Their leaving had caused a lot of pain, and she hated that. Rick might suspect the things they believed, or hoped, or feared hoping, and support their efforts. But this trip might not yield answers, which would mean they'd hurt Jessica and Donna for nothing. And now, those answers had as much potential to be very bad as they did to be very good.

"Dad will take care of them," Brady murmured, his eyes closed but his face tight. He clearly didn't like the excuse she'd made.

She clamped her teeth on defensiveness. Maybe it had been the wrong thing to say, but she hadn't exactly had time to consider her options. She'd been trying to spare him the burden of lying to his parents, and her thought processes had been compromised by the huge shock she'd still been recovering from.

A shock, she acknowledged, that must still be reverberating in Brady.

He rolled his head and tilted it closer to her. "Shae."

"I know." She did the same, so they were face to face and no one else could hear them if they talked low. "She's the spitting image, Brady. And yet, I don't know if I'd have seen it if she hadn't stood right next to his photo like that."

"I don't get why." His voice cracked. "Why didn't we know?" He laced his fingers through hers again, something he'd been doing a lot lately.

She didn't mind. She would gladly be his anchor as much as he needed her to be. She just wished she could convince her body that was all it meant.

"Maybe *he* didn't know." She let her mind drift into speculation about the girl. "She was about fourteen," she started, and stopped when Brady's arm jerked under hers.

"She was? How do you know?"

She wasn't sure how to answer that. "I…can just tell."

"How?"

She made a face. She wasn't about to say she judged the girl's age by the development of the girl's hips and chest along with the combination of softness and angularity in her face.

"I have to know," he insisted. "Just in case —"

Molly sighed. "I'm a girl. I was fourteen once. Just trust me on this."

"But girls develop faster now. I read an article about hormones in milk —"

"If they do," she said levelly, "maybe she's thirteen. But not younger than that." She understood why his need to know was so strong. "Don't worry. It was before Jessica. I'm sure of it."

"How can you be?" He shook his head and rubbed his eyes. "Never mind. I'm flogging you about something we can't possibly determine now. Do you think Chris found out in May? And that's why his behavior changed?"

She blew out a breath. "Maybe. I'd have thought he'd have told Jessica, but we've already learned things weren't as perfect in their marriage as they seemed. And it might not have been up to him."

"What do you mean? I'd never keep a secret like that."

"Maybe he was ordered to. It could have been a court thing. He could have known since the beginning, maybe even had visitation rights but only as long as he didn't tell his family about her, or something like that."

"She seemed to know him, didn't she?" he mused.

Molly thought about the way the girl had knelt next to the coffin, the grief twisting her delicate features. But her eyes had been dry. "I think she at least knew who he was to her. But that doesn't mean he knew her. She could have found out who he was but never approached him."

"How did she find out about the funeral?"

"Obituary in the newspaper, most likely. Or a Google alert. Reading online papers. Whatever." She was tired of playing Q&A. "What are you thinking?"

He gave a hollow laugh. "I'm thinking I have a niece, and maybe it will be better if Chris really is dead, because once Mom finds out she's a grandmother and she missed out on the kid's entire childhood, she'll make his life a living hell and then kill him herself."

Molly managed to give a chuckle of agreement. But too many things were rushing through her all at once. Brady's statement was the first time any of them had dared even to come close to indicating there was a chance Christopher was alive. And he'd said it without thinking, so she knew he'd stopped trying not to hope he wasn't dead.

An image flashed into her head, of the Fitzpatricks this Christmas, all together—Chris and pregnant Jessica, Shae and her newfound grandparents, Brady and Molly, as a couple instead of best friends...and her secretly pregnant, too, about to announce it to everyone.

The vision was so vivid it took her breath away, and longing dug deep, carving through the scars she'd laid when Brady opened his heart to Jessica and was rejected, then rejected Molly and everyone else in return. Since finding him in South America and spending so much time right up against him this week, her yearning had fluttered against the scar tissue, but she'd refused to let it break through. But with the vision, the claws of her hunger for more opened new wounds, and that intense longing gushed through.

But she wasn't pregnant. She couldn't be. Wrong time of the month, stress, intense emotion, and she was on birth control in addition to the condom they'd used.

That vision was pure fantasy, and fantasies didn't come true.

Tears stung her eyes. She aimed her gaze out the window, at the clouds reflecting brilliant sunlight. If Brady noticed, he would think her eyes were just watering from the light.

"I've been thinking," he said.

"About?"

He stroked his fingers against hers. "About you. Us."

Oh, no. No, no, no. *Hell* no. That was way too cliché. Brady suddenly willing to talk about his feelings, hard on the heels of her own thoughts? She couldn't handle that.

But a deep-down part of her that had never stopped hoping, that sang in joy at his words, compelled her to ask, "What about us?"

His hand tightened. He turned his body more toward her, though he didn't raise his head to look in her eyes, thank God. He kept his gaze glued to their hands.

"Mostly about how I never would have gotten through any of this without you."

Molly made an involuntary noise in her throat. Wow. What was even worse than a treacly declaration of love? A sincere expression of gratitude.

He was damned lucky she was stuck on this plane with him.

She managed a smile. "Don't thank me. You're my best friend, and I'm doing what best friends do."

She watched his brows dip in a frown. "You're more than a best friend. You've gone way above and beyond this week, and I know none of us have appreciated it nearly enough."

For God's sake.

She pulled her hand from his and banded her arms over her body. "Yes, you all have. And these circumstances haven't been normal. You've never had another best friend, you don't know what we're supposed to do in a situation like this. I know you'd do the same for me."

But he was shaking his head. "You know it's a lot bigger than that, Moll. We've had a unique bond since the day we met."

She couldn't even remember the day they met. They'd been so young, all she really had was a collection of impressions. Her parents fighting, her escaping, Brady—and to a lesser extent Christopher—always ready to distract her, their parents always willing to take her in. She wasn't sure she remembered what the days had been like before the Fitzes moved in behind her house.

Okay, so maybe it was a rare bond.

"Fine, it's bigger. So?"

"So maybe it—"

"Drinks?" The flight attendant appeared at Brady's side, a practiced smile on her face.

Molly would have declined, but the woman wasn't going anywhere, so they both asked for water and waited until she'd finished their aisle and moved away. Once she had, Molly seized the opportunity to change the subject.

"Which do you think is more likely?" she asked Brady before he could speak. "That Chris is alive or that he was murdered?"

Brady had sat up straighter to open his snack and water, so now he loomed over her, not at all distracted. The tenderness in his eyes as he looked down at her unnerved her, but she forced herself to keep her own gaze steady and not falter under her discomfort.

Brady, probably understanding how confused he was suddenly making her, settled back and finally looked away.

"Honestly, the odds seem pretty even at this point." He offered her his nuts. She declined, and he went on, "I'm afraid to concentrate too hard in either direction."

"I know. Going through all this once was bad enough, but to have to do it all over again..." She reached for her water, trying to block out an alternative to her earlier vision, of the Fitzes destroyed, fragmented, full of dark pain.

That made Molly think of Jessica, which brought her back to her own feelings for Brady, and what he'd been trying to say to her. She tried to turn her brain in another direction, but she couldn't help herself. She had to ask.

"Jessica's not doing very well," she began.

"No." Brady heaved a sigh, and cradled his water bottle

against his torso. "I don't know how to help her. And if she finds out about Shae—"

"She seems to be clinging to you."

"Yeah." His tone revealed nothing. It made Molly want to growl at him. Maybe poke him for good measure. Hard.

So she'd just go for it. "It looks like you're getting a second chance."

"Does it?" He actually sounded amused, damn him, and his eyes twinkled when he turned his head to look at her.

"Don't act like this is funny," she spat out. "The past twelve years might be worth all the pain if you actually end up with her. It's all you've wanted since the instant you laid eyes on her."

The twinkle faded. "The past twelve years will never be worth it. I did too much damage, to all of us." He drew a deep breath and faced forward. "If I'd been more mature, spent some time with them as a couple, or even with Jess on her own, I might have realized things a little more quickly."

Molly's heart rate picked up. Brady declaring feelings for her was a tangled mess of issues. But Jessica was the knot in the middle. Was he really starting to untie it?

"What kinds of things?" she managed to ask with a little more whispery hope than she'd have liked to show.

"Things like…she's very high maintenance."

Her heartbeat slowed. Big shock. That didn't mean anything. "We're all high maintenance."

Brady gave her a lopsided grin. "*You're* not."

"Of course I am. You just haven't been in a relationship with me to find out."

His gaze went soft. "Moll, I've been in a relationship with you my entire life. You are the lowest-maintenance chick I've ever met."

She shook her head, wondering what perverse devil's advocate in her drove her to protest, but he didn't give her a chance.

"David Scott."

"Who?" But she blushed, knowing exactly who he was talking about.

Brady knew it, too, and didn't bother with reminders. "You know why he really broke up with you?"

She knew damned well why. "Because Laurie Hatterly shook her booty at him at the frat's Monopoly party, and she had a better ass than I did."

"Nope. She was just an excuse because he didn't want to hurt your feelings." The corner of his lip curved. "You made things too easy."

"No, I didn't," she scoffed. "I was anything but clingy, and I didn't mother him or anything."

"Yeah, that's what I'm saying. You were comfortable hanging out with him, doing whatever. You didn't care what it was. You didn't make demands or force him to do what you wanted to do. If he wasn't interested in something you liked, you did it without him. He wasn't used to that."

"That makes no sense at all," she grumbled, but of course it did. She knew guys wanted to be needed, and she had never been very good at needing anyone but herself. Wanting, yes. Needing, no. It was probably why her few attempts at dating since That Christmas hadn't progressed very far.

"Anyway." Brady shook his head with a hint of wonder. "If I'd stuck around, my crush on Jessica might have died a natural death."

"Crush?" Molly was getting sick to her stomach with all these ups and downs.

He turned to her again. She kept her eyes on his mouth, unable to meet his gaze.

"Yeah. Crush. I love her like a sister-in-law, Molly. I want her to not be hurting. Not be alone. But I don't want to be the one to make it that way for her. I don't want to be with her. Not anymore."

And with those words, Molly's world shifted irrevocably.

Again.

Chapter Twelve

Customs went smoothly, but slowly, so Molly and Brady barely had time to get to the café where Dixson had sent them. Dix hadn't told them how to identify the man they were meeting, so Molly hoped he knew to look for them. She was glad Brady had experience with this kind of stuff. When people came into her store, a defined set of code phrases helped her identify who people were and why they were there.

It was like a symphony, where every musician knew their own parts and how the sections came together, but didn't have to know the details of the other sections.

Brady's work was more like improvised jazz, where the players followed each other and made things up as they went along.

As they settled onto chilly iron chairs at a cold bistro table on the deserted sidewalk, Molly decided she was much better off as a conduit. She'd leave the field to Brady. Symphony was definitely a better fit for her.

About ten seconds after they sat down, a waiter came out to take their order. He looked annoyed that they were forcing him to come outside where it was too cold for al fresco dining.

They ordered coffee, and he quickly went back inside.

She stifled a yawn and tried to look like a tourist instead of someone waiting for a rendezvous. It was Sunday in the business district, so things were pretty darn quiet. Few people were strolling along the sidewalk. Traffic was also light. The fountain in a cement courtyard across the street danced in the sunlight, but no one sat around enjoying the sparkle.

She shivered and wrapped her arms around herself. She hoped the waiter didn't dilly-dally with the coffee to punish them for being outside.

"We should call your mother," she said to Brady, so they looked normal, engaged in conversation.

He grimaced. "I don't think so. Better to ask forgiveness—"

"Yeah, I don't think she likes that saying."

Their shared smile was interrupted by a man dropping into the third seat at their table.

Molly couldn't believe she hadn't seen him approach. He was a few inches taller than Brady sitting, and his knees touched the top of the table, so his legs were long, too. Unlike most very tall men, though, he wasn't lanky and bug-like, but broad and solid. He wore khakis and a denim jacket over a T-shirt. Nothing that would stand out. But his close-cropped hair was bright blond, his face rugged with a prominent brow ridge. In short, not the kind of guy who blended into any crowd. Yet Molly, who'd been paying attention, hadn't noticed him until he'd appeared at their table.

"You're Code 11." He looked at Brady, then at Molly, after giving the designation Dix had provided for them.

Since he was still looking at her, she nodded once. "So you must be T-59."

His nod was even more abrupt than hers, and he said nothing more. A moment later the waiter came out with three mugs of coffee. Brady handed him some cash he'd exchanged at the airport and told him to keep the change. Looking less disgruntled, he thanked them, hesitated as if about to ask if they wanted anything else, thought better of lingering, and went back inside.

There were no pedestrians for a block around, but T-59 didn't say anything. He leaned forward and sipped his coffee, making a pleased noise that made Molly try hers. It was good coffee.

Finally, Brady said, "You have information for us."

T sat back. "I may."

"You work for Global." Brady named their cover employer.

"I do."

"In what capacity?"

T gave him a *you-know-better-than-that* look, but his hand twitched toward Brady. She took that to mean he was a field agent, or had been.

"You knew what Fitzpatrick was working on?"

At the use of Chris's name, T's eyes went dark, and though his forehead didn't move, the brows seemed to have grown. Molly shivered at the subtle glower, but Brady appeared unperturbed. He waited patiently until T nodded.

"And?"

T shook his head. She figured he was afraid of being overheard. No one was close by, sure, but parabolic microphones didn't have to be. She surreptitiously scanned the rooftops all around them and didn't see any silhouettes or glints of light, and no open windows in the buildings. But that didn't necessarily mean anything, either.

Brady set a small device on the table. Molly had no idea what it was, but T visibly relaxed. He leaned in and motioned them closer. She shifted her chair and rested her forearms on the table, as if she was simply huddling around her hot coffee.

T kept his voice low. "Fitz was investigating someone in Global. Someone high up."

"Stationed here?" Brady asked.

"No. HQ. But the trail led him here. Fitz was good. I was suspicious about the accident, but couldn't be sure someone had found out what he was doing and taken care of him."

"What made you suspicious?" she asked.

T shrugged. "Where it happened, the injuries on the report. I saw the car. I was curious," he answered Brady's unspoken query. "I managed to get a look at it before it was crushed. The impact zone didn't really match the injuries on the official in-company report."

"No police report?" Brady asked.

"None."

"Why not? Don't they have to report to a fatal accident scene?" Molly didn't know how things worked in Canada, but that seemed like a no-brainer.

"Normally, yes." T didn't elaborate, leaving them to make their own interpretations.

"Do you think he was murdered?" Brady asked outright. Molly held her breath.

"I do."

She jolted, even though she'd expected that answer. But Brady didn't react at all, just continued seeking answers.

"And you think they retrieved what they were after—the evidence he'd gathered on them." That one wasn't a question.

"The originals, yeah." He drank more coffee. "Any agent worth his salt would have kept copies."

"But for copies to be of any value," she mused, "he'd have had to let someone know they existed."

Brady grunted, his body jerking as if something had hit him, and yanked his phone out of his pocket. After a few seconds of hitting buttons, he cursed. "I need a computer."

T drained his coffee. "Anything else from me?"

"Do you have anything else to tell us?" Molly asked.

He didn't crack a smile. "Just to watch your backs. If the person he was investigating gets wind that you're on the case—"

She stood when he did, blocking his path. Brady was still fiddling with his phone and hadn't caught the hint. "Do you know who that is?" she demanded quietly.

All hint of wariness dropped from T's face, leaving only sincerity. "No. But it's someone high enough to have a lot of power, and either no conscience or a wealth of desperation." He slipped past her, and seconds later, she couldn't tell which person on the street was him.

"I need a computer," Brady repeated, getting to his feet. His expression was twisted, anguished.

"To use, or to buy?"

"Buy."

"There's an Apple store up the street. I saw it on the way here."

"That'll do." They started walking. Molly found it tricky keeping up with Brady's long stride without looking like a little dog trotting next to its master. He didn't seem to notice, and she didn't think it was a good time to question either his pace or what he'd found.

"What was that device you put on the table?" she asked instead.

"High-frequency disruptor. If anyone was using mechanical means to listen to us, they'd only get feedback, whether it was from a distance or something planted near us."

"You field agents get all the cool toys."

Brady rewarded her with a smile, slowed his pace a little, and took her hand so they could walk side by side.

An hour later, they were set up in a random hotel room with Brady's new top-of-the-line laptop. He'd also taken them down an alley to a small electronics store that he'd heard about, where he'd bought some software and more gadgets that were clearly not meant for the general public. The gadgets were now set up and working to jam any signals in or out of the room, and he paced while the laptop installed the software.

"We're good for now," he said, "but I'm going to need to shut the jammers down while I download the software updates and then go online, because I'll need the wi-fi for that. So start talking. Spill whatever it is eating you."

So he *had* been paying attention.

"Just tell me what you thought of at the bistro that made you so grim and desperate for a computer."

His smile faded. "Chris and I had a secret system of communication. A way to leave each other messages we didn't want to risk anyone else seeing."

She stretched out on her stomach on one of the double beds so she didn't get in the way of his pacing. "Why? You guys didn't know you both worked for SIEGE."

"He might have known. I don't know." He rubbed his forehead. "But anyway, it started when we were kids. And lately, we've used it to talk about gifts and stuff, and for family discussions he didn't want Jessica to see, or whatever. I usually check it when I come back from a mission. I never thought—"

His last mission had ended with the news that his brother was dead. There wouldn't have been reason to check after that.

"Why couldn't you just check on your phone?" Molly doubted method was important, but Brady was getting increasingly agitated the longer this took. Keeping him talking seemed like a good idea.

"The mailbox I use for him has a login for an encrypted site. E-mail isn't safe."

Hence the laptop, and the encryption software he'd bought. "How long before the laptop is done updating?"

He checked the progress indicator, which didn't seem to be moving. "At least an hour. This stuff is heavy duty."

She groaned. "I need something to do. Maybe I'll go shopping." Not her favorite task, but they needed clothes and toiletries.

Brady knew it and threw her a bone. "No sense shopping until we know if we're staying. We might head straight to the airport after we read what he's sent. If he's sent anything."

The thought of getting back on a cramped, stale airplane so soon made her slightly queasy. She reversed off her belly and scooted back to lean against the headboard, grabbing the TV remote off the nightstand. "All right. Option two it is."

He came over and sat on the edge of the bed next to her thigh. He pulled the remote slowly from her hand and replaced it on the table. "Or option three." His voice rumbled through her body, and her eyelids drifted to half-mast.

"Brady…"

It was only half a protest. She was so tired. Tired of staying rational and protective. Of trying to make sure they didn't let the situation dictate feelings that weren't real.

Fuck it. *Her* feelings were real, and had been for decades. Maybe Brady was honestly, finally seeing her differently.

"Molly." He shifted up the bed. One arm crossed over her body, his fist bracing next to her hip. "Even with everything that's happening, I can't stop thinking about your mouth."

"Ha!" slipped out before she thought it through. But Brady only smiled a slow, lazy smile that sent desire rolling through her gut. "Seriously," she snarked out of pure desperation. "You *never* stopped?"

The smile became less predatory, more genuine. "Okay, I stopped. Occasionally. But it keeps popping into my thoughts. And right now it's either think about your mouth, or about what message Christopher sent me that I can't access right now."

That hurt. Almost as much as it did to pull away from him. "So, I'm just a distraction." She shoved at his arm and wiggled off the bed on the opposite side. "TV is a more appropriate way to take your mind off your brother, Brady."

She stomped off toward the bathroom, but he caught her before she got halfway there and swung her around into his arms.

"That is *so* not what I meant." He held her easily, even as she pushed against his chest. His rock-solid chest. "Moll, come on. Stop and listen to me."

It would have been very easy to do that, but capitulation meant losing herself to him. She'd been on the verge of that their whole lives, and had always known that wasn't the way to get what she longed for. The vision she'd had on the plane, the family—that was *real*. Fantasy, maybe, but worth holding out for. Worth ensuring that if Brady chose her, he did it deliberately and 100 percent.

She'd almost lost the struggle, almost accepted what little she could get as better than nothing. But with a few words, he'd flipped her from lethargic acceptance to panicked resistance. If she gave in, she might never get the fantasy. And Brady might never decide that was what he really wanted, too.

She kept pushing and twisting until he let her go. She backed up a few steps, her chest heaving, eyes burning again. "I can't play with you, Brady."

Now hurt glimmered in his eyes, but he quickly masked it. "That's not—"

"It's what you implied. I don't know if it's proximity, or convenience because Jessica's morally unavailable, or—"

"I didn't mean to imply that," Brady said, cutting her off, his tone hard now. "You inferred it because you won't talk about it. About us. You won't listen to me. You'd rather—"

"Don't tell me what I'd rather!" she half-shouted. "You have no idea what you're slicing open."

The silence rang in the echo of her admission, and regret flowed into those slices. *Too late.* She'd flung away the barrier keeping Brady oblivious to her feelings, and she knew there was no way he'd let her get away with ignoring or denying what she'd just said.

He stood stock still, his blue-hazel eyes intent on hers. "Tell me, then."

Molly pushed an unsteady hand through her curls. She didn't try to dissemble. "My world crashed to a halt the day you told Jessica you were in love with her," she admitted. Brady's mouth fell open. She held up a hand and didn't let him respond. "I'd known, of course, since that very first day. But she wasn't available, and I thought you'd get over her and move on. Instead you were open and honest with her." Her throat started to close, the words quavery, but she forced herself to continue. "The bitch shattered you, but left the door open. She let you believe she cared about you more than just as her fiancé's brother. So you know what? I don't think you'd have gotten over her any faster if you'd stuck around. She'd have strung you along, manipulated you. Maybe not intentionally, maybe out of misguided kindness, but the result would have been the same."

"Moll—"

"I would have done *anything*," she cut him off with a whisper, "to take that pain from you. But what she did to you— it didn't just hurt you. It didn't just damage your relationship with your family."

Brady gazed at her, regret saturating his eyes. "I knew I'd hurt you. That pulling away from everyone, sealing myself off, was unfair to you. I just didn't—"

"Think I cared that much?" Her eyes burned, but the pain went too deep for tears. "It was more than a sister losing her brother, or a woman losing her best friend," she said, hurt crushing her voice to soft dust. "I lost even the hope of you. I knew Jessica would never, ever, release her hold on you."

"But she has," he told her, his tone solid with certainty. His hand lifted, palm up. An invitation. "Molly, I don't love Jessica."

Truth rang in his words. He believed them, Molly could tell. But that didn't mean he loved *her*, and she wasn't stupid enough to let him in now, so soon after his apparent epiphany. Jessica was still needy and would still turn to Brady for help. He'd never be able to deny her. She was carrying his fatherless nephew, for cripes sake. And she might not even know about Shae. How much damage would that revelation do?

Molly's one hope, so tiny and fragile she could barely acknowledge it, was that Christopher was still alive and could return to his wife. That could finally, fully free Brady.

Maybe.

"That's good," she told him. "But it's not enough."

. . .

Brady let Molly escape into the bathroom this time. He had to. She'd knocked him completely off balance, revealing a vulnerability he'd never seen in her before. He couldn't risk making the wrong move and blowing his chances with her forever.

Because for the last few days, he hadn't quite been able to label his growing feelings for Molly. He'd questioned their origin, their reliability, even what they actually were. He'd wanted to explore them, see what happened when he tried to name them, share them with her. But every time she'd blocked his clumsy attempts...and he'd been kind of glad. It was safer, easier, that way.

Yet those emotions wouldn't relinquish their hold. He kept coming back to poke and prod at them like a sore tooth.

But as soon as she'd implied that his feelings weren't real, that they weren't enough for her, they'd exploded over him in a rage of *how-dare-you?* And he suddenly *knew* what they were.

The shower came on, flashing him back to that other hotel room, the one where Molly had given herself to him because he needed her. He realized now she never would have done that if she hadn't loved him. The depth of that love had been apparent in her outburst just now.

He was the luckiest son of a bitch in the world. And the stupidest. The question was, what was he going to do about it?

The computer beeped its completion before she came out of the bathroom. He deactivated the signal disruptor, accessed the hotel's wi-fi, engaged basic encryption, and started downloading the updates to the software he'd bought. With nothing better to do, he lay down on the bed, hands behind his head, and stared at the ceiling, wondering how best to approach Molly.

She was rational to a fault, so he could try appealing to her that way. Lay out the facts. Problem was, they weren't all facts. And women tended to get pissed off when men tried to factualize emotions.

Or he could tell her what he'd just figured out. But what would stop her from saying the same things as before?

She didn't believe he felt what he felt. And she didn't trust that Jessica wouldn't enthrall him again. And who could blame her? Twelve years of evidence was tough to argue against. And yet, he knew to the depth of his soul that it was true. Jessica was firmly in the past, his feelings for her completely gone.

Molly was his future. He wanted her, and only her.

But he'd never convince her of that with words.

So he'd just have to show her.

• • •

Molly took as much time in the bathroom as she possibly could. She wanted Brady to be caught up in the computer, his focus on his brother and off of her by the time she emerged. She also needed to work through her own tide of emotion before facing him again.

Her goal had been to stay in the shower until it went cold, hoping that would stem the urge to run out into the bedroom and throw herself on Brady. Her body hummed, ignoring her mind and egging on her heart. If the need had been mostly physical, she could have taken care of things herself, so she could concentrate on Christopher.

But the physical was only a side effect.

The hard part was believing that Brady wanted her, loved her, and was truly over Jessica. There was no way he could honestly assess how he felt about *anything* while they were mired in this hellish mystery. Let them get through this, get back to their normal lives, and see how he felt then.

Molly's feelings wouldn't change. They hadn't in two decades. But if Brady's did—again—she'd handle it. Again.

The water never went cold. Lost in her thoughts, she'd also lost track of time. So once she was dressed, hair mostly dry, steam fully dissipated, she braced herself and opened the door to the bedroom. She was relieved to find Brady sitting at the desk, staring intently at the laptop screen. His fingers pounded away on the keyboard.

"Did you get to it yet?" she asked, hanging her towel over the back of a chair.

"Just about." His eyes tracked back and forth, rapidly reading. He frowned and hit a few more keys. She started to sit on the end of one of the beds, keeping her distance, but then Brady clicked to open a file and she couldn't help herself. She surged forward and leaned over his shoulder to read.

The file opened into a pop-up window, which held a few lines of text. An address in Washington, DC, and the words "Dix ten twelve full doc asap."

"Dix?" Molly exclaimed. "Was he helping Christopher?" A slow burn ignited. Dix had acted as if he didn't know anything, that he'd taken risks to get the information he'd provided them. He'd been suspended… "Oh."

"What?" Brady half turned toward her, his attention still on the file.

"Dix didn't get suspended because of me. Or not because of *me*." She waved a hand, dismissing his romantic interest with a pang of regret. "He was on to something." And now she and Brady were on to it. "We've got to get out of town." She straightened and looked at the door, adrenaline flowing, half expecting someone to come through it. She'd forgotten the signal suppressor was off. Someone could be listening to them right now, and that was the perfect line to burst in on.

Yeah, in the movies. When nothing happened, she laughed at herself and sank onto the bed, watching Brady shut down and pack up the computer. "Did you recognize the address?" she asked him.

"Yeah." He clicked on his little black device and leaned against the desk facing her, arms folded. "It's a drop Chris and I have used before." His mouth quirked up on one side. "We probably both thought we were so clever, pretending to play at spies when we really are spies, but thinking the other didn't know it." The wry amusement faded, his face sinking into the familiar lines of grief he'd worn all week. He rubbed his hands over it, then grabbed his stuff and stood. "So, let's go to DC."

. . .

Brady stood under a tree in a quiet DC neighborhood, pretending to smoke a cigarette while he watched the building across the street. The tree shaded what was supposed to be a grassy square where residents of the block could walk their dogs or sit on a bench on nice days. The barren patch of dirt he stood on and the scattered cigarette butts attested to a different use.

Molly was driving around in a car they rented at the airport. She would pick him up again when he sent a text he'd already typed into his phone. It was still dark, early enough in the morning that traffic was light, both vehicle and pedestrian. No one had come out of the building since Brady started his cigarette ten minutes ago, and only two people had walked by, neither even glancing in his direction. There was no reason not to go in.

Except avoidance. He wasn't sure he wanted to find out what Chris had been after. Already, his death had brought so many revelations. Not only that his brother was also SIEGE, but that Molly was, and even his father. Who seemed to be retired now but had probably been high up enough in the organization before that to get all his kids recruited.

What if the information Chris had obtained revealed something bad about their father?

"You're being ridiculous," Brady scolded himself. Dropping the cigarette on the dirt and mashing it with his toe, he checked the street and sidewalks again, then headed across the four lanes to the small apartment building. His shoes scraped against the worn concrete steps. The hunter-green painted door was locked. He dug out his key and winced at the creak when he went in. But it was okay. No one was inside.

He stood still in the small foyer, listening. The frayed carpet runner over warped wooden boards only muffled sound slightly. No one moved on the stairs or overhead, and Brady couldn't detect movement in the apartments on either side of him. This was the kind of old building that telegraphed every step with creaks and groans and thumps. It was why they'd chosen it.

After a ten-count, he walked as quickly and silently as he could to the far end of the bank of metal mailboxes on the wall. The last mailbox had no name or number on it and appeared to be rusted shut. Unusable. Brady slipped another key into the tiny lock, turned it, and pulled on the door. He breathed a sigh of relief when it glided open on oiled hinges. It had been a long time since they'd used this drop. They'd come up with the idea after their mother had guessed their Christmas present for the fifth year in a row. It became a game—her guessing, them trying to come up with something she'd never guess, then keeping it secret. They'd resorted to nonelectronic means, suspecting her dim-witted approach to computers was put on. It had worked two years ago, and the new car they'd splurged on shocked her so much she reportedly burst into tears. After that, he and Chris had stopped using the drop. But they hadn't let it go.

Another glance around, another pause to listen, because this was the crucial part. If someone discovered him looking in the mailbox, he'd say he was apartment-sitting for his brother. But if they discovered him working at something *under* the mailbox…

He pried up the metal floor of the narrow rectangle and leaned to look beneath. Something white gleamed deep in the cavity. He reached in. It was a smooth packet, like a large envelope around a half inch–thick sheaf of papers. Feeling a little paranoid, he probed around the envelope and touched the bottom of the cavity, making sure nothing was wired or rigged. But it was empty except for the packet. He pulled it out. On the outside, his name was written in black Sharpie. Chris's scrawl was obvious. Unexpected tears burned Brady's eyes for a few seconds before he could blink them back. He quickly secured the mailbox's loose floor and locked the rusty door.

Down the hall, blocked from his view until now by the open mailbox door, stood a motionless figure. He was a silhouette in the dim light, legs braced wide, hands in jeans pockets, a big coat and stocking cap blurring the body and head shape. But still—

Brady blinked, hard, his free hand reaching for a weapon he wasn't carrying, much slower than his trained reflexes should have had him reaching. Half his brain reeled from the truth of who stood there. The other half rebelled, claiming impossibility. Then the figure spoke.

"Took you long enough."

Chapter Thirteen

Molly couldn't believe Brady really thought she would circle the block endlessly in the rental car and let him go to meet Dix at the drop site by himself. Sure she'd agreed to his plan, but hadn't bothered taking the time to advise him of hers. She did drive around for a few minutes while she called Dix and ordered him to the park two blocks up the street. Once she spotted him approaching, she double-parked—you never got a parking space at this time of night in a residential section—and hit the flashers. On her last pass, Brady had still been "smoking" while he cased the building he needed to enter. She figured she had five to ten minutes before he texted her. Brady had wanted to retrieve Chris's package before they talked to Dix, but Molly felt a weight of urgency on the back of her neck and thought they should do both at the same time. Brady would never have agreed to let her meet Dix alone, but instinct told her he was not their enemy.

Dix stood behind a bench, hands in his pockets. The streetlight hit him square in the face. No skulking for her handler. She let two minutes go by before getting out, but nothing moved for a block in any direction, except one car that passed, full of club-hoppers judging by their revelry and shiny clothes.

Dix didn't move when Molly opened her car door. He must have known it was her sitting there. It didn't take a genius to figure that out. She hurried over, her attention still split between their surroundings and Dix.

"What did you find?" he asked as soon as she got close enough, his low voice cutting through the cool, clear air.

"We found out that you haven't been truthful with us." She tried not to sound accusing, but stopped well out of his reach. "You didn't simply discover what Chris was after."

"What makes you think that?" His tone was wary but resigned. He didn't move out of the light into shadow, though, so Molly assumed he wasn't trying to hide. Either that, or he was a very good agent. One or the other.

"Chris sent Brady a message with your name on it." It was all she was going to give him.

It was enough. Dix's shoulders fell an inch. "What did it say?"

"I don't know." She held her tongue about the fact that Brady was retrieving it as they spoke. "What do you expect it to say?"

Dix sighed and rubbed a hand over his forehead. A couple of days ago, she'd have said he was a happy-go-lucky guy who was exactly as he portrayed himself. But now she saw the toll this had taken. Whatever "this" was. He'd been carrying it for a while, and that meant he had a better poker face than he'd allowed her to think.

"I sent Christopher on that mission," he confessed softly.

As shocks went, that one was lighter than just about every other one she'd had recently. "Why? And how?" Handlers didn't assign missions, they only helped make sure they were completed successfully. They were communicators, not decision-makers.

"The how was easy. Handlers have access to the mission

software. No one really had to know he was on a mission, especially when an approved request in his personnel file said he was taking the week off."

Dix had to have been Chris's handler to fake a vacation approval, but Molly asked the question anyway.

Dix nodded. "He was doing me a favor, Molly, and I got him killed." Torment roughened his voice. "I need to get the information he found. I have to know—"

"It was worth it?" Molly finished for him. She flexed and curled her hands, shifting her balance onto the balls of her feet. The answers were almost within reach—at least some of them were. But when Chris had gotten close to answers, he was killed.

The sense of a burning gaze on her made her suppress a shudder. She twisted to look behind her for Brady. Stupid move, because anyone watching would read her movements and know she was expecting someone else. But the need to see what Chris had sent him overwhelmed her caution.

The night remained silent and unmoving. She didn't even know which building Brady had gone into. She turned back to Dix.

"What was Chris investigating?" she asked again. "Someone dirty on the inside?" Dix nodded but didn't speak.

"Who?" she demanded, but he didn't answer. Didn't even move.

That wasn't going to cut it. "Someone high up, I assume."

He nodded again, his eyes intent on hers. The dread in them reminded her of how she'd felt facing Chris's casket. "Someone...close to you?" she asked.

"I don't know," he whispered. "That's why I asked Chris to check into it. I don't know if I'd have been brave enough—" He swallowed. "I don't know if I'd have had the courage to look into the discrepancies if I didn't think my father was the one responsible."

• • •

Brady turned and leaned against the bank of mailboxes, a casual pose totally belied by the slamming of his heart against his ribcage.

"What took me long enough? Coming here?" He pretended the taunt had come from a stranger, one of the goon types he frequently dealt with on the information trail. When the figure dipped his head—Brady assumed it was a nod—he shot back, "I was a little preoccupied. I don't know if you heard, but my brother is dead. Don't say it." He threw up a hand, not wanting to hear the "greatly exaggerated" line. "I went to your fucking *funeral* today. I don't know whether to hug you or break your jaw."

Chris pulled his hands from his pockets and held them out at his sides. "It's a no-brainer, bro."

Brady strode down the hall, his right fist clenched, the edge of the envelope digging into his left. A definite no-brainer. But instead of hauling off and slamming his fist into his brother's face, he halted a foot away. "Do you have *any* idea what you've done to Mom? To *Jessica?*"

"God, yes." The wry amusement disappeared, replaced by anguish that sounded familiar. "It was the last thing I wanted to do to any of you. Almost the last thing. The last thing was really dying."

Brady shoved a hand through his hair. "How did you do it? The police report—"

"I'm not going to tell you. Most of what I did was very illegal, and if I'm lucky, no one will ever find out the details." He jerked his chin toward the envelope in Brady's hand. "You need to give that to Conrad Dixson. No one else. He's—"

"I know who he is. He's Molly's handler, too."

Chris's body jerked. "*Molly's* handler?"

Brady took perverse pride in shocking his brother. "Yeah. You didn't know she was SIEGE? She knew you were. And me." Chris didn't react to that one, so he must have known Brady was, dammit.

"What's her job?" Chris demanded. "Not an agent." It was more a statement of hope than certainty.

"Conduit."

His brother nodded and looked down. "So she—"

"Look, we can't shoot the shit all night. I could spend an hour asking you questions, and I haven't decided not to hit you yet."

A ghost of a smile slid across Chris's mouth.

"Why did you even show yourself to me? I already knew you wanted Dix to get these." He raised the envelope. "Something you need to tell me about what's in here?"

"No. I just—needed to see you. It's been—" He seemed to think better of describing what it had been like, but Brady imagined it wasn't much better on his brother's side of things than it was on his.

"I get it. When can you come in?"

"Dix will tell you. You can signal me the same way I did you." He started to fade back into the dark hall.

Brady was going to let him go, but at the last second, he lurched forward, grabbed his brother's arm, and pulled him into a hug, his fist twisting the back of Chris's jacket and his eyes screwing shut against the prickle of relieved tears. His brother was *alive*.

An instant later, chips of plaster flew off the wall and pelted Brady in the hand. Chris jerked out of the hug and touched his face, his eyes going unerringly to a fresh hole in the wall.

A fresh *bullet* hole.

· · ·

Molly was still trying to figure out what to say to Dix's revelation that he thought his own father was dirty when her subconscious caught a faint, familiar-yet-not sound. She wouldn't have even paid attention to it except that Dix stiffened and stared straight at the building Brady had gone into.

"What?" Molly spun and stared, too. Why hadn't she

positioned them so she could see the building and Dix couldn't? Her conscious caught up to what they'd heard. "Was that a—"

"Suppressed gunshot? Sure sounded like one." He glanced down at her. "Fitz in there?"

She nodded and swallowed. Maybe she couldn't trust Dix—he'd lied to them, and even what he'd told her could be false. But *he* hadn't fired a weapon.

A weapon. Brady was in there. He could be shot. *Oh, God, no. Not Brady*. Déjà vu held her paralyzed for a few seconds.

Molly was a conduit, Dix a handler. Neither had field experience, no matter what their training. She was certain the last thing they should do was run into that building. But it was also the only thing she wanted to do. "We have to—"

But Dix had already started forward. She was a few steps behind him when two people ran out of the narrow brick apartment building. She recognized one of them immediately as Brady. The other was—

She gasped. Dix halted in the middle of the street, but she kept going, fueled by joy and fury and fear.

"No!" Brady shouted, throwing up a hand to make her stop. Another person came out the door, arm raised, and Molly threw herself behind a car, her mouth glued closed in sudden terror. She wanted to yell at Dix to get down, but didn't want to call the gunner's attention to him. She wanted to scream for Brady and Christopher—dammit, he *was* alive!—to get away. Scream for police, for the killer to stop. Just to scream. It built in her chest, jumping in size every time she heard the ever-louder, but still muffled pops of the gun.

Pop. Pop. Pop pop pop.

She covered her ears and buried her face in her knees, more terrified and helpless than she'd ever been in her life. This was nothing like South America, and everything like hell.

And then suddenly it was silent. Heavy now, not the anticipatory, sleepy silence of before. The kind of silence that meant horrifying things. She loosened her hands and lifted her head the tiniest bit. The lack of sound rang so loud she didn't trust it. Maybe she'd gone into shock, and chaos surrounded her. When she opened her eyes, though, there was nothing. Dix wasn't where he'd been standing, not even lying in a heap on the ground.

Twisting, she got to her feet but stayed low, eyes skipping right past where she'd last seen Brady and Chris and zeroing in on the position of the shooter. He was gone. She couldn't see a single person anywhere.

Taking a chance, she stood. That brought them into her line of sight, and as soon as she could see them, she could hear them. Moans. Pleading in a gaspy, pain-filled breath.

She ran to where Brady knelt next to his brother. Chris lay in the gutter, the ground moist around him, glistening under the streetlight.

"Hang on, bro," Brady begged. He had one hand against his right shoulder, the other pressed hard on Christopher's chest. Chris was the one moaning.

Molly dropped down next to Brady and elbowed him out of the way, replacing his hand with both of hers. "I've got it. How bad?" She asked it of Christopher, to give him something to focus on. His head rolled toward her, his eyebrows furrowing as he tried to focus his vision. "Wha—? Two. One flesh. One still in. Brady—shoulder."

"I know. Call 911," she ordered Brady. Her terror had subsided, oddly, once she knew their status. She wadded Chris's T-shirt with one hand and shifted it to press harder on the wound and stem the way-too-fast flow of blood.

"Dix already did. They're on the way."

She looked up at him again. "How bad?" she repeated.

"I don't know." He wouldn't take his eyes off his brother, had only moved back far enough to give her room to apply pressure. "Bad." She must have made some kind of panic noise, because Brady turned to her. "No, not me. I'm—I don't know. Not dying. But Chris— Molly—"

"I know." She looked down into the scarily blank face of her surrogate brother. "Hey! Look at me! We are *not* losing you for real, you hear me? You have a lot to answer for, mister."

Chris actually managed a smile. "Thank you, Molly." He gripped her wrist with his left hand, and its strength encouraged her. Until he added, "Take care of my brother," and the hand fell limp to the ground.

Chapter Fourteen

Attempts had been made to make the room comfortable and warm, with soft chairs, carpeting, muted paper on the walls, even flowers centered on the magazine-scattered table. Lilacs. Out of season. Molly stretched out a hand to touch them. Yep, fake. Good fakes, though.

The distraction lasted only a few seconds before the grief, fear, and overall misery swamped her again. She slumped over and buried her head in her arms so she didn't have to see the empty waiting room. Normal procedure for anyone else would have been to call the family, who'd have rushed over to wait for news. But how did you tell someone who'd just buried their eldest child that he'd been shot in the chest?

Footsteps started down the hall outside, and she lifted her head to watch two more cops, this time detectives, walk by with a nurse. They weren't hurrying. She didn't know what that meant. No rush, the victim died on the table? Still being operated on, or in recovery? Awake, but we caught the guy, so there's no urgency.

Molly had no idea what was going on anywhere. After Brady had bellowed his anguish, Molly had managed to convince him Chris had just passed out. Brady hadn't been in his right mind after that. Molly had monitored Christopher's breathing and thready pulse and kept pressure on the wounds and her eye on Brady, who thankfully waited to do his own passing out until the paramedics showed up. Luckily, Dix had seen enough to convey they needed two ambulances. The cops hadn't been far behind, and when Dix didn't return, one of the officers had given Molly a ride to the hospital, where she'd cleaned up before being shown to the OR waiting room. Both brothers were in surgery. Contrary to Hollywood convention, the shoulder wasn't a safe place to get shot. The bullet had done damage to Brady's brachial plexus and possibly the joint. No one had come to talk to her in three hours. Her cell phone was off, and she didn't want to leave the room to go check messages or make calls and risk missing the doctor or the detectives, who'd certainly want to talk to her.

Where the hell was Dix? Had he caught the shooter? Been shot himself? He hadn't called her when she was on her way to the hospital, and hadn't answered when she'd tried to call him.

What the hell had happened in that building? When the paramedics first arrived, she'd taken Brady's keys from his pocket and sneaked into the dim, narrow foyer. Not until she was in there, staring at a hole in the wall, the only evidence anything had gone down, did she think of the information Brady had been picking up. Why was Christopher there? Had there been any information at all, or just Chris? She hadn't thought to check Brady's coat or pockets for papers or a flash drive. She hoped to hell the shooter hadn't gotten it. If it had meant losing the guys or losing the info, she'd choose the information every time. But this was no-win, and the need for vengeance burned in her. She wanted to—

A figure appeared in the doorway, and she jerked her head up, her breath catching. But it wasn't the doctor. It was Dix.

Hatred exploded, surprising her enough to extinguish itself. She hadn't realized she blamed him for this. Hadn't thought far enough past Brady's and Chris's wounds to put blame on anyone. But right now, he was the only target she had. *Dix* had been suspicious. *Dix* had sent Chris for incriminating information someone was willing to kill for. *Dix* had torn her and Brady away from the worst moment in his family's lives to send them on a trip that had led to this horror.

He watched her from the doorway, obviously uncertain of his welcome. She thought of the years he'd been her handler. When she'd wanted extra training, he made sure she got it. When she'd faltered in that training, uncertain if she had the skill or ability necessary, he shored her up. Encouraged her, supported her, fed in her a conviction that they were doing the right thing as members of SIEGE.

Surely, he couldn't have faked it for so long. She'd trusted him for years. Unless she was a total fool, there was no reason to change that.

She nodded, and he came over to sit next to her, taking her hand. She hadn't known it was so cold until he folded it between both of his.

"Any news?" he asked, though he had to know the answer already.

"No. Both in surgery."

He let out a slow breath. "Okay. Molly, I'm so—"

Dark emotion flared again, defying her attempts to logic it away. "Do not apologize," she gritted out, "or I'll want to kill you."

He stayed silent for a full minute after that.

"Where did you go?" she asked after she'd gotten herself under control. The heat of his hands helped. She shivered, the rest of her suddenly cold compared to that one hand, and Dix wrapped his arm around her shoulders, leaning back so she was fully up against his side. He was still steamy. She wondered how far he'd chased that guy.

"Did you catch him, or at least get something on him?"

"Yeah." Dix's voice rumbled through his chest into her ear.

"You did?" She lifted to look up at him. She hadn't expected a positive answer. "Which?"

"Caught him. Saw who it was. Beat him up a little, then took a good one on the chin and lost him."

"Did you tell the police?" she asked, straightening fully. Dix removed his arm reluctantly.

"Yeah, I saw the detectives on the way in. They caught a full elevator and I had to wait for the next one. I assume they're up here?" He slumped further on the chair and rubbed his face. Molly marveled at how much older he looked from when she first met him, so short a time ago. Face lined, eyelids drooping, and the happy, bashful guy completely gone.

"Yeah, but I haven't talked to them yet. Or the doctor. Or the Fitzpatricks," she said miserably. "I don't know what to tell them."

"Smart to wait," Dix agreed. "Hey." He waited until she turned to look at him. "They're going to be okay."

"You don't know that." She managed a small smile. "But thanks."

"No, thank *you*." His sudden tension belied the words. "You have no idea what you guys have done for me."

He didn't really sound that grateful. "You got the information Brady was after. That Chris retrieved?" She frowned when he nodded. "When?"

He sighed. "I knew you'd want the full sequence of events."

She tried to withhold judgment. "Why does it sound like I'm not going to like it?"

He barked a laugh. "Because I left your boyfriend bleeding on the ground and his brother at death's door? Again."

Completely still and cold again, Molly said, "I assumed you went after the shooter because you knew I was there for the guys. You called 911."

"I did. But I'm not sure I wouldn't have acted the same way even if you weren't there."

Molly couldn't respond to that. Part of her understood. The

mission was priority, don't let them sacrifice in vain, and all that. But the part of her that loved Brady more than herself didn't want to forgive Dix for his admission, however hypothetical.

After a moment, Dix continued. "Brady told me to go, that the shooter had the packet Chris had left. So I went. I chased him a few blocks. A car turning a corner slowed him down, so I was able to catch up. We fought, and when I grabbed the packet, that's when he clipped me and got away." He wiggled his jaw with his right hand.

"So you still have it?"

He nodded wearily.

"So what's next? What do we do with it?"

Dix considered. "There's an oversight committee. I don't know much about it, not even who's on it. But they were formed for just this kind of thing. We need to find out who's on it, to make sure we don't hand the information right back to the enemy."

That was a good plan in theory, but they had no idea who the enemy was. She didn't even know what "enemy" meant. Since SIEGE dealt in information, it could be assumed that someone had sold some of it to the wrong people. How had Dix discovered that? What made him think his father was the culprit?

But she was too exhausted to ask those questions now.

"What did the packet say?" she managed.

"I haven't had a chance to look. I came straight here."

"Not straight here." He didn't have the packet on him. "Where is it?"

"I hid it. It's safe for now."

"We thought it was safe where it was before." Misery thundered down on her. But the waiting room was as silent as any ever got in a hospital.

Dix's warm hand rubbed her back in comfort, and she folded over onto her lap again. "God, Dix, I can't do anything. I can't call people or give insurance details or even give blood.

I'm not compatible."

"They donate their own blood, and SIEGE keeps it banked. I'm sure it's in the system."

She turned her head. "Chris lost more than what would be banked." Tears suddenly welled and seeped out to dampen her sleeve.

"I'm a universal donor. I'll go donate some now." He patted her back. "Hang in there, Molly."

One of the detectives came into the waiting area as Dix was exiting. The cop stopped the handler and murmured something. Dix told him where he was going, and the cop nodded before coming in and sitting next to Molly.

She forced herself to sit up and meet his gaze but didn't bother swiping her eyes. "Is there any news?" she asked listlessly. She didn't think there would be any yet, and wasn't surprised when he shook his head.

"I'm sorry. All I know is that they're both still in surgery." He flipped open a small notebook and twisted the tip down on a silver pen. "I need to ask you some more questions."

"Of course."

He started with the hardest one. "Can you tell me why one of the victims had a funeral yesterday?"

"Reports of his death — ?"

"Do not say it." He shook his head.

"Sorry. It's easier." She heaved a big sigh. "I don't know much. I didn't know he was alive until I saw him get shot."

"But you were investigating his death."

Surprise shivered up her body. It must have showed, because he said, "You and the other victim just returned from Canada, the location of Mr. Fitzpatrick's fatal accident." He didn't put verbal quotes around the words, and Molly appreciated his restraint. She didn't bother to confirm his statement but waited for him to get to a question.

He suppressed a sigh and looked down at his blank notebook. "Did you recognize the person who shot them?"

"No. I barely saw him."

"Him."

"Probably. Moved like a him. But Dix—I mean, Conrad Dixson, the guy who just left, saw him better. He said he talked to you."

"He did. I'm gathering as much detail as possible."

"Well, I can't tell you much, I'm sorry. I was standing in the little park with Dix when Brady and Christopher came out of the building and the gunman followed them." She didn't explain about hearing the suppressed gunshot. That would mean also explaining how she or Dix recognized the sound, and the less they said about SIEGE, the better. "I saw the gun, Brady yelled to me, and I hid until it was all over."

The detective scribbled on his pad. Though she could see it, the words were indecipherable. A sudden thought struck her, and she said, "I'm sorry, I didn't get your name."

"Detective Mike Wiszowski." He reached into the inside pocket of his trench coat and showed her his ID, all his movements automatic and smooth.

She relaxed, at least back to her previous state of tension. "Thanks."

"No problem." He asked a few more questions, dipping into areas she didn't feel comfortable talking about without guidance, but Dix was the only one who could have guided her. She managed to get through without referencing SIEGE, and the detective took her contact information, not raising an eyebrow at the Boston area codes.

"Will you be in DC for long?" he asked as he tucked his notebook away.

"A little while," she replied. "As long as they need me." She jerked her chin in the direction of the operating rooms. Detective Wiszowski nodded and rose to leave.

Molly let her vision go fuzzy and floated in numbness until someone nudged her shoulder. She looked up, and the detective had returned. He held out an insulated paper cup with a muffin perched on top of it. She automatically took it and said thanks, but raised an eyebrow at the unexpected consideration.

"You looked like you were going to keel over onto the floor. I know you won't feel like eating, but you need it." He stood for a second, then added, "I can stand here for a while, make sure you eat it."

She managed a smile and set the coffee down so she could unwrap the plastic around the muffin. "Thanks. That was very nice of you."

"Yeah, don't tell anyone." He winked and left.

She thought she'd have to choke down the food, that it would taste like sawdust, but as soon as the blueberry scent hit her nostrils, her stomach growled. For a vending machine muffin it was pretty good. She chewed and swallowed, with only a few crumbs getting stuck. She gingerly tried the coffee, which wasn't horrible. By the time she'd finished both, she felt better. Not nearly good, but not collapsing in on herself, either.

She got up to throw her trash away in a can in the corner. As she did, a man in pale blue scrubs stepped through the doorway. He was looking at the chairs where she'd been sitting. She stood out of his immediate line of sight, so it gave her a second to analyze his look, prepare herself for whatever he was going to say.

The scrub cap had been pushed back on his head but not off, and he still wore the mask around his neck. He was probably in his late 30s, but deep grooves at his temple and the side of his mouth spoke of exhaustion. He stifled a curse and consulted the clipboard in his left hand, flipping papers and mumbling over them.

"Excuse me," she said as gently as she could. He didn't startle, but looked relieved when he spotted her in the corner.

"Molly Byrnes?" He walked over to her.

"Yes."

"I have an update for you." He gestured for her to sit. She'd have taken that as preparation for bad news, except he sank down next to her, his body in such obvious need of relief that she couldn't freak out.

"About which one?" She laced her fingers to harness her tension.

"Both. Interestingly, we have a consent to release privileged health information to you for both of them, so I'm able to convey all the details of their health status to you."

It didn't surprise her that Brady's records would have a release with her name on it, but that Christopher's did, too, made her press her lips together and blink back more tears.

"Mr. Fitzpatrick—" He caught himself and smiled wearily. "Sorry. Brady's injury was the least severe and not immediately life threatening. We repaired the damage done by the wound, with an orthopedic consult. I wasn't the actual surgeon on his case," he cautioned, as if anticipating questions he wouldn't be able to answer. "Dr. Midrick was called to another emergency and asked me to relay her notes." He flipped a few pages on the clipboard again. "He'll need extensive rehabilitation, and we need to keep him for a day or two for observation post-op, but otherwise he's fine."

Molly's breath came out in a long stream as half of her insides loosened. But she couldn't inhale again, not until he told her the rest.

"Christopher…" He made a "Wow, that was a rough one" kind of face, but it didn't project a look of "This is the worst part of my job, why can't someone else tell her?" She sipped in air, the pain in her lungs generating tiny lights at the edges of her vision. The doctor noticed and put his hand on her shoulder. "Breathe, Molly. It's okay."

She obeyed, and her vision cleared. "He's alive?" she croaked.

"Yes, he's alive. And he'll stay that way, if I have anything to say about it."

"Oh, thank God." The tears that had threatened for hours sprang to her eyes again. "I couldn't handle telling Brady a second time."

He gave her an odd look, but waited for her to collect herself before giving details. "I think you know that one wound was superficial, a through-and-through that caught his side but hit nothing vital. The second wound was far more serious, and he's not out of the woods. We had to do major repairs and there's a possibility of additional surgery in the event of internal bleeding. But despite organ damage, all are still functioning, and I'm fairly certain we closed or cauterized all open vessels. He's under strict observation in the ICU and it will be touch and go for a while."

"Okay." Molly could draw a deep breath again. She could manage the fear and despair now, too, but anger began to take over. She clamped down on it, afraid to see how hot it would get. "Can I see Brady?"

"He's in recovery. We'll let you know when he gets moved to a room." He stifled a moan as he pushed to his feet. Then he looked down at her hesitantly. "Do you mind if I ask…the files didn't say. What's your relationship to the patients?"

Damned good question, Molly thought, and gave the simplest answer. "I'm like a sister."

He nodded as if her response was normal and walked out of the waiting room, checking the pager clipped to his waistband.

More waiting. But at least this time it was easier. Anticipation rather than anxiety. Should she go make some calls and let the Fitzpatricks know what was happening? Her stomach roiled at the idea. Not yet. She'd wait and talk to Brady and see what he wanted her to do.

A while later, Dix returned, a Band-Aid over a wad of gauze in the crook of his elbow. He carried a cup of orange juice and had a cookie crumb in the corner of his mouth. He looked even more tense and worried than before.

"Any word?" he asked as he sat next to her again.

Molly relayed everything the doctor had said. "I'm waiting for Brady to be moved to a room so I can go see him. I don't know if they'll let you—"

"They won't. I'm not family, and these nurses are sticklers. I tested them." He sipped his juice, his lip curling slightly.

"What's the matter, you don't like OJ?" she teased, pleased at how much lighter she felt, at least temporarily.

"Hate it. It was all they had, and they insisted I drink it or they'd tie me down and force me."

"That might've been fun." But the joke fell flat, and she shrugged. "Want me to scrounge some apple juice for you?"

Dix scrunched up his face. "Ugh. That's even worse. But thanks for offering."

They sat in silence for a few minutes, but when the back of Molly's head throbbed, she realized the tension had been growing since he returned. She studied him, and he didn't notice. He fidgeted with his hands and shook his head in a tiny jerk, as if arguing with himself. She could practically see the conversation going on in his head.

"What is it?" she finally asked, when it was clear he wasn't making the decision to share.

Dix flicked his eyes toward her, then the door, then the sign on the wall proclaiming death to anyone who used a cell phone. He watched the door while he pulled out his smartphone and thumbed it on. "I got this a few minutes ago." After a few thumb swipes and taps, a video started.

"I'm okay."

Molly's entire body jerked when she recognized the girl on the screen. "Shae," she murmured involuntarily, barely registering Dix's sharp look as the video continued. Tears streamed down the teenager's face, and her voice shook.

"But I've been taken. They want me to tell you to bring the information to Connecticut now, and they'll let me go. If you don't…" She trailed off, and a pistol entered the frame, aimed at her head. Molly gasped. "Send a text reply with your ETA," Shae rushed on. Her eyes were crammed sideways, staring at whoever held the gun. Her breathing was ragged and fast, but she didn't stumble over her words. "You have until morning to get here, or I—"

The image froze, and so did Molly.

Chapter Fifteen

"That's it," Dix said. "No details. No accompanying text message. No way to trace it without equipment and time we don't have."

"I can't believe you weren't going to show this to me." Molly wanted to scream. She couldn't look away from the small screen. Shae was wearing the same hoodie she'd worn at the funeral. The T-shirt peeking out the top of the zipper looked the same, too. Someone had been at the funeral home. Had they been inside and seen Shae's exchange with Brady and Molly? Or had they been outside and simply spotted the girl, recognized her significance, and taken advantage of it?

"You're dealing with enough already," Dix protested. "I should show the detectives and let the authorities—"

"*No.*" Molly knew she was being stupid, but this wasn't a typical kidnapping. Her mind raced. They didn't have time to deal with the authorities.

She bent over the phone again, scrutinizing the frozen shot. The background was completely white, a wall or sheet or something. No reflective surfaces to enhance for clues. Though again—no equipment, no time. The gun pointed at Shae's head was obscene, heavy and black and sinister beyond the obvious.

Molly sat, momentarily paralyzed with indecision. She was three hundred miles away, and both men she could rely on for direction were incapacitated. Could she trust Dix to help her with this? He had the video — Wait. *Why* did he have the video?

"Why did they send this to you?" she asked. "You don't know who she is, do you?"

"I can figure it out. But no, I didn't know she existed before I saw this video."

"So the threat can't be meant for you. You wouldn't care."

"Hey." Dix looked down at her indignantly. "I'd care."

"Okay, but not like we would. Me, or Brady, or especially Chris. So why wouldn't they send it to them?"

"We don't know they didn't," Dix pointed out. He swiped away the video and turned off the phone. "I could just be insurance."

"No." Nausea waved through her. "They know Brady and Chris are in the hospital. They had to have hired the shooter, as well as whoever grabbed Shae." Did any of this matter? *Why* didn't lead her to *who* or *where*. She was bracing herself to ask Dix for the information packet, or at least to go with her to Connecticut, when a nurse came in and said Brady was awake and insistent that she be brought to him immediately.

A warm knot formed in her chest as they made their way through the maze of corridors. She'd lost him emotionally when he declared his love for Jessica, and more concretely when he'd pulled away from everyone. Tonight, she'd come so close to *actually* losing him, irrevocably, forever. She had to take a chance, tell him how she felt, and stop wondering if the risk was worth it. The words crowded her throat and filled her mouth. Until she left the bright, cheery corridor for the dim sickliness of his hospital room…

She nodded her thanks to the nurse and made sure the door closed behind her before crossing over to Brady's bed. He lay with his eyes closed, probably drifting from the anesthesia and apparently unaware that she'd come in. She stood for a while, swallowing repeatedly against the burn in her throat.

His body hadn't changed. He filled the bed, his feet nearly reaching the bottom, the border on either side not wide enough for her to sit next to him. His uninjured arm wasn't paler or less muscled. But the nasal cannula and the giant white bandage on his left shoulder still managed to diminish him.

She had never thought him or anyone else invulnerable or immortal, but it was a whole different thing to have it shoved in your face.

"Hey," Brady said without moving or opening his eyes.

"Hey." Molly stepped closer and slid her hand into his. The intense need to declare herself had subsided, and she held back on asking him how he felt to avoid the typical "How do you think I feel?" response. More important was, "Did they tell you about Christopher?"

Brady opened his eyes, then, and calm settled through her. They were as distinctive a blue-hazel as always, not dulled by pain or despair or even drugs.

"A little. I was still pretty groggy, so they didn't bother with details." His hand tightened around hers. "Nothing's changed, right? He's still alive."

"Yes." She covered his hand with her other one, an automatic gesture to reassure him. "He's in ICU. They have to make sure there's no internal bleeding post-op. Dix donated some blood. I wasn't the right type…" She trailed off when she realized how close she'd come to rambling.

"Sit." Brady pulled his hand free to reach for the chair by the bedside.

She quickly stepped in his way and scowled. "You weren't going to try to pull that over here, were you?"

One side of his mouth curved and he settled back against the pillows. "Of course not." He waited until she sat and had taken his hand again. This time, he stretched his fingers to curve over her palm and around her wrist, anchoring their hold more firmly. As if one of them was falling.

"What did you tell them?" he asked.

"Who?" She wasn't sure if he meant his family or the police. "Anyone."

She sped through her conversation with Mike Wiszowski, knowing she couldn't put off the worst news very long.

"I didn't call your family," she admitted, working up to Shae, prepared for him to be angry at her decisions. "I didn't know how to tell them that Christopher had been shot."

Brady's chuckle turned into a cough, which made him wince and work his shoulder a little. "That's good. My mother will kill us, but we need to wait until he's awake at least. The fewer people who know he's alive, the better. In fact—"

He started to lean forward as if to get up, but Molly lunged to her feet and pressed a hand against the good side of his chest. "Don't be an idiot. Wiszowski's putting a uniform on his door."

Brady subsided but didn't look less concerned. "I hope that's enough."

"Dix saw the guy, too. The one who shot you. Hell, they could already have him in custody." She waited to be sure he wasn't going to try to go anywhere again, then perched on the edge of her chair, throat closing.

"We need to get that information to the right people." His voice was weaker, with slightly squeaky cracks.

They needed to do more than that, but how the hell was she going to tell him about Shae? He already wanted to leap out of bed. Finding out his niece had been abducted would catapult him out of the building.

"You need to rest," she told him. "Dix and I will handle it."

Brady didn't seem to like that idea any more than she did. "What are you going to do?"

"We don't know yet," she admitted reluctantly. No way would Brady let her get away with telling him not to worry his pretty little head over it. "Dix thinks the best thing to do is get the file to someone on the oversight committee, but I've never heard of it, and he has no idea who's on it or even who we could trust if we did know." She remembered what Dix had told her in the park about his reasons for investigating in the first place.

"What?" Brady said.

Molly glanced up to find him studying her.

"There's something you're not telling me."

"No, it's not—" She had to tell him, but couldn't yet. "It's Dix. He's afraid his father is involved."

"Did you read the packet?" He scowled. "Do you *have* the packet?"

"Dix does. He got it from the shooter after he ran. But no, neither of us has had a chance to read it. Or at least," she amended, "he says he hasn't."

"Presumably the information will say who's dirty."

"But that doesn't mean no one else is." She rubbed her temple. Her headache had intensified again. "We need to find out who's on the oversight committee, and from there, determine who might be okay."

Brady slid his hand out of hers again and motioned, palm up, fingers flicking toward him, in a "give it up" gesture. "Cell phone," he said.

She pulled it out but warned, "It's off. Like it's *supposed* to be."

"You're such a rule-follower." He snagged it, waited for it to boot up, then used the speed dial. He waited while it rang, then, when someone answered, said only, "Oversight."

She could hear the one-word answer clearly: "Me."

He hung up and held down the button to shut off the phone. "See? Thirty seconds. Less. They'll never know."

She absently took the phone back and shoved it in her pocket. "That was your father?"

Brady nodded.

"So I guess he's definitely in the business." She sighed. "A lot of years of secrecy have been destroyed this week."

"Maybe for the better. Molly…" He toyed with her fingers

and didn't meet her gaze. "I want to talk to you."

"We are talking." Her heart skittered through several beats before settling into a quick rhythm.

"No, I mean *talk*. About us."

Terror seized her lungs. She couldn't do it. Couldn't put it all out in the open when everything was so complicated, when she was driven by fear instead of hope. Maybe fear was stopping her as much as it had propelled her a short time ago, but the sheer selfishness of putting her feelings over Shae's situation dwarfed it all.

"Brady, they have Shae."

He froze. "Who has her?"

"Whoever we're after. They sent Dix a video."

Brady cursed and started to get out of bed again, but stopped when a loud beeping sounded outside the room, loud enough to have penetrated the closed door. Commotion followed.

"That sounds like an alarm at the nurses' station." Molly stood, hands curled into fists, watching the door. There was no reason to think it meant anything, but the ICU was on the other side of this floor. It shared a central desk with the step-down unit Brady was in.

"Wait here," she ordered him in a voice strong enough that he obeyed. Or maybe the pain in his shoulder, enough to make him gasp when he moved, convinced him to stay. He motioned his agreement, and she went to open the door and peer into the hall. Health personnel rushed around, some toward the ICU octagon, some to the central nurses' desk to back up the ones running to the alarm. A few others hovered, either waiting to see if they were needed or just watching.

Molly asked the nearest nurse what was happening, but wasn't surprised when she got a polite demurral. She looked back over her shoulder to Brady, who shooed her to go, his face tense and one leg out of the bed. She'd better go check it out.

"Where's the rest room?" she asked the nurse, hoping

it wasn't away from the commotion, but the nurse motioned toward the crossroads of hallways.

"Down to the right a little way," she said without looking at Molly. "On the left side of the hall."

"Thanks." Molly walked in that direction, snaking between people and behind the nurses' station. No one was paying attention to her, so she passed the hall with the rest rooms and went through the archway into the open ICU section.

Family members stood around the edges of the central area, some watching from inside their loved ones' rooms, some right outside the door. All faced one room across the way—the one with the cop standing outside.

No longer caring about stealth, Molly hurried over to him. "What's going on?" When he turned to her, hands raised as if to grab her shoulders and bodily move her away, she said, "I'm on his HIPAA." She showed him her ID instead of saying her name, because she didn't know who might be nearby.

"I'm sorry, Ms.—" He stopped when she said *pssht* and made a cutting motion with her hand. "I can't tell you anything."

Molly looked past him into the room. Chris's surgeon and a few nurses worked over his still body on the hospital bed. The alarm had been turned off, and the machines measuring his vitals still beeped. There was no crash cart evident. The doctor barked orders and made statements that sounded like he was intubating Chris, based on Molly's occasional watching of medical dramas, but all the bodies around the bed blocked her view.

"Can't because you don't know, or can't because you think you're not allowed?"

He didn't blink. She took that to mean the latter.

"Have you called Detective Wiszowski yet?"

Now he blinked, but he schooled his surprise quickly and didn't give her an answer.

Frustrated, Molly eyed the nurses and staff around the hospital bed, trying to decide who was doing the least and could be approached. But more important than the what was the how.

"What happened?" she asked the officer again. "I don't mean what's wrong with him. Did someone go in there?"

He looked uncomfortable. "Just medical personnel."

"Or people dressed like medical personnel?" she guessed. Again, the blank stare. "Crap." She needed to find out what was wrong. Forget being tentative. She strode over to the nearest nurse and touched her arm. The woman immediately turned to usher Molly out. She didn't try to hold her ground, knowing the woman had a lot more experience at ushering than Molly did at holding. But she made sure the woman came with her.

"What's happening?" she asked yet again. "I'm family. You have his permission to tell me his status." She said it loud enough to catch the doctor's attention. He glanced up, nodded, and said, "Tell her."

The nurse pursed her lips but let go of Molly's shoulders. "His airway is swelling, and it cut off the tube supplying him with oxygen. We're replacing it with a stronger tube to keep air going into his lungs."

That sounded very odd to Molly. "How often does this happen post-op?"

"Not very often." The nurse's eyes darted to the side.

"Like never." Molly's own throat tightened. "Someone did this to him."

Now the nurse looked to the cop, who was probably preparing himself to lose his job. "Yes," she said in a low voice. "We think they injected something that—"

"Shellfish."

"What?"

"He's allergic to shellfish," Molly told her. "That's probably what they injected." It would have been in his file at SIEGE, but who knew how long it would have taken them to dig it up here? "Is he going to be okay?"

"He will now." She bustled back over and talked to the doctor, who met Molly's gaze before firing orders at the crew.

Molly left the room, urgency tightening her body as she headed for fight-or-flight mode. She stopped briefly to tell the officer, "Call it in, and make sure they send someone else out here. There had damned well better be a uniform inside the room at all times, as well as one out here." She waited for him to nod, then headed down the hall. Once she was past the nurses' station she broke into a run, skidding into Brady's door. When she pushed through, he was standing next to the bed. The IV still held him in place, but the nasal cannula was lying on the sheet. He was trying to figure out how to unlock the IV pole's wheels when she entered.

"What happened?" he demanded. "It was Chris, wasn't it? You were gone too long."

"Yes. Let's go." She opened the cubby next to the sink, relieved to find his clothes there. "Someone injected him with shellfish, or whatever's in it that he's allergic to. Closed his throat. He's going to be okay," she assured him, tossing his jeans and shirt on the bed and grabbing a wad of gauze from a tray by the sink. "I told them to put more uniforms on him."

"It's not enough."

"They blew their best chance. They won't risk going after Chris again, and the police are on higher alert. They know he doesn't have the information, which makes you a bigger target, and maybe Dix, if the guy who shot you recognized him. So keeping you safe while we get Shae is our priority." She grabbed his hand and pressed the gauze over the IV insertion point.

"What are you doing?"

She didn't bother explaining, just pulled the needle out.

"Ow!"

"Be quiet. Hold this."

He scowled but put pressure on the mild bleeding until she secured the gauze with a bandage.

"Get dressed," she ordered next.

"How?" Brady gestured to his shoulder.

"All right. Hang on." She checked the door for a lock and

twisted it. It was probably more of a privacy lock than a real one, but that was all they needed. "Lean down a little."

"You've gotten bossy," he grumbled, leaning. He flinched when she yanked the gown off his shoulders and dropped it on the floor, leaving him naked. Before he straightened she had his shirt over his head. He was able to put the right arm through, but she had to twist and pull the shirt to get the left arm in. The body in front of her didn't make the job any easier.

He was supposed to seem frail and weak after getting shot, not strong and virile. She closed her eyes when she knelt to hold his jeans for him, and escaped around to the back to pull them up. She had no choice but to do the fly, though. She made short work of it, ignoring his squeak at her speed.

"Shoes." She knelt again, this time with a lot less tension, and held the shoes so he could shove his feet into them. "Let's go."

"I'm not leaving Christopher," he protested, his good hand on her shoulder to keep her from opening the door.

She kept her voice low so no one outside could hear through the door. "The fastest way to save your brother is to get that information to your father. Once oversight has it, there won't be any way to hide it anymore, and *all* of us will be safer, including Shae." She hoped. These people would go far enough to kill an agent. Would they kill a kid, too? "We have to find Dix—before they do—and figure out our next step. They're desperate, Brady, and we have to stay ahead of them. They could be in here any second, coming after you." When he didn't move, she resorted to pleading. "*Please*, Brady. I can't do this without you.

He stared at her as seconds ticked past. She struggled not to push him; she could see his brain working over what she'd said and looking for alternatives. But then he smiled and slid his hand under the curls at the back of her neck, the warm, strong fingers curving against her skin.

"You're fantastic, Molly Byrnes," he murmured before lowering his head to give her a soft, intense kiss that sent heat zinging through her body, awakening everything she'd been tamping down for days. *Years.* Tears pricked her eyes when he pulled away. She turned quickly and opened the door, blinking as she peered out. They didn't have time for emotion.

Dix wasn't in the waiting room where she'd left him. She shoved her hair back, trying to think. He might be with the detective, or he could have gone to get the information. They couldn't figure that out from in here.

Brady was scouting the hallway, listening for buzz among the staff, when she joined him.

"Nothing," he told her. "They contained the attack on Christopher and nothing could have happened to Dix here."

"Okay, good. We need to go outside and call him." She snagged Brady's arm and hurried him to the elevator. Once they were on it, she scowled at the grin playing over his mouth. "What?"

"You. You've gone all commanding officer on me."

"I—" She shut her mouth. He was right. "Sorry."

He laughed. "Don't let me stop you."

"Seriously, though, you're the field agent, and this is really your mission. So to speak. So…" Her cheeks flamed and she watched the numbers above the door.

"You'd make a good field agent. I don't know if I've told you that, but you've proved it over and over since South America."

His quiet sincerity cooled her embarrassment. "Thanks."

She thumbed the power button on her cell phone as they hurried through the lobby, so it was ready by the time they got to the sidewalk past the loading area. Dix answered on the first ring.

"Where are you?" She asked him. She motioned to Brady to come closer so he could hear, but he shook his head, his shoulder obviously paining him. He actually sat on a nearby bench and propped his elbow on the arm, a sigh escaping him as he relaxed.

Crap. She should have found him a sling.

She didn't sit. She kept turning, watching cars moving

through the nearby parking lots, looking for people walking toward them, glints of light where there shouldn't be any.

"I'm on my way to get the package," Dix told her. The rushing noise of the highway backed his statement. "How is everyone?"

"Aside from someone trying to kill Christopher—*again*—" She couldn't finish the sentence. "We'll meet you."

"We who?"

"Me and Brady."

"No way, he just got out of surgery! Don't let him out of that hospital, Molly."

"Too late. We weren't safe there, Dix. Brady's mobile. But we don't have transportation. We know what to do with the package, but—"

Dix clued in that she wasn't going to say on an unsecured line. "I'll come get you. Lot C, there's a bus kiosk. It'll provide some shelter and a place to sit down. Give me twenty minutes."

"Or fewer," she told him, and he chuckled.

She relayed the plan to Brady after she hung up, and he nodded. But he was chalk white, and the relief he'd gained from propping up his arm had been momentary. Pain pinched his mouth and showed in the awkward way he sat.

"I'll be right back," she told him, nerves building a lump in her throat at the idea of leaving him like this. He nodded, and she dashed back inside the hospital and followed the signs for the gift shop. They had a wall of sample-size toiletries, and she snatched half a dozen packets of painkillers before pacing the little shop, looking for something she could use for a sling. She spotted a rack of hats and gloves and beelined for it. Hopefully…yes. Perfect. She paid for the painkillers, a couple of bottles of water, and a scarf with the Capitol building embroidered on it, then rushed back out to Brady, relieved he was exactly where she'd left him.

Relief turned immediately to fear when she reached his side and found him slumped over.

Chapter Sixteen

"Brady!" Molly shouted, and his eyes snapped open.

"What?" he yelled back, jerking upright. Then he grabbed at his shoulder and moaned, leaning forward.

She dropped to her knees in front of him. "Are you okay?"

He nodded, but his jaw was tight, teeth clenched, and he'd squeezed his eyes closed. "What the hell did you shout for?" he ground out.

"I'm sorry. I thought you were…" She trailed off, visions of him being shot or injected or stabbed, all in a drive-by, snapping in and out of her head.

"I didn't pass out or get knifed." His eyes opened and he managed to look amused at her chagrin. "What's that?" He indicated the bag.

"Let's go over to lot C first, then I'll get you taken care of." She felt too exposed here. Not that they would be any safer there, but the bus shelter should be less open. "Lean on me."

"I've been doing that a lot." But he did use her shoulder as support to rise and let her wrap her arm around his waist to help him across the macadam. Lot C, thankfully, was to the side of the building and therefore not as far away as it sounded.

Once they'd reached the bus kiosk she gave Brady some of the painkillers and a bottle of water, then tied the scarf into a sling to support his elbow. When he guzzled the entire large bottle of water, she gave him the second one, too.

"Better?" she asked, holding her breath.

"Much. Thank you." He reached for her to sit beside him and took her hand. "When will Dix be here?"

"Any minute."

"And then?"

"Hopefully he'll have the package and we'll all take it to oversight. If not, we'll go with him to get the package, and then take it to oversight." She was careful not to specify location or person, just in case. In case what, she didn't know, but it felt safer. "We have until morning to get to New Rochelle. That's plenty of time to come up with a plan." God, she hoped. She was sure she was going about this all wrong, but doing what the bad guys wanted felt even more wrong.

A silver performance sedan pulled into the lot from the access road and sped in their direction. Molly watched it, her heart racing. Dix, or the enemy? Damn, she wished she had a gun, even if she didn't know how to use it. She sat clutching Brady's hand and waiting for rescue or attack.

• • •

Brady fumed as the car took a corner too fast. The tires squealed and the engine growled as the driver goosed the gas. Instinct told him it was Dixson, but what if it wasn't? With this bullet wound, he'd be unable to protect Molly. Hell, he'd be unable to stop *her* from protecting *him*.

Molly's phone rang. They stood, and she pulled it out and answered on speaker.

"Get in," Dix's voice echoed from the phone as the car screeched to a halt in front of them.

Brady opened the back door and started to slide across the seat, but Molly closed the door behind him and jumped into the front. Dix raced off before she had her door closed. Brady burned with jealousy that she chose to sit with the handler instead of him.

"Why the bat-out-of-hell act?" Brady growled, annoyed that the guy's driving sent him tipping all over the place so he couldn't get his seatbelt on, already difficult enough with one hand. He glowered at the back of Molly's head. She could have helped him.

"I was followed," Dix said. "I think I lost them, but they could be doing tandem, so I don't want to take any chances."

"Do you have it?" Molly asked. Dix handed her an envelope she assumed Brady had retrieved from the drop. She started to open it.

"Hey." Brady reached his good hand forward. She immediately handed him the envelope. "Did you read it yet?" he asked Dixson.

"No chance." Dix's voice had tightened. "Where are we going?"

"North," Brady said, already focused on the papers he'd pulled out. "Molly will direct you."

They drove in silence for a little while, the only conversation ramps and route numbers. Brady skimmed the papers until he hit on one name. "You know Howard Ellison?" he asked Dixson. It rang a bell for Brady, but he couldn't think of why. Maybe because he was ready to pass out from exhaustion.

"He's one of SIEGE's founders. A tagalong, not the guy who originally had the idea. And…he's my father's best friend."

"Ouch," Brady said under his breath, grateful he hadn't seen his own father's name in the file.

"What's inside?" Dix tried to sound cool about Brady reading it, but whatever he thought it said was tearing him up.

"Hang on, I'm not done." The pages described a breakdown in standards, to the level of criminality. As an agent, Brady never knew who he was collecting information from, nor to whom it was going. SIEGE was a private enterprise. But it was understood that the majority of the intelligence was to be used by either the US government or in cooperation with other agencies and countries friendly to the US. Every so often, Brady was pretty sure they also did business with corporations.

But some of the missions listed here, sanctioned by Howard Ellison and another so-far-unnamed party, were with nonapproved countries. If SIEGE had supplied them with sensitive intelligence and the government found out, it would be the end of SIEGE, and everyone involved would be in deep shit. No wonder Christopher had become a target. Ellison had to be watching things carefully in case anyone caught on to his illegal activities.

"How were you alerted there was a problem?" Brady asked Dix as he neared the end of the papers. "What made you send Chris up to Canada?"

"It wasn't just Canada," Dix said. "That was just the last place. Christopher has been digging for me for the past year."

Molly gasped a little. "That long?"

"Yeah. You were the first hint, actually," he told Molly. That made Brady scowl even more.

"How?" she asked. "I never have any idea where things are coming from or where they're going."

"Officially, you don't. But you figured out a lot, didn't you?"

She didn't say anything, but neither did Dix. Both men looked at her until she cracked. "Okay, fine, I could sometimes tell who was from what agency, or private, or a SIEGE agent. But I never had anything to confirm what I thought, and we never talked about that, so how did I clue you in?"

"You made a joke once about globalization making it difficult to tell who our enemies are."

"Seriously?"

Dix nodded. "It struck me odd. So I looked up who'd had a pickup from you that day, and they seemed off. The more I dug, the more things didn't match up. So I asked Chris to help me."

Brady was in shock. How many of the missions he'd been on

had been illegal, or feeding enemies of the state? He thanked God SIEGE didn't do wet work. Living with innocent blood on his hands... He thought back, way back, to college, when SIEGE had recruited him. Part of the appeal had been the idea of doing patriotic duty in a way that fit who he was. He wasn't naïve. He was sure plenty of the information he'd brokered had led to deaths of some kind or another. But at least he'd believed he was doing work that would save American lives.

Dix continued, "Slowly, Chris gathered enough hinky details for me to start to trace things up the line. It got higher and higher, until I knew it had to be one of the guys at the top."

"It's more than one," Brady said. "This information wasn't compiled by a suspicious manager. This was—"

"Yeah, I know. One of the crooks." He said it with a bitter twist. "If it names Ellison, then—"

"The evidence you have must implicate two people," Brady said. "This stuff only names one, but indicates there's another. So they were probably planning to frame someone innocent."

For some reason, he thought of his father. If he was on the oversight committee, he had to have been positioned highly in SIEGE before he retired. *If* he'd retired. He hadn't exactly confirmed Brady's educated guesses.

"How did you know about oversight?" he asked Dix.

"It's in the handler training manual." Dix laughed in disbelief. "A buried, brief mention of a committee created to monitor the integrity of the agency. But there's nothing anywhere who says who's on it, so..." He trailed off, clearly wanting them to say who they were taking the information to, but Brady still wasn't confident of Dix's innocence. They only had his word for anything he'd told them.

Bile churned in his stomach. Who better to frame for corruption than one of the people charged with maintaining SIEGE's integrity?

No, he couldn't think about that. It was bad enough that Chris was still in danger and that Chris's daughter was in enemy hands. One thing at a time, and the thing immediately in front of them was how much to trust Dixson.

Christopher had told Brady he was working for Dixson, and obviously trusted him. But Dix could have been using him to retrieve whatever implicated him, or to betray the unnamed partner before he betrayed Dix.

That didn't really jibe for Brady, though. It wouldn't be necessary for any handlers to be actively involved in the corruption. Ellison and his partner could use them the way Dix had described, without the risk of anyone else knowing their secrets.

An exit sign flashed by. "Hey, Molly, we should drop you at my apar—"

"No."

Brady didn't bother trying harder. Yes, her safety was more important than catching these guys, but the argument would take forever, and she'd make valid points, no doubt stronger ones than Brady's protective instincts.

She directed Dix off the beltway onto I-95 north, then turned to look over the headrest at Brady. "Why don't you get some sleep? Do you need more pain pills?"

"No." The pain was a dull pull-and-throb, and it hadn't been that long since he took the last ones. "I want to see the video." He'd barely had a chance to think about poor Shae, and guilt ate at him. She was the only innocent in all of this. She had to be their first priority.

"I couldn't see any identifying—"

"Show me." He didn't apologize for cutting Molly off. He didn't have the energy to spare.

She took the phone Dix handed over and set up the video before passing it back to Brady. His jaw clenched as he watched, and he wanted to rip the pistol from her captor's hand and beat him bloody with it. His vision blurred. She was so tough, despite her obvious fear. So much Chris's daughter.

He sniffed and ran the side of his hand across his eyes.

Damned pain meds. After watching the video three more times, he had to admit Molly was right. There was no way to tell where it was taken or even when, except that it had to be after the funeral.

"This was the only communication?" he asked Dix.

"So far."

Molly held out her hand, but Brady shook his head and tightened his grip on the phone. "We have to find her."

"I know. We will."

But he could tell she was saying it automatically and couldn't really believe it. He eyed the information packet the abductors had demanded. They could skip oversight and trade for Shae. But he didn't consider it for more than a second. It went against all his training, everything he stood for.

Except what was worth standing for more than family?

He caught Molly watching him, furrows curving across her brow, and knew she'd somehow guessed what he was thinking. She didn't say anything, just waited for his decision.

"Last resort," he told her.

She nodded. "Try to sleep."

He had to admit he didn't have much choice. He reached out and stroked his thumb over the dark circle under Molly's right eye. "You need sleep, too."

"I'll catch a nap between navigations," she assured him. Then she did something astonishing. She caught his hand and kissed the pad of his thumb. "Go to sleep."

He tucked his thumb into his fist and closed his eyes, unable to wipe the smile from his mouth.

· · ·

Molly only meant to doze for twenty minutes at a time. She didn't want to give Dix directions for much more than that, even though the route was a fairly straight shot. Brady hadn't told Dix who they were going to see, which meant he wasn't sure he could be trusted. Molly would have to quit SIEGE if her instincts were that off, but she wasn't going to go against Brady's caution.

Her plan worked exactly twice. By the third set of twenty minutes, her fatigue took over, and when she woke up again, they were taking an exit off I-95, about half an hour from their destination.

"What the—" She held back her curse and checked the time. "Fuck. Dix!"

"You were both exhausted, and it didn't take a genius to figure out where to go."

She twisted to look at Brady, hissing a little as the tight muscles in her back stung. He was sprawled across the back seat, tilted so his bad shoulder was supported behind him and he lay on his good arm. They went over a bump, and Brady's body flopped, evidence of his level of relaxation.

"Has he woken up?"

"Nope."

She turned back around, blinked hard, and yawned. "Did you stop at all?"

"No. We'll need gas in about two point three minutes, and if I don't get a bathroom—"

"I got it." She smiled at him. "Thanks, Dix."

He didn't return the smile.

"What's the matter?"

"I never stood a chance, did I?"

She wasn't groggy enough to miss the nuance of his question. "Of course you did." *Huh*. She'd meant to say "do." "I really like you, Dix."

"But you love him." He gave a short head jerk to the back seat. "It's okay. Any fool watching you together can tell that's what's meant to be."

Molly sighed and slumped in her seat. "It's more complicated than that." She frowned and changed the subject. "Where do you think we're going?"

Dix shook his head, as though he didn't want to say it

out loud, but took a left turn that made it obvious. They were definitely going to the Fitzpatrick house.

He pulled into a gas station with a big convenience store/ fast food counter and stopped at the pump. "You fill the tank, I'll go to the bathroom and get some food. Any requests?"

She shook her head and unbuckled. Dix popped the gas cover and hustled inside. She yawned again and got out of the car to check on Brady. When she opened the back door, the night's chill air drifted across his face and he stirred, blinking groggily. Not the way, she suspected, he usually woke up.

"We there?" he asked, groaning as he pulled himself upright. "Fuck, that hurts."

She reached for the pain pills tucked into the back pocket of the car's front seat. "Here, take—"

The car door jerked toward her and knocked her off her feet. Her head slammed into the edge of the roof. As she hit the ground, grit scraping her palms raw, Brady flung himself out of the car. Molly was so shocked at seeing him move so fast when he'd just been moving gingerly and groggy, she didn't immediately register why he'd done so.

A booted foot came within inches of her already throbbing head. She scrambled backward, out of the range of Brady and the man he was grappling with. A second later her head had cleared a little. She gasped—the other man gripped a knife in his right hand. Brady held off his wrist with his own right hand, but with the awkward angle and his existing injury, he was going to lose within seconds.

Molly pushed herself toward the attacker's feet. She wrapped her arms around his ankles until he twisted and fell, grunting as he bounced off the pavement.

"Call 911!" Molly yelled. No one was outside, but maybe the clerk or Dix would hear inside. Brady staggered against the side of the car, half collapsing on the hood, coughing and groaning.

She scrambled up the big man's body until she could step

on the knife, now loose in his hand, and dropped her knee onto his chest, knocking out whatever air he'd recovered in the last few seconds.

"Who are you?" she demanded. Blood roared in her ears. She was so freaking sick of being attacked. "Who do you work for?" She balled her fist in his shirt and shook him hard. She'd have knocked his head against the ground a few times, but he'd rolled partly to his side and stiffened his body.

She *thought* he'd done that to protect himself while he recovered, but she learned differently with a flash of silver and a cold burn across her chest. The only reason his second knife didn't slit her throat was because Dix yanked her back just in time. He flung her to the ground and started battling with the attacker.

Instantly Brady was kneeling at Molly's side. She leaned on one elbow, gaping at the well of blood through the slit in her shirt. "It doesn't hurt," she said, her voice irritatingly wondrous. "Does that mean I'm going to die?"

"It's shock." Brady flung his scarf-sling over his head and struggled to peel off his shirt. "It means it's a deep cut. It'll start—"

Fire blazed across her chest and she choked off a scream.

"Right about now." Grim-faced, Brady laid her back and pressed the balled-up shirt against her chest. "Fucking déjà vu. Wasn't I doing this last night?"

"Not with me," Molly wheezed. "I need to see how bad it is."

"No way. Leave the pressure on."

"You can't do it with your shoulder." She tried to push his hand away, but she had no strength. She ducked her chin, trying to see. The shirt didn't seem too stained with her blood. Then again, it was a dark shirt.

Crap. She was getting lightheaded. "Dix."

"He's a little busy," Brady quipped.

She squinted up at him, surprised at his composure. "You

were a lot more hysterical last night," she said. "Does this mean you don't love me as much as you love your brother?"

He smiled, but his face was ghostly white against the dark sky. Almost green. But maybe that was the fluorescent lighting. Was it because of his injury, or what she'd said?

The pain subsided, making her suspect the slice wasn't as deep as Brady feared. She pushed away his wrist and sat up. He wasn't doing well, if he was weak enough to let her.

Several feet away, Dix had gotten the upper hand with their attacker. He zip-tied the guy's hands behind his back and added ties to his ankles for good measure. He was reaching for his cell phone when Molly braced herself and tugged her shirt away from her skin. The lighting wasn't good, and the cut was high, just below her collarbone, but she could tell it wasn't bleeding very fast, even removing the pressure and sitting up. She brushed her fingers against it.

"It's superficial," she told Brady. "I think I can get away without stitches."

"Good." Dix came over and helped them both up. "Police are on their way for this guy. I gave the clerk my contact information, but we've got to go."

"How did he find us?" she asked as she climbed into the back seat with Brady, who looked strangely satisfied. "What if there's a tracker on one of us, or on the car?"

"We'll have to take that chance," Brady said. "The faster we get the information to my father, the faster we can end this."

"You want to risk leading them to your parents?" she questioned. "To Jessica?"

He didn't answer, but he didn't change his mind, either. That made Molly feel strangely satisfied, and she had to look out the window to hide her grin. Brady had taken her hand again, and his thumb stroked over her knuckles. Shivers raced through her, making her cut prickle, but she didn't care. This was the greatest swell of hope she'd ever felt. If Brady had still been ga-ga over his sister-in-law, he would never have considered taking this fight anywhere near her.

The tension in the car increased with each mile. Brady watched out the rear window to be sure no one was following them, including cops, while she sat and fretted about how clammy his hand had become. He really needed to be in the hospital, or at least a bed.

Taking the package to Rick would create other complications, too. Hopefully, he'd be able to do something to give Howard Ellison and his unknown partner no reason to harm anyone else. But they were going to descend on the house after two days with no word, a strange person with them, myriad injuries—and the news that Christopher was still alive, but in critical condition in a hospital hundreds of miles away. Not to mention a kidnapped granddaughter.

Molly fervently hoped she wasn't going to have to be the one who imparted all that information.

A phone rang. All three of them checked theirs reflexively. It was Dix's, in the front seat. He pulled it out and glanced at the screen before staring back out the windshield, handling the phone as if unable to decide whether or not to answer it.

"Do you want me to—" she started to offer before Dix cut her off.

"No." He thumbed the speakerphone button and held it so they could all hear the conversation. "What?"

"Son. Where are you?"

The voice was familiar to Molly, but she couldn't pinpoint it. Obviously Dix's father, but he was the only Dixson she knew.

"I think you know where I am," Dix said.

His father hesitated. "I know where you're supposed to be." He sounded confused. "Or were supposed to be, a few hours ago."

Dix cursed under his breath. "I forgot. Things are a little hairy today. A friend got shot. Is Mom furious?"

As natural as his words sounded, Molly had a feeling they were calculated, that his father's response would reveal something to Dix. When he immediately asked about the friend, the concern in his voice as sincere as she could detect without being face-to-face with him, Dix relaxed a little.

"He's okay," Dix told him. "He'll be able to complete his mission."

"Good, good. So I guess we won't be expecting you for dinner in the next few days." He chuckled. "I'll tell you, your mother does not miss me doing field work. Bet you'll be glad to get back to the desk, too, huh?" He didn't wait for Dix to answer. "Okay, I can hear you're driving, so I'll let you go. Call us in a couple of days if you don't want your mother descending on you."

"Sure, Dad. Couple of days. Thanks." He disconnected the call and dropped the phone onto the front seat.

"You think he's clean?" Brady asked.

"I don't know." Dix sighed and rubbed his forehead, then checked the rear and side mirrors again. Molly twisted to check, too, but there were no lights or moving shapes that could be cars with their lights off.

"He said the right things and didn't sound like he was fishing," Dix said. "But he *was* a field agent, and a cofounder of the company, so he could just be that good. I've been watching him with a lot of suspicion, paranoid about what every little thing meant. It's exhausting and I've lost any objectivity I might have started out with."

She let go of Brady's hand to lean forward and lay it on Dix's shoulder, squeezing with comfort. "You've done more than most would have," she told him. "That's a lot of integrity."

When she sat back, Brady took her hand again, this time lacing his fingers firmly through hers and shifting so their shoulders touched. She closed her eyes and let her mind release everything external and just soak in his warmth. After a few seconds, she was breathing in tandem with him, slow and deep, and she sensed the tension draining out of them both. For the moment, she didn't care what happened when this was all over.

If moments like this were all she'd ever get, as long as Brady was alive, she'd take it gratefully.

The car lurched sideways, the back end slewing left. She whiplashed with it, the seatbelt cutting into the side of her neck. She belatedly registered the smashing noise of fiberglass and metal, and the shattering of glass that rained over her and Brady. Dix was shouting and fighting the wheel. She got a glimpse of a vehicle bigger than theirs as they spun before Dix slammed on the gas and they were racing down the road again. Over the roar of the engine she heard the now-familiar report of a handgun. She and Brady shoved against each other, both trying to cover the other. Molly unsnapped her seatbelt and rolled to the floor with a grunt. The longer she fought Brady, the longer he'd be exposed. Then his body was over her, his shoulders wedged between the seats, his legs heavy on her knees. She felt herself whimper, the sound smothered by all the other noise. Dix was still in the line of fire. But as long as the car kept moving in a straight line—or fairly straight, she corrected herself as they slewed left again, apparently around a corner— he had to be okay.

"Gun." Brady's voice rumbled through her as he reached between the seats. Dix complied, and Brady shifted to drag himself up and aim through the space where the rear window used to be. He fired three times before sinking back down over her, his breathing ragged.

"Are you okay?" She put her hand on his shoulder gently, and felt moisture on his shirt. "You're bleeding. Let me—" She reached for the pistol.

"No." Brady set the hand holding the gun on the seat, out of her reach. "You're not exposing yourself."

"Hey, maybe that would work!" She reached for the collar of her shirt. Brady laughed, but his eyes tracked her movement. He spotted the blood on *her* shirt as she touched it and felt how much wetter it was than before. *Oops.*

"We need to get out of here, Dixson!" he called over his

shoulder.

"I know what we fucking need!" Dix shouted back. "You shot one of the tires, but they're still coming! I don't know these roads well enough. Do you? You grew up around here."

Brady's eyes met Molly's, and even in the dark, she could see what he was thinking. They hadn't grown up here, but that wasn't the point. He *would* know the roads better, if he'd spent any time with his family after they moved to Connecticut. He hadn't spent enough. But she had.

"Move." She struggled to get out from under him.

"Molly, no."

"I'm just going to navigate." She dragged her body from under his and squeezed between the front seats onto the passenger side, keeping herself as low as possible. She looked out the front window to figure out where they were.

"Okay."

"Okay, what?" demanded Dix.

"I'm thinking." They were about four miles from the Fitzpatrick home, but they had to lose these guys before they got there. This main road took them into town, but there should be— Yes! She pointed to a farm road, its entrance marked by three-foot-tall reflectors on either side. The burst of inspiration solidified into a real idea, the needed steps laying themselves out in her mind.

Dix waited until the last second, then spun the wheel and swerved onto the narrow dirt road. The sedan bounced over ruts. In the back seat, Brady grunted and cursed.

"They're closing in again," he told them.

"This doesn't seem like a good idea," Dix said through gritted teeth as he fought the wheel. "They've got an off-road vehicle."

"I know. It's okay." She hoped. The vehicle following them was more powerful, but also bigger. As long as things hadn't changed too much... She inhaled slowly when the buildings came into view. "There. Go between the barn and silo."

It was Dix's turn to curse. The gap wasn't meant for vehicles, and it would be a tight fit. "They'll go around and meet us on the other side."

"No." She didn't try to explain. "Just go. Hard."

Dix mashed the accelerator to the floor and braced his arms straight out, gripping the wheel tightly to keep the car pointed that way. They zoomed through the gap like an arrow through the window slit of a castle, and both men whooped as they came out the other side.

And—*yes!*—the pile of hay was still there, as tall as the barn and filling all of the space between the building and the forest on the other side.

"Turn left!" Molly shouted as the car's momentum took them toward the trees. Dix turned and they ran parallel to the woods, on rutted tracks made by farm vehicles. The car's engine made odd noises now, protesting its rough handling.

"Okay." Dix's elation had been short-lived. "What now?"

"Are they back there?" she asked Brady, who was still watching out the back window.

"Not yet. They'll have to go back around the buildings."

"As fast as you can," Molly told Dix. "We're almost to it."

"To *what*?" But then he saw it, a gap in the trees, and swung the car wide left to make the tight right turn. This road was still dirt, but hard packed and littered with pine needles.

"Still nothing," Brady said. "Kill the lights, Dixson."

"That's going to slow us down." But he did it, slowing to a crawl. It was late enough in the season that the deciduous trees had lost their leaves. Soon their eyes adjusted, the moonlight sufficient to see the path. A few minutes later their sedan came out onto a regular road. She gave directions, and soon they were in town, with no sign of their pursuers.

"We've got to ditch this car." Dix pulled into the first big parking lot they found, in front of a small grocery store with enough cars in the lot to hide the sedan. "In case it's being tracked."

"And the cell phones," Brady added, dumping his onto the seat. "They have the GPS data for the company phones."

"What good will that do?" She pried the back off of hers and popped out the battery. "We have to take Dix's with us. It's our only contact with Shae's captors. And if we have his—"

"The rest don't matter." Brady powered down Dix's phone and took out the battery, looking grim.

"What about our clothes?" Molly patted herself randomly. "They could have hidden trackers on any of us."

Dix shook his head and turned the car off, dropping the keys under the seat. "This is real life, not spy TV. Trackers small enough to hide are still rare and expensive. Just check all your pockets and stuff."

They did, then left the locked car to be retrieved later and started walking. They only had about a mile to go and agreed stealing a car or calling a cab would be counterproductive.

"Can you make it?" She tried to tuck herself under Brady's good arm, but he shook her off and took her hand again instead. Dix noticed, quirked a sad smile at her, and moved to walk in front of them in the direction she'd indicated.

"I'm fine," Brady insisted. "How did you know about that place, and the hay and everything?"

"I worked for the census one summer, and we had to go explore lots of remote spots like that. I'd talked to the owner for a few hours and took a chance that his 'biggest haystack in the county' was still there

Brady whistled. "Big chance. That was a long time ago."

"Yeah, but he wasn't very old. Something like that, people don't let go of easily." She shivered when Brady's hand tightened around hers, as if to punctuate her last few words. "I'm just glad it popped into my head."

"They know we're here," Dix pointed out. "And that we're not heading to the rendezvous point. What's that going to do to the kid?"

"Hopefully nothing," Brady said. "They gave us until

morning. We have time to meet that deadline."

"Unless they figure out what we're doing." Anxiety danced over Molly's nerves. "If they think we're copying the information, or taking it to someone, they might—" She stopped, because what the hell else could they do at this point?

They crossed a road into a residential area. It was late now, and quiet, and the stillness of the streets had them all silent as they got closer to Brady's parents' house. He wished he'd been able to call his father, alert him that they were on their way and being tailed. They could have met somewhere else instead of in front of his mother and Jessica, perhaps still leading the bad guys to his innocent family. He wished, as they turned down his parents' street, that it felt more like nearing safety and less like dooming everyone.

"Hold up," he murmured, reaching out to stop Dix before they reached the driveway. "This doesn't feel right."

Dix and Molly waited while he did a 360, checking the neighborhood for any tiny thing out of place. A fluttering curtain or glint of light, shadows where there shouldn't be, vehicles that didn't match the homes they were parked in front of. But nothing jumped out at him. Nothing alerted him to the presence of any danger. So all he could do was lead them up the walk.

Assuming everyone was asleep, he headed for the kitchen door. But as he lifted his foot to the bottom step, his father loomed out of the shadows of the back porch.

He gave a silent head jerk toward the detached garage behind the house and started down the steps. Brady shrugged at the other two and they followed. How long had his father been outside, waiting for them? He pressed his arm against the package inside his shirt and hoped whatever was about to happen next would put an end to the lies and the pain.

His father eased open the barn-style door, let them all go in, and closed it behind them, sliding a two-by-eight board into an iron frame to secure the door. Brady relaxed and reached into his shirt as his father lit an oil lamp on a heavy wooden table.

"Everyone okay?" Rick asked. Experienced eyes assessed each of them in turn—Brady, then Molly, then Dix.

"No," Molly said in contrast to the guys' nods. "Brady was shot last night and was barely out of surgery when we had to flee the hospital. Dix's driving—and my navigation," she added before Dix could get too huffy, "aggravated the wound."

"Molly took a knife slice to the chest," Brady countered, not caring if it made him sound ten years old. She hadn't let him look at it when they left the car, and he'd been worried enough about being out in the open to let it go until they were safe. "It hasn't been treated yet," he added as his father came to him instead of Molly.

"Surgery, huh?"

Brady rolled his eyes when his father motioned for him to remove his shirt but obeyed, trying very hard not to wince as his movements pulled at the stitched-together flesh. His father assessed the amount of blood staining the bandage. "Looks okay, considering. We'll need to get you antibiotics. That the information?" He reached for the packet sticking out of Brady's waistband.

At that exact moment, two bodies burst feet-first through the wooden slats over windows on the back and side of the building. Brady tried to do too many things at once—reaching for a gun he didn't have, crouching to present a smaller target, pulling Molly down and trying to get her behind cover, and protecting the packet.

The men must have swung down from the roof. Black ropes dangled through the shattered wood. One of the black-clad figures leapt on Brady's father, while the other dove for the packet that had fallen to the floor. Dix lunged, too, knocking Guy One off the envelope, but his momentum took him out of reach of it. Brady would have gone after it, but his father had lost the upper hand.

"Help Rick." Molly scrambled for the packet, too close to where Dix grappled with Guy Two.

Brady hesitated for a crucial second before rushing to his father's side. He had no upper body leverage or strength, so he balanced on his left leg and slammed the bottom of his right boot at Guy One's head. Guy One fell sideways, stunned enough for Rick to get out from under him and finish him off with a knee to the chin.

Brady spun to find Molly. She huddled—and looked furious about it—behind the massive table, several feet now from where Dix still exchanged punches with Guy Two. Brady stepped to go help him, but his father caught his arm and shook his head. Two hits later, Dix stood panting over Guy One.

"Nicely done," Rick said in an authoritative voice. "Now, let's see who we have here." He bent and pulled the knit hood off the guy at his feet. "I don't know you." He looked to Brady and Dix, and they both shook their heads. Rick bent to check pockets, found a wallet, and tossed it to Brady.

He flipped it open and found a DC driver's license. It looked legit. Not a field agent, then, or one not trained very well. His eyebrows went up when he read the name. "Dad. It's John Ellison."

"Howard Ellison's son." Rick studied the groaning man. "Not part of SIEGE, but obviously working for his father. Secure him." He pulled a handful of zip ties from the thigh pocket of his cargo pants and tossed them onto the table before striding over to Guy Two, whom Dix had already secured and kept on his knees with a hand on his shoulder.

Brady took a moment to absorb the absurdity. He'd always seen his father as a standard middle management type, and here he was engaged in hand-to-hand combat and giving orders. By the time Brady moved toward the zip ties, Molly had already picked them up.

"I got him." She handed the information packet to Brady. "You guard this."

He bristled at the implication that he couldn't handle Ellison Junior, but then pain burst through his shoulder, the abuse it had taken making itself known. "All right. But be careful." He watched closely as Molly rolled Junior to his stomach, ready to intervene if the guy so much as flinched. But though he was fully conscious now, he made no effort to get away. With quick, sure movements, Molly ringed his wrists with the ties and hauled him to his knees. She didn't even blink at an effort that would have been difficult, if not impossible, if the cut on her chest had been deep.

He was so busy watching her that he didn't notice another presence in the room until he heard the distinctive click of a revolver being cocked. Right by his ear.

"I'll take those, thank you very much." The woman's soft voice was an even bigger shock than the weapon. A long, slender hand tipped with crimson nails reached around him and plucked the envelope from his hand. After a few beats, everyone else in the room froze.

"Ramona?" Molly asked incredulously. "Aldus, right? But...you're a facilitator."

"What? No, she's not." Dix looked from Molly to the woman behind Brady, puzzled.

"Yes, she is," Molly insisted. "She's the woman I met with about Christopher. She's, like, public relations." But she sounded less certain by the time she finished speaking. Brady could follow her thoughts. The woman could be a simple facilitator working for Ellison or his partner...but she seemed much too confident and in charge.

Brady's father was the only one who didn't look confused. In fact, he looked...amused?

"Dad." Brady couldn't believe it. This woman had had Christopher killed! Twice! "What's going on?"

Rick shrugged. "It's obvious, isn't it? Ramona, one of SIEGE's top executives, and Howard are the bad guys. They think that information"—he motioned to the packet Ramona held—"is all they need to destroy, to eliminate the evidence against them."

"Evidence of what?" Ramona scoffed. "There can't be anything in here too incriminating. Certainly not my name."

"But it is!" Molly rolled her lips inward after her outburst, clearly regretting revealing her knowledge. But then she shrugged. "I mean, if you're exposing yourself, threatening us at gunpoint, you must believe it is. But I don't know your endgame. You gonna kill us all? That would just set more people on your trail."

Brady smiled at her, pride and love filling him up until he almost forgot about the muzzle behind his ear. Molly was smart and tough and understood him better than anyone, but more than all that, she was the strongest person he'd ever met. Man or woman, agent or not.

How the hell could he have been stupid enough not to see it before now? How could he ever have wanted Jessica, and all that weakness and self-centeredness?

"I don't need to kill anyone," Ramona said. "Without evidence, no one can prove anything. They can't—"

"Get you tried for espionage against the government?" Rick asked conversationally. "Are you sure the only evidence is in that envelope?"

The sullen silence behind him told Brady that no, she wasn't sure. She was probably trying to decide whether or not to call their bluff.

Except… *Fuck*. She didn't need to call it. She had everything now. The information and Shae. He was surprised she hadn't used her leverage already.

He fumed, unable to come up with a plan. Normally her position, with the gun up against his skull, wasn't a strong one. It was too easy for him to spin and disarm her. Easy when he wasn't hobbled by a pre-existing bullet wound.

"SIEGE isn't a government entity," she said. "All we do is move information. We don't act on it."

Rick scoffed. "That defense won't even get you in the door. And that information isn't all we have on you. Sorry, but you're toast."

"Then I guess I should kill you, after all."

The gun shifted against Brady's skull. He tried hard not to flinch away from it and cause a reflexive shot. His eyes narrowed at the sudden glint in his father's eye. But he didn't move.

In his peripheral vision, he saw Molly shift onto her heels, out of the ready stance she'd taken as soon as Ramona put the gun on him. What the hell was going on?

The silence in the building crackled with tension. Something was about to break, and Brady didn't want it to be him.

"Treason's the least of her worries," he said. "She tried to kill Christopher. *Twice.* They'll start with murder one."

The glint in his father's eye deepened, a dark, satisfied amusement. "You know, Ramona, your field agent skills still suck ass."

"My field—" The woman's indignant retort ended abruptly with a dull thump. The gun fell away from Brady's head and he spun, bracing himself to take Ramona out with one punch. That was all he'd get, the way he felt right now. But she was already on the ground, cold-cocked by baseball bat, her revolver held—in his mother's free hand.

Chapter Seventeen

Donna Fitzpatrick stepped around the heap that was Ramona Aldus, uncocked the revolver, slipped on the safety, and tucked it into her waistband without a hint of hesitation. Then she set her bat on the table and dried her hands on a dish towel. His disconsolate, wet mess of a mother was gone, replaced by a steady rock displaying as steely an edge as her husband.

"You're losing your touch," she chided Rick as she walked across the barn. "Ten years ago she'd have never gotten the jump on you."

"I had it fully under control," Brady's father said as if this was banter they were used to exchanging. But it fell flat under the circumstances, and Brady couldn't wrap his head around one important point.

"Mom?" His voice came out thin. "You're— You can't be—"

"SIEGE? Why not?" She checked the ties around the wrists of the man Dix stood over. "I'm guessing this is Howard." She pulled off the hood, leaving the man's white hair fluffed on top of his head. Ellison scowled and stared straight ahead.

Brady had no answer for why not. Hell, everyone else was

working for SIEGE. But... "You were always home. You never went on missions."

"Not after you kids were born, no." She leaned against the table and folded her arms. "We can talk about this later, sweetie. The police are on their way. Then it looks like you all need some patching up."

A siren wailed. Brady shook off his incredulity. This wasn't over. He strode to Ellison, since Ramona was out cold, and fisted his hand in the guy's shirt. "Where is she?"

Ellison's gaze never wavered, but his mouth twisted with smugness. Rage had Brady hauling back, oblivious to the surging pain in his shoulder, but his father intervened.

"Hey! Hold on. Where's who?" Rick looked grim. "Jessica—"

"No." Brady took a step back. His chest heaved, frustration tearing at him. He wanted to hurt Ellison, make him give up Shae's location. "Not Jessica. Shae. Chris's daughter." The words came out hard and intense, but only when he heard them did Brady realize what he was doing. He shifted to look at his father, whose face had drained of all color.

"Chris's...what?"

"What did you say?" His mother came around from behind Brady and stared at him.

Crap. He shoved his right hand through his hair. This was the opposite of how he had wanted this to come out. There wasn't time to explain, and possibly even less time to get to his niece. Dawn was moments away. But words twisted and jumbled in his brain, pounded down by the throbbing pain in his shoulder.

Then Molly stepped forward and put her hand on his arm. A balm, even if it barely took the edge off.

"At the funeral," she explained quickly to his parents, "we found a young girl trying to pay her respects. She was the spitting image of Christopher. Ramona was there, and she must have seen the resemblance, too. She abducted her and sent

Dix a threatening video. They implied they'd trade her for the information, but since all the players seem to be here—"

Behind them, Ramona laughed. Brady and the others turned to watch her roll gracelessly onto her back and sit up. Her laughter didn't match the mingled fury and fear in her eyes.

"Let me go," she said, "and I'll tell you where the girl is. Keep me, and she dies within the hour."

"How?" Brady demanded, advancing on her. "Where is she?"

Ramona gave him a disdainful look. "I *said*, let me go."

"Not gonna happen."

Brady's parents hadn't said anything yet, out of shock, he figured, but as the police approached the garage and called out, his father took charge again and opened up the main door to let them in. Uniforms and plainclothes swarmed the building, weapons ready, and it took a few minutes—too many minutes—to sort out who was whom. Every beat of Brady's heart measured the time passing. Maybe the time Shae had left. Aldus had given them just an hour.

Rick handed over the materials to the detective in charge, who admitted it was outside his jurisdiction and would have to go to the feds. But it was in the right hands, so Chris should be safe, even if Ellison and Aldus had other people working for them, still out there.

Brady didn't bother stopping the officers leading Aldus away. He wouldn't get anything from Aldus now, not when she didn't think she had anything left to lose. But they had no other leads, and no *time*.

When Brady saw Molly slip back into the garage, he skirted a cluster of cops to get to her. "Where did you go?"

She pulled him further away, toward a shadowy corner. "I checked the GPS on Ramona's car. I was hoping she didn't know how to get to the house and keyed in the address from wherever she's holding Shae."

Hope flared. "And?"

"I don't know if that's where she was, but she did use it. I got an address." She waved a piece of paper. "Can we sneak out of here?"

Brady glanced over his shoulder. He didn't want to sneak away without backup, with both of them injured. But his parents and Dix were all engaged with the cops right now, and the heartbeats measuring seconds had become thuds. Nearly half an hour had passed already since Aldus had given Shae an hour. Molly was right. "Okay. Let's go. I'll call my father from the road, and he can send backup just in case."

They hurried out to the street.

"What are we going to drive?" Molly asked, surveying the crowded neighborhood. Her car was still at the airport, the rental getting ticketed in DC. Dix's, of course, they'd ditched. Ramona's was the easiest to get to, but they had no key.

"I'll get my keys. Car's down the block. I don't think it's locked." Brady hurried inside the house, trying to look purposeful but not in such a hurry that he drew attention from the cops dotting the yard. When he came back out the front door, Ramona was being led to a squad car by one of the detectives. She sneered at him, defiant even as she was lowered into the vehicle.

He ignored the urge to go plow his fist in her face and instead walked to his car, where Molly was already in the driver's seat plugging the address into his GPS.

"It's only a few miles," she told him when he got in the car. "We'll make it."

Assuming they were going to the right place. He handed her the keys and braced himself for whatever they were about to find.

. . .

The address turned out to be in a residential neighborhood, a small Cape Cod–style house. Molly was glad it wasn't a warehouse or something else huge, with too much area to search. But as innocent as the house looked, she had a feeling this wasn't going to be easy.

"What if it's wired?" she asked as they got out of the car.

"I'm sure they've got something set up." Brady scanned the sidewalk but saw no evidence of a trap. "They wouldn't have risked harming a stray pet or random local. If they did anything, it will be to the house."

They made their way carefully to the top of the front stoop. "Is the front door too obvious?" Molly asked. "We should check out all the entrances, right? Look in windows?" She could see from where she stood that the front windows were covered with solid curtains.

"No time." Brady's hand went to his hip, as if reaching for a weapon. "We're down to ten minutes."

"We can't just open the door."

He frowned, examining the doorjamb and latch. "She can't have booby-trapped everything. She had to be able to get back in."

"So there's probably a timer?" Molly guessed. Man, she wished she'd had more field training.

"It could be anything. We probably don't have to worry about explosives. That would call attention. She'd want to handle everything quietly." He slowly pushed down on the latch and nudged the door. It moved half an inch.

"Not locked," he said. He moved it a tiny bit more and called through the crack. "Shae? Are you in there? We're here to help you."

Sobs broke the waiting silence. "Who are you?" The voice was young, female. Molly let out the breath she'd been holding. The girl was still alive.

"I'm Brady Fitzpatrick. I'm your—I'm Chris's brother—we met at the funeral."

The sobs grew louder, harsher. Broken words came through, but Molly couldn't understand them.

"Sweetie, we need to know what's going to happen when

we open this door," she said.

"Nothing." Shae gasped back her tears. "That's not the problem."

"You're sure?" Brady said. "The door's not rigged to do anything?"

"No. It's just me."

Molly's blood ran cold. Brady's face hardened with fury. His head moved slightly in a three-count, and then he burst through the door, rolling right as he did. Molly lost sight of him and squeezed her eyes shut, her shoulders hunching, but nothing happened.

"It's clear," Brady called to her, but he didn't sound relaxed.

She slowly crossed the threshold. Shae sat in a comfortable-looking upholstered chair in the center of the room. Molly frowned at the oddity. The girl wasn't even tied to the chair. But she sat extremely still, her eyes locked on something above her.

"Don't move," Brady ordered. Like either of them was going to.

Molly followed Shae's sight line and bit back a curse. Three wicked-looking knives hung above the front door, tied to fishing line looped through eye hooks in the wall and ceiling and connected somehow to Shae. It was clear that if the girl moved too much, it would release the knives, which would come swinging down at her. Molly thought a skilled adult could guess at their trajectories and duck or dive wide, but no way an inexperienced teenager could figure it out or move fast enough. Or have the courage to try.

"Can we disconnect them?" Molly asked.

Brady moved closer and squinted, trying to see the nearly invisible fishing line holding them in place. He shook his head. "They're barely held up here. If we touch the line, they'll release."

"How are they connected to you, honey?" Molly asked Shae. The girl had to fight herself to take her eyes off the knives and look at Molly, and only lasted a second before her eyes whipped back to the knives.

"I don't know. They gave me a shot and I went to sleep, and when I woke up I was here, and they told me if I moved…" She couldn't finish the sentence.

"Did they do anything to the rest of the house?" Molly tried to keep Shae talking, calm her a little, and distract her from Brady, who was now prowling around, trying to follow the lines. "Were there areas they avoided, or maybe they used extra caution in some places?"

"I don't think so," Shae said. "They moved around normally, like there was nothing to worry about."

"What else did they tell you?"

"That if they weren't back in an hour, I'd—" She choked, more sobs bursting from her.

"Is there a timer?" Molly asked Brady. She didn't understand the whole hour thing.

"I'm looking."

"What did the people look like? Did they use any names?" Molly kept asking questions, but her mind raced. Why would they rig the knives to drop at a certain time? It was gruesome and cruel, and seemed overly melodramatic compared to everything else they'd done. Even with the desperation factor…

"It was two people," Shae said. "A woman and a man. The man was younger, and called the woman Mona, I think. She called him Junior."

"There's no timer." Brady stood from where he'd been examining the base of the chair. "The time thing seems totally arbitrary. But we're not getting her off that chair without those knives dropping." He rested his hand on Shae's shoulder when she cried harder. "It's okay. I have a plan."

He talked them through the plan and made them both recite it back to him. He was outwardly calm and direct, but Molly could see the anxiety underneath.

God, she loved him so much.

"Okay, ready?"

She took a deep breath. Brady stood next to her with an end table. She eased around behind Shae's chair, being careful not to touch any of the lines coming down to it. She crouched and dug her fingers behind the upper cushion, getting as much of a grip as she could on the back of the chair. "Ready."

"Okay." There was a scrape against the floor as Brady picked up the table, grunting with the effort of using his damaged arm. He counted to three, then yelled "Now!"

Molly yanked on the chair, pushing her feet hard at its base to make sure it tipped backward instead of sliding. Shae screamed. There was a faint *twang*, more felt than heard. The chair fell back on Molly and she rolled, shoving hard to flip it over onto the girl. Her brain belatedly registered two *thunks* and a clatter. Breathing hard, she pushed herself up.

Brady was crouched behind the upturned table. How did he fit his whole big body behind there? The points of two of the knives were visible from the underside of the table. Molly scanned until she spotted the third, on the floor next to the upholstered chair. She scrambled to lift the chair off Shae. Brady helped, his good arm as strong as both of hers.

Shae lay curled tight into herself, not crying, not moving. There was no sign of blood.

"Honey." Molly crouched and touched the girl's shoulder. "We've got you. Everything's okay now."

Shae exploded up into her arms, hugging the breath out of her, whispering, "Thank you, thank you, thank you."

Molly hugged her back and stroked her hair. Her eyes met Brady's. His mouth was tight around the edges, meaning his shoulder hurt again, but his gaze was soft and satisfied. Molly had to suppress a shiver at the message he sent her: *It's over, and now we can focus on us.*

Suddenly, she felt like the danger was just beginning.

• • •

Brady drove back to his parents' with Molly holding Shae in

the back seat. She'd asked the girl about calling her mother, but she'd refused to give them any information, even when Molly reminded her the woman had to be frantic with worry. She and Brady silently agreed to wait until they got back to the house and let the police take care of it.

Two detectives were still there when they got home. Brady wanted nothing more than to find a pain pill and a horizontal surface, but by the looks on the guys' faces, that wasn't going to happen. They separated him and Molly as soon as they walked in the door. Brady's mother took over Shae, leading her to the kitchen for food and comfort and, Brady was sure, gentle interrogation.

"Where's Jessica?" he asked his father before following the cop to the dining room.

"She's resting. The commotion woke her, but she didn't see anything until it was over, and they let her go back to her bedroom."

Brady nodded and limped into the dining room. Funny how a shoulder injury could affect how you walked. His entire body ached now, radiating from the bullet wound. He didn't wait for permission to sit.

"There's a lot I'm not going to be able to answer," he warned the detective. A sigh of relief escaped him as the table took the weight of his injured arm. "I don't know everything that's been going on."

"Yeah, I got that." The detective looked down at his notes. "I've been given three different names. One DC Metro cop, two feds. They'll take over the case, I'm sure. So don't expect this to be the last set of questions."

Brady's eyes burned. "Hit me."

The detective actually went easy on him, surprising since he'd skipped out on the scene. He made Brady tell him about the events leading to today's incident, and asked more questions about Shae than anything else.

Brady described what had happened, how they knew she

was abducted and how to find her, but added, "I don't know anything else. I believe she's my niece, but I don't even know her last name. I'm not sure my brother knows about her. The rest of us didn't."

Ten minutes later, the detective let Brady go and went to the kitchen to talk to Shae and convince her to let him call her mother. Brady stayed behind to call the hospital to check on Christopher. He wasn't sure if his parents had gotten the implication of him saying Aldus tried to kill Chris—twice. But he was going to have to tell them now and didn't want to have to say, "I don't know" about his condition.

After being transferred three times, he got the nurses' station nearest where they'd moved his brother. The woman asked him half a dozen questions to confirm his identity and her freedom to give him information.

"Mr. Fitzpatrick is stable and awake and…um…resting comfortably."

Yeah, right. "He's making threats, huh?" Brady would be, in Chris's situation. He took the woman's silence for confirmation. "Can I talk to him?"

"I'll transfer you to his room."

There were a few *clicks*, then a ring, then a barked, "Hello."

"It's me," Brady said.

"What the hell is going on? No one will tell me anything, no one answers their frigging phone, and the cops just stare at the wall. Is everyone okay?"

"Yeah, everyone's fine. But tell me how you are. Mom will want to know that first thing."

That calmed Chris. "I'm okay. Good pain meds, lots of adrenaline. Doc said I'm out of the woods, but I'll be here for a few more days, at least. Did you tell them yet?"

"No. But I'm about to." Brady gave him the rundown of events since the shooting at the drop site. He kept his voice level when he talked about Shae, as if they'd known about her all along.

But Chris exploded into curses. "How the fuck did she get to Connecticut? She shouldn't have even known I was dead! Where's her mother?"

Brady chuckled wryly. "You're not the only one with questions, bro."

Chris went silent for a moment. "Yeah. I guess I have some explaining to do, huh?"

"Does Jessica know about Shae?"

"Hell, yeah. She always has. It's been…complicated."

Brady couldn't believe he'd told Jessica and not the rest of them. "You'd better start explaining," he ground out.

Chris sighed. "All right. Basic rundown. I dated Shae's mother briefly in college. She was graduating and had already entered the Peace Corps. I had been recruited by SIEGE. We both thought it was over, until she discovered she was pregnant. She'd just told me when something happened where she was serving. She went into witness protection and I didn't hear anything else for six years."

"Jesus, Chris." Brady noticed Chris didn't mention Shae's mother's name. It was possible Brady knew her, since they'd all been at school together.

"I cultivated contacts at WITSEC and was able to keep tabs from afar, until the threat was neutralized. She decided not to come out of the program, but since I was an operator, she let me make contact." His voice grew raspy, and he cleared his throat. "I missed out on a lot. I only get to see her once or twice a year. Her mother is still afraid and refuses to let me tell anyone. I thought it would be easier if Mom and Dad didn't even know she existed."

Brady couldn't believe how much his brother had kept hidden. What a strain it must have been. "Well, it's out now. I don't think those conditions are going to hold. Mom's filling Shae with food and love as we speak."

"I don't care. I just—she's okay?" His anger must have been spent, and now the fear was belatedly seeping through.

"I think so. Physically. She won't let us call her mother, but a detective is trying to convince her."

"I want to talk to my daughter."

"Sure. But you know I've got to tell Mom and Dad you're alive, if they haven't already figured it out. They'll be down there on the next plane."

"Yeah. I'm ready." He sighed. "Thanks, Brady, for everything. I'm sorry I put you through all this."

"You did what you had to do. And God knows I have my own apologies to make." He rubbed his hand over his face again. He was so fucking exhausted.

"No, you don't," Chris surprised him. "I get it. I think everyone does."

It was Brady's turn to sigh. "Doesn't matter. I stayed away too long. Caused too much pain. Wasted too much time."

"Yeah? With Molly?" Chris sounded excited.

"Yeah." Brady pushed himself to his feet with a groan. "Let me get Shae. I'll see you in a day or two."

"Thanks, bro."

When Brady entered the kitchen, he stopped for a moment to watch his mother and niece. They were hunched over mugs of hot chocolate, a plate with sandwich crumbs set off to the side. They talked in low murmurs he couldn't hear even from the doorway. But Shae giggled, apparently already recovering from her ordeal. Maybe living a secret life had made her resilient. But being a Fitzpatrick made her strong.

"Did it work?" the girl asked his mother.

"In a manner of speaking. The roof was so slick, they landed on their butts, slid down to the edge, caught the gutters with their feet, and flipped off into the snowbank. They were grounded for a month."

"Hey, now." Brady walked around the center island to the breakfast nook where they sat. "No fair telling her all our misspent youth stories right off the bat. Let her get to know her manly uncle first."

Shae grinned up at him. "Can I call you Uncle Brady?"

Her words pierced his heart with a sweetness he'd never felt. "Of course." He cleared his throat when it came out husky. He quickly handed her his phone. "Your father." And didn't *that* sound weird.

She stared at him. Then her face lit up. "Dad? He's— He's not—"

Crap. He couldn't believe he hadn't told her. And now he'd told his mother, too. What was wrong with him?

"He's fine. He wants to make sure you are."

Shae jumped up and dashed out of the room, the phone already to her ear. "Dad? Is that really you?"

Brady sat across from his frozen mother and eyed her warily, not sure what reaction he'd get when she finished processing what he'd said.

She slowly turned to face him. "Did you just say Shae's father is on the phone?"

He nodded.

Hope and sorrow flickered over her expression, as though she wasn't sure which to feel. Hope that her son was alive, or sorrow that Shae wasn't her granddaughter after all. "Who is her father, Brady?"

"It's Christopher," he said gently.

She burst into tears.

"Mom, it's okay." He quickly slid around to her side of the table and pulled her into his arms. "He's okay." Her sobbing didn't lessen. "Where's Dad?"

Just then, he came into the room.

"Who's the girl talking to?" he asked before noticing that his wife was uncharacteristically hysterical. "What's going on?"

"Chris is alive." Brady said it flat out, so there were no uncertainties. "Aldus and Ellison tried to kill him when he got too close, so he pretended they'd succeeded. Unfortunately, he came out of hiding too soon, and he was shot. He's in the hospital in DC, but he'll be okay."

Rick wobbled over to the table and sat, his eyes watery. "I can't believe it. What a crazy…" His hand shook as he reached across the table to take his wife's. "Donna. He's alive. And we have a granddaughter. And we're going to have —" He glanced at Brady and stopped, just smiling.

Speaking of which…

"Where's Molly?" Brady released his mother and stood, working his way around her because she didn't seem to want to let go of his father's hand.

"She's still in with the detective."

"Still?" Brady echoed. Dammit. He wanted her now. Everything was settling into place for everyone else, and he wanted *his* share.

But maybe it was better this way. He should tell Jessica about Christopher first. Then everything would be taken care of, at least for now. He wanted to know more about how everyone had wound up in SIEGE, and who knew what when. Then he'd be able to concentrate on convincing Molly that they needed to be together.

He walked down the shadowy hallway to the room Jessica was using and tapped on the door.

"Come in." She sounded dull, drained. When he opened the door, he found her sitting on the side of the bed, her pose listless. His heart went out to her. She wasn't equipped for this. Luckily, he had the cure, and then he could hand her back to her husband to manage.

"Jess, I have news."

Her head came up, color flaring into her cheeks and anger into her eyes. "How dare you come in here to talk to me? You *left*. You walked out on your brother's funeral! On *me*."

"That's what I'm here about." There was no chair to sit on, and he wasn't comfortable sitting on the unmade bed, so he leaned against the wall in front of her. "I want to tell you where we went. Why it was so urgent to leave."

"I don't want to hear it! You betrayed us! All of us! For

years, Chris was so depressed that you stayed away. And now you couldn't even watch his body get buried."

"Hey." Brady bit back self-defense. It wasn't important now. "Jess, he's alive. Okay? I didn't betray anything. Molly and I went to find him." He spared her details. It was up to Chris to tell her what had happened and why. "He's hurt, but he's okay. He's going to be okay," Brady repeated when she didn't react. Was she even listening?

"You and that whore," she growled, looking around her as if for a weapon. "She had to take you away when I needed you most." Apparently giving up on finding what she was looking for, she launched herself off the bed at Brady, fists landing first, bouncing off his chest. He gasped when one landed on his wounded shoulder, and tried to catch her wrists.

"Jessica, *listen*. He's—" He had to duck when she aimed at his head. She didn't stop, so he wrapped his arms around her, pinning hers to her sides. "Stop. Jess. Chris is alive." He said it directly into her ear, and she froze. He repeated it more softly, and she sagged against him.

"Really?" When she tilted her head back, he saw how ravaged her grief had made her.

"Really."

"Oh, my God." She backed away, her hand over her mouth. "How? Where is he? I need to get to him."

"My parents are probably making those arrangements right now." He explained that Chris was in the hospital, but not the details. Again, it was up to Chris how much he'd tell anyone.

"Thank you, Brady." She leaned up to kiss him on the mouth, a quick, shocking press before she dashed out. He stood there, frowning, flashing back to the one other time they'd kissed. He remembered the roiling, burning, destructive longing, such a complete contrast to the utter cold he felt now.

He became aware of a presence in the hall and turned quickly. "Molly."

"I know." She came in and reached for his hand. "Come on.

You must be exhausted."

He was. He'd known he was, but now it sank on him like a blanket of snow, or fog, enveloping his whole body. He trudged up the stairs behind her, his legs so heavy he could barely clear each step. "I need a shower," he murmured when they got to the hall and approached the bathroom.

"You're not supposed to get your wound wet. And even if you could, you wouldn't make it through that." She did pull him into the room, though, and sat him on the toilet. "But we can clean you up some."

Brady sat in a daze as she removed his shirt and bandage, sponged him down as clinically as any nurse, and re-covered his wound. The inevitable spark of interest when she stripped off his jeans snuffed out almost immediately, even before she helped him into a pair of boxers.

He must have dozed off standing up, because in a blink they were next to his bed. A pillow had never looked so inviting in his life. But when Molly would have lowered him to the bed, he resisted and pulled her into his arms, burying his nose in her riotous hair. She smelled like her. Like home.

"Stay with me," he begged.

"*I* need a shower." She pulled away and coaxed him onto the bed. "I'll come back, okay?"

"You better," he grumbled into the pillow, and then he was out. He woke a little when she did return, making sure she spooned against him, not even caring that draping his arm over her made his shoulder ache. "I love you," he whispered, and fell asleep.

* * *

Molly slept far more soundly than she'd expected, but she woke early. The house was deadly silent. Before her shower, she'd talked to Brady's parents and Jessica. They'd gotten an emergency fare for the next flight out of New York and were almost packed. She'd offered to drive them to the airport, but they refused. Since she actually was as exhausted as they accused her of being, she didn't insist.

Jessica had been eager to leave. Her demeanor had changed drastically, the tragic widow gone in a seeming instant. The ravages of the last few days were still apparent in her red eyes and haggard complexion, not to mention how frighteningly skinny she'd become. But there was a glow of happiness as she urged Rick and Donna to hurry, and kept checking the flight status on her smartphone.

She hadn't said a word about Shae, or about Molly and Brady's role in getting Christopher to safety. Maybe she was just too focused on her husband, but Molly briefly wished Brady had been able to see her self-centeredness so vividly. Just as reinforcement.

After Molly woke, she lay in bed for a long time, thinking. Brady still slept deeply, his possessive arm flung across her. She was right where she'd longed to be for so many years.

She'd watched Jessica kiss Brady, and his reaction had been contemplative, not devastated. It hadn't sparked memories or his old feelings, she was sure of it. So she could be sure of him, couldn't she? As they dozed off last night, he'd whispered that he loved her. The words had sunk into her and taken root, a more solid binding than even a lifetime friendship.

If she and Brady were together now, she'd have to banish any concern that he could backslide, or that he was lying to himself about his feelings for Jessica being gone. Molly wouldn't jeopardize their relationship because of jealousy or fear.

But that wasn't the only element in the equation. Brady's feelings had changed during the most painful and high-tension period of his life. A very *short* period, too. Maybe he didn't really love her, but only *thought* he did because of what they'd been through. Hell, maybe it had affected *her*, too. How could either of them know what they wanted when their entire lives had been flipped upside down?

She turned her head to look at him. His face was half-buried in the pillow, so she could only see one side of it. One thick-lashed eye. The sweep of one cheekbone and jaw line. Half of a full, firm mouth. But his gorgeousness tore at her. The urge hit her to roll over and dip her tongue into the corner of his mouth. Heat erupted all over her body, driven by desire. She had to smile at herself. Her life might have changed, but her feelings were as constant as they'd ever been.

Brady's eye blinked open, then sank closed again. He sighed and pulled her closer, a whimper of pain escaping him. "Holy fuck, that hurts," he muttered into the pillow, but didn't let go.

"What does, your shoulder?"

"Everything." He gave up and rolled onto his back, letting out his breath in a long groan. "Please tell me I can take a shower."

"You can take a bath. We'll have to cover your shoulder, though." She pulled herself up and flung back the covers. "I'll go get a trash bag and tape." She stopped when Brady grabbed her wrist. "What?"

Sleepiness was gone. He gave her a very intent look like he was trying to pin her to something. "I want to kiss you, but I've got sick morning mouth."

Molly smiled. "Me, too. It can wait."

"Toothbrushing, showers, and then I want you back here in this bed with me. We'll pretend to be waking up again."

She laughed and agreed. When she'd retrieved the supplies from downstairs and met him in the bathroom, he'd already started the water and was ready to get in. She steeled herself and made efficient work of covering his bandage, able to remain clinical until he wrapped an arm around her waist and hauled her up against his naked body.

"Come in with me? Make sure I keep it dry?" He waggled his eyebrows.

She laughed again but shook her head. "I need to brush and stuff, too. You can handle it."

"Fine." He pouted, but climbed into the tub and let out a long, ecstatic moan that set her pulse racing.

"Fuck, that feels good." After a pause, he said, "You still there?"

"Yeah." She moved to the sink and wet her toothbrush. Brady yelped as his water briefly went cold.

"Any word from my folks?" Water splashed, and she heard the click of the shampoo bottle being opened.

"Not that I saw. They got a quick flight and were leaving immediately." She checked the little clock on the shelf above the toilet. It had been several hours. "They've probably been to see him and gotten a hotel room already."

"They won't be back until he's ready to come home."

"That could be a while. They might be willing to let him out of the hospital, but not necessarily to travel that distance." She scrubbed the fuzz off her teeth and brushed her tongue for good measure.

"That gives us an empty house for a few days."

She winced at the teasing in his voice. "Brady, I have to get back to my shop. Even without my SIEGE responsibilities, I can't afford to leave it closed or under someone else's management."

His response came slowly. "Yeah, okay." Water splashed, less vigorously than before.

She said, "I'm going to go use the other shower. I'll be back in a few minutes."

"I'll be in bed waiting for you."

Her heart thumped hard for a couple of beats. She grabbed towels and went downstairs to use the tiny shower off Jessica's room. Her shower was quick and far less satisfying than Brady's bath. Partly because he'd used most of the hot water, partly because her mind was in his bedroom, already engaged in whatever he had in mind. She didn't want to assume the obvious but...

A few minutes later she walked into the bedroom wrapped

in her towel, her hair still damp. She hadn't had the patience to do anything with it, so the curls rioted around her head. Brady grinned when he saw her and held up the covers.

"Come here."

He was naked.

She could barely breathe as she dropped the towel and slid in next to him. He lay on his good side and raised his bad arm just enough for her to slip under it. Their knees alternated, and she tucked herself close to his chest. He smelled incredible. Clean, but hot, too. She licked her lips. His eyes tracked the movement but lifted again to meet hers.

"We have to talk," he said.

Her heart sank. "I always have to be naked in a bed to do that," she snarked.

His hand stroked soothingly between her shoulder blades. "We have to talk *first*," he clarified. "Last time —"

"I don't want to talk about last time," she said. The pain of that day flared before she could squash it. "I don't think we should ever talk about last time."

He frowned. "I used you. I just —"

She sighed hard. "Brady, I *offered* myself to you. I would have done anything to help you. And you feeling guilty about it is just as painful." She blinked against the prickle of tears. Dammit! This was exactly what she wanted to avoid. "Can we let the past stay there and move forward, please?"

"Yeah." He pulled her closer, but not so close they couldn't see each other's faces. "I just want to know we're on the same page. That we understand each other and want the same thing."

She stayed silent. He could go first. But she realized the way her fingertips were tracing over his pecs and smoothing the line of hair down his abdomen probably gave a hint of what she wanted. She smiled a little when his muscles jumped.

He caught her hand before it went lower. "Stop that." Pulling her fingers up to his mouth, he kissed the pads. "I love you, Molly. I think it's been obvious to everyone but me, both before I first saw Jessica and now." His brow furrowed, as if he wasn't sure how to say what he wanted to say. "It seems so obvious now that we belong together, I feel stupid for not seeing it."

She sighed and rolled onto her back. "Brady, I don't want you doing this because of logic or anyone else's opinions."

He yanked her back around and trapped her, not even wincing this time despite how it must hurt his shoulder. "That's *not* what's happening here. Can you feel this?" He flattened her hand on his chest. His heart thudded rapidly against her palm. "It always does this when you're near me. When you're not, I'm looking for you, feeling something missing. I'm not *whole* when you're not around. It took being with you again to discover how empty my life was without you in it."

God, that sounded good, but she wasn't sure he was reading himself right. "You felt empty because you weren't with *Jessica*."

"No. I *thought* that was why I felt empty. But if it was, why didn't being with her fill that void? Even affected by Chris being dead." He chuckled. "God. So much easier to say that now that he's not."

She managed a smile. "What if some of the emptiness was just because we didn't see each other? We were close friends for a really long time."

He scowled at her. "This is not—" He shook his head against the pillow. "I'll have to convince you a different way." And before she could react, he rolled forward and kissed her. Not the slightly stunned, exploratory kisses from before, and nothing like the raw, pain-driven need of their first time.

This time, his mouth landed on hers with a core-deep confidence. Perfect pressure, perfect fit. His lips glided across hers as he adjusted the angle, clung as though they were magnetized just for each other. His arms wrapped around her, under her, and lifted her body against his. And again, they fit. Despite the damp-at-the-edges bandage on his shoulder, despite their height difference, they met in all the right places.

Chest, belly…pelvis.

She went soft and began to ache. He parted her lips by opening his mouth, then touched his tongue to hers. Not tentative, but an invitation. A promise. She whimpered. Her hand plunged into his hair and pulled his head down to her, raising her own to suck his tongue into her mouth. Desire drenched her. She shuddered, the move making him groan deep in the back of his throat.

His hands started to move. They stroked her back, down to her ass, where they dug in enough to tilt her up to him. His rock-hard cock fell into place as her legs parted slightly. She bowed up, wanting him *there*, but he held back. His lower body settled between her knees and he supported himself on one elbow while the other hand swept up to cup her breast. The caress contrasted with the sharp pinch to her nipple. She gasped and arched into his hand, breaking the kiss. He buried his face against her neck. His mouth suckled and nibbled the sensitive skin. She cried out and writhed under him. God, she needed him. Inside her. Engulfing her. She bit at his good shoulder and demanded with her hands, tugging, squeezing, until they were low enough to wrap and stroke. Brady gave a long, low moan and pumped into her grip, once, twice, before pulling back.

"I love you, Molly," he gasped, raising his head until his mouth brushed hers again. "I want to marry you and make babies with you and, God help me, I want to start now." He teased her with the tip of his cock. "Tell me no, and I won't."

But she tilted her head back to look into his eyes. They burned, not simply with lust but with fervent intensity. She knew he meant what he said, and she had to close her eyes against the longing that overtook her. She pressed her cheek against his shoulder and held him, keeping her body still, until the desperation faded and they relaxed into each other. He whispered her name, so softly she might not have heard it if it hadn't fluttered her hair.

And she knew. The longing hadn't faded with the slow

relaxation of their desire. She wanted everything he'd just said. Her birth control prevented the "now" part, but she didn't bother to explain. She nodded against his good shoulder, and seconds later he slid into her with a long, relieved sigh.

"I love you, Brady." She couldn't let him be the only vulnerable one. "I've loved you my entire life."

The next stroke was harder, his body no longer languid but tense and straining again. He grunted. "This isn't going to go the way I wanted." He leaned back, and the motion pressed him upward against her clit. Pleasure flared, making her gasp.

"It's— Oh." She couldn't turn thought into coherent words. "Brady, I— *OhmyGod*." The faster he thrust, the higher she climbed, the pleasure taunting, tantalizing, so close.

"Yes, sweetheart." He slowed again, his hips quivering with the effort. "I love you." He kissed her and moved slowly, but pushing himself deep and hard into her, his tongue matching the movement, as if trying to bury himself so deep in her he could never be removed. He'd stopped trying to support himself and crushed her into the soft mattress, but she didn't care. It just meant more of them touched. She laid one hand against his face and held him to her with the other, lifting her hips to meet him as they rocked. Fused like that, they climbed together, their breathing in sync, hearts pounding against each other's chests, and then exploded. Golden glass shattered behind Molly's eyelids, the rest of her body echoing the sensation. Brady kept moving, and the ecstasy went on and on until she'd been completely depleted.

With a moan, Brady rolled onto his back. He tried to take Molly with him, but she resisted. "That must hurt." She settled on her side and placed her palm gently on his bad shoulder.

"You have no idea."

She started to get up. "I'll get you some pain pills."

"Not yet." He sighed and the tautness in his face slipped away. He ran his good hand down her back and tucked her against him. "I'm okay. I don't want you to leave."

She kept her head on his biceps, trying not to put too much pressure on his shoulders, but she couldn't stop tracing his torso. Her fingertips outlined each rib, floated over his nipples, tugged at the little bit of hair on his chest. "I'm not going anywhere, Brady. I never have."

• • •

Brady couldn't believe this much happiness could fit inside him. It was almost as effective a pain reliever as Demerol. They lay quietly, touching, feeling. Being. He'd lived so long with his immature yearning that he hadn't realized how dark and lonely his life was.

"I can't believe you waited for me," he said after a while. "All this time."

She shifted closer and draped her arm across his torso. "I didn't, really."

He scowled, "What do you mean?"

Her laugh put an immediate damper on his jealousy. "I mean, I had boyfriends. I was even proposed to once."

"Seriously?" He couldn't turn his body, so he twisted his head to look at her. She seemed to realize it wasn't comfortable and rose to rest her chin on her hand on his chest. "You never told me."

"It was when I was in Europe. He was French. Sweet, talented, passionate. But..." Her eyelashes fluttered down to hide her eyes. "He wasn't you."

"See? You waited for me."

"Fine, if you want to see it that way." She kissed his skin, sending ripples of warmth through him. "What do we do now?"

He heaved a growling sigh. "I don't know. I guess we talk about it." He lived in DC, she lived in Boston. They had options, but it would be a trade-off no matter what. "Do you want to stay in SIEGE?" he asked her.

She shrugged. Her breasts bobbed against him, perking up the one fully uninjured part of his anatomy. "Do you?"

He'd forgotten the question. "We'll figure it out." He coaxed her up onto his body. "We have more pressing matters now."

She straddled him and sat up, grinning.

"What?"

Her curls bounced when she shook her head. "Nothing. Just...I love you. And I never thought I could be this happy."

"Me, neither." He reached up to cup the back of her neck and pull her down for a kiss. "Let's see how much brighter the future can be."

For the record: a *lot* brighter.

Epilogue

Brady cursed as the big box of ornaments slipped and he lost his grip on the back door, which slammed on his hand. Already sweaty from wrestling stuff around in the loft in the garage, he banged his way inside the house and hauled the dusty, flimsy box down the hall to the living room.

Laughter rolled out to meet him, and he paused in the archway. His mother, Jessica, and Molly stood by the tree, all as wrapped in strung popcorn as the tree was, and in such a fit of giggles none seemed to have the ability to unravel the mess.

Chris sat on the couch grinning, and their father stood on a stepladder at the tree, watching them all indulgently.

"You could help us," Jessica shot at her husband, ducking and spinning while Molly lifted a strand over her head. Bits of popcorn crumbled to the floor and turned to dust under their feet.

"I'm still recovering," Chris tried, but that excuse had stopped working about eight months ago, when he was released from physical therapy.

"I got it." Brady set the box on the floor and strode over, scooping up a pair of scissors on the way. With three quick snips, he had them all free. When the women protested, he shrugged. "I don't know what the heck you were trying to do, but we can't have popcorn on the tree, anyway. Della would pull it off and try to eat it."

Donna tsked at him. "Like any of us would leave her unsupervised near the tree. Where—oh! That's it!" She'd spotted the box he'd hauled in and beelined for it. "Molly, come here. Remember those awful ornaments you and the boys made in second grade? Here, Rick." She handed a battered, sequined angel to her husband, who dutifully topped the tree with it and climbed down the ladder.

"You're not supposed to put that on until the end," Chris pointed out. Holding his beer out of the way, he hauled Jessica into his lap and nuzzled her neck.

Brady felt his wife's eyes on him and realized he was smiling a little. He met her gaze and was relieved to see affection and gratitude there. He retrieved his own beer from the end table where he'd left it and sauntered over to Molly, wrapping an arm around her waist and leaning down to kiss her temple.

"You okay?"

"Fine. You?" She looked back at his brother and the woman he'd wasted so many years idolizing.

"Just dandy."

Molly chuckled and pinched his side.

"Honestly, Moll, I am. I'm happy that they're happy. And I'm happier." He closed his eyes and kissed her mouth. She'd been sampling the popcorn. He nipped, and they smiled into the kiss. When he raised his head, both his parents were watching them. His mother sniffled and went back to her box, swiping her hand under one eye.

"This stuff brings back such memories." She launched into a story about a rocking horse ornament she pulled out of the box. Jessica was the only one listening, but his mother didn't seem to notice.

Brady back-walked Molly into the nook between the tree

and wall. The lights glowed over her face, dancing in her eyes. He kissed her again, this time deeply, letting all the love filling him spill over. Molly's arms tightened around his neck and she pressed her body against his.

Something was different. He broke off the kiss and frowned down at her. She smiled, such a knowing smile he knew instantly why her abdomen had felt so hard. His mouth fell open.

Before he could say anything, from behind him came "Ew! Not in front of impressionable children!"

He turned as Shae walked by, carrying Della, her half sister, on one hip. The six-month-old baby babbled at him in the same disgusted tone, making him laugh. Shae deposited the baby with Chris and Jessica and went over to her grandmother, kneeling next to the box and pulling something out, asking questions Brady knew would keep his mother going for hours.

He turned back to Molly. "Are you pregnant?" He tried to whisper, but his joy was too strong. His mind raced back, looking for clues. She hadn't spiked her eggnog, but he hadn't seen any morning sickness, and she hadn't been overly tired. No more than a three-hour drive from Boston normally made her. Her appetite had been fine. This morning she'd eaten about a dozen of his father's sour cream pancakes. Well, that was probably a clue, too.

He realized Molly hadn't answered him. She was watching him fly through his thoughts, clearly amused. "Well?"

"Yes. Test was positive this morning."

"And you didn't tell me?" That came out louder, and the conversations behind them faltered before they went on, stilted enough that he knew they were listening. He almost turned to shout the news, but Molly grabbed his arm and yanked him out to the kitchen.

"They're going to think we're fighting," Brady said. "Do you need to sit?" He pulled out a bar stool.

"Knock it off." Molly slapped his hand away and leaned against the island. She had no trouble keeping her voice down.

"Don't you dare start with that invalid crap. I can still take you."

He grinned. She could, but usually only because their weekly sparring matches turned into hot crash-mat sex whenever he got the upper hand. "So why can't I tell them?"

"I want to do it tomorrow. I have a present all wrapped up for your mom to open."

He made a face. "So she can go all shrieky and we can film it for *America's Funniest Home Videos*?"

"Something like that."

"Okay. If that's what you want to do."

"It is." She folded her arms and eyed him sideways. "So? What do you think?"

Brady didn't give his instinctive response, which was to whoop and spin her around. He thought about the past year, the happiest of his life. On New Year's Eve they'd celebrate their first anniversary. His mother hadn't argued against their civil ceremony by the local justice of the peace, not after the roller coaster of Chris's supposed death and the shooting. He hadn't wanted to wait, and Molly said she was locking him up before he changed his mind again.

The fallout from the arrests had been massive. SIEGE had nearly shut down while the oversight committee called in all their agents, conduits, facilitators, carriers, and suppliers and tried to determine who was knowingly working with Ellison and Aldus. There were more arrests and plenty of dismissals, and in the end, the company was starting over with a damaged reputation and a new generation of leaders, including Chris and Dix. Brady had chosen a move to a job as a facilitator and a station in Boston, so Molly could keep her shop open and maintain her conduit role.

There'd been a big family meeting, and Brady's parents finally ended all the secret keeping. They'd retired from field work when the boys were young, but Rick had kept his old connections and friendships. He eventually got pulled back in to join the oversight committee and learned his sons had been recruited. He'd recommended Molly, himself.

Dix hadn't been the only one suspicious of some of the missions being assigned, but Brady's father admitted to being blinded by friendship and looking in the wrong direction. Dix's father hadn't been involved, much to Dix's relief, but the older man stepped down anyway, playing scapegoat for the government in an attempt to smooth the path for the revamped company.

Despite the upheaval in their work life, Brady and Molly had settled easily into their personal one. Every day with her was a gift, and Brady had yet to take it for granted. A baby would obviously disrupt that again, but it would also make their life complete.

"I'm not ready to share you," he admitted, stealing another kiss. "Give me, what, about seven and a half months?" A wail from the living room punctuated his words.

Molly laughed. "Exactly seven and a half months." She sighed. "I was worried you'd think it was too soon."

Brady pulled her into his arms and rested his head on top of her soft curls. "No. It's just right." The wail returned, this time escalating. "Come on. Let's get upstairs before they try to pass her off on us." He chased her up the steps to his old bedroom and showed her exactly how happy he was.

The next morning, Shae woke everyone with breakfast in bed. She dashed from room to room, rushing them all through their scrambled eggs and bacon, then chasing them down to the living room to open presents.

When the floor was invisible under shredded wrapping paper and everyone had *ooh*ed and *aah*ed over their gifts, Molly pulled a slim, gold foil–wrapped package out from under the tree skirt and handed it to her mother-in-law.

Brady should have known this wouldn't be the typical spectacle shown on *America's Funniest Videos*. His mother eyed Molly with spy-like intensity, turned her laser eyes on Brady, and started to undo the ribbon. But her wary anticipation turned to puzzlement when she saw the mission folder inside the paper.

"What's this?" She read the numbers on the folder label and shrugged. "Are you trying to tell us you finally got promoted?"

Molly smiled and slid onto Brady's knee. But her grip around his hand ground his bones. "Nope."

Donna opened the folder. Rick stood and went around the back of the couch to read silently over her shoulder. They laughed together after a couple of seconds and went back to the beginning to read the coded information out loud. By the time they got to the end, Donna was crying, Rick was pretending not to be, and Chris had done the whoop-and-swing with Molly that Brady had been tempted to do the night before.

"What?" Jessica pulled a bow out of Della's hand just before it hit her mouth and scowled at Shae, dancing in the middle of the floor. "I don't get it!"

Brady, abandoned by his wife, went over to help Jessica off the floor. "We're having a baby." He watched her reaction carefully. She'd changed a lot since Della, finding her old self and then improving on her. She was less dependent and needy, more compromising and giving. But every so often, Brady sensed a hint of the feelings she'd confessed to during that other, long-ago Christmas. He, of course, wondered how he could *ever* have wanted Jessica over Molly, but he was a dumb jock. It sometimes took them a while to figure things out.

Jessica grinned and congratulated him with a hug. "I'm so happy for you guys!" Her voice flowed with sincerity, and Brady relaxed.

He worked his way back to Molly and stood behind her, his arms wrapped around her waist, his chin propped on her shoulder, watching his family. He tried to swallow. It was a struggle, the lump in his throat swelling by the second. His parents on the couch, cooing at Della about the cousin she'd have soon. Shae, nearly sixteen, chattering about how glad she was that they were doing this before she went away to college.

Jessica cuddling with Christopher, whole and content and toasting his brother from across the room with a bottle of water.

And Molly and their child in Brady's arms. It had taken a long damned time to get here, but they'd made it. And he'd spend his entire life making it up to all of them.

Acknowledgments

A big thank you must go to Kim Law, who critiqued my first chapter with a completely unbiased eye and gave me an entirely new perspective. Another goes to McKenna Damschroder, for helping ensure I used my music analogies correctly. And one more to Tracy Madison, who not only critiqued the opening of this book once, but twice. Tracy, you always know what's wrong, and you always know the exact right places to praise. Thank you.

This may be my favorite of all the books I've written, and Nina Bruhns deserves a tackle hug for loving it for the same reasons and helping make sure all areas of the book are strong. My editorial experience on this book was blissful, and for that, Nina, I thank you.

One final huge thank you is in order to the editorial and publicity team at Entangled Ignite and to the Entangled Ignite authors, who are the most supportive in a world of extreme support. I couldn't be happier to share an imprint with all of you.

About the Author

Natalie J. Damschroder is an award-winning author of contemporary and paranormal romance — Love with a Shot of Adrenaline. She sold her first book in 1999, and 2014 will see the publication of her 15th novel. She grew up in Massachusetts and loves the New England Patriots more than anything. (Except her family. And writing and reading. And popcorn.) When she's not writing, revising, proofreading, or promoting her work, she does freelance editing and works part time as a chiropractic assistant. She and her husband have two daughters she's dubbed "the anti-teenagers," one of whom is also a novelist. (The other one prefers math. Smart kid. Practical.) You can learn more about her and her books at www.nataliedamschroder.com.

DELETED SCENE NUMBER ONE

His father, unlike his mother, seemed to believe Brady and Molly belonged together, and Dad was afraid Brady was going to succumb to Jessica's neediness and lose his best friend. But Brady didn't know what he wanted, except not to hurt either woman. So he stuck to half the truth, the half Molly already knew, or thought she knew.

"About Jessica. I spent all that time with her, and then suddenly stopped, and she didn't eat well today, or sleep, even though she spent most of the day in her room. I guess tomorrow's eroding any progress we made, getting her through the grief."

Molly nodded. "It's going to be hard, no matter what. But I hope she can hold it together. She needs this closure if she's going to heal. If she's sedated through it, or can't go because she's too distraught, she'll be stuck here, emotionally."

Brady nodded, his brain already moving on. "Uh, Moll, he said some things—you told them, right? About that Christmas? What happened with..." She was nodding, so he didn't have to spell it out. Good, because the memory still pierced him with embarrassment and the residue of the shattering pain.

"Of course I told them." She lifted her chin a little defiantly. "Not details. But I told them why you were acting the way you did. They were so hurt when you left immediately after the wedding toast. So was Chris."

Horror swept over Brady. "You told Chris I wanted his wife?"

"Jesus, no. I never said anything to him. But he probably figured it out. I mean, he'd never believe it was just work keeping you away. Unless..." Her eyes went wide.

"Unless he knew I was SIEGE. Which he could, since he was recruited first." Brady shook his head. He couldn't believe the secrecy in his family, in his company, and didn't understand the reason for it. They weren't the CIA, for cripes sake, they were private sector, even if they worked with the government. It made sense to keep it secret from uninvolved family, like his parents, but not another active agent.

"I don't think he did." Molly shifted, pulling one leg under the other.

"Why?"

She shrugged. "I don't know. I just don't."

DELETED SCENE NUMBER TWO

They'd uncovered both traitors, and hopefully enough information to put them away. Certainly, enough witnesses to go to trial. They were all safe. Christopher could—

Chris. He supposed it was possible they'd known everything that was going on, but he really didn't think they could have been so convincing in their grief. Telling them was priority one. But before that, he had to call the hospital and find out if he was okay. He'd been out cold for most of the drive up here, and used the chaos and urgency to hide the fact that he was too scared to call after that. Hell, he was still too scared.

The police called out from outside the barn. Within minutes, they'd taken control of the prisoners and started segregating people to take statements.

Brady had his phone out, but couldn't seem to push the buttons. He automatically looked to Molly, who nodded and faded to the rear of the garage. How did she do that? Always know what he needed?

He craved her, suddenly. Wanted her by his side. Somehow, he had to convince her he meant it when he said that was where she belonged.

• • •

Molly tried not to let resentment swell as she hovered in the shadows, watching the police and listening to modulated voices ask her to hold while they transferred her sixteen times. She understood why Brady had been unable to make the call. She could practically read his mind, and definitely read his emotions. He couldn't handle the risk of hearing bad news again. She got it. And of course she didn't mind doing it for him.

But dammit, she was tired of being his solid, supportive best friend. This was it. When this was all over, she was cutting ties. Yes, she'd gone twelve years without him, but she had never let go. Now, she would.

Her heart laughed at her.

"Ward One," someone said on the other end of the phone line.

"This is Molly Byrnes calling for a status on Christopher Fitzpatrick." She kept her voice low, even though no one was paying attention to her. Certain words caught attention, and it would be better to tell the Fitzs later.

"Yes, Ms. Byrnes, Detective Wiszowski said you'd be calling." After rapid keyboard clicking, the woman said, "Mr. Fitzpatrick is in stable condition and has been moved out of the ICU. He's still under observation, but there's no sign of internal bleeding, and his vitals are strong."

Molly let out a long breath. "And the allergic reaction?"

"Fully recovered."

"Thank you." She hung up as a uniformed police officer approached, pen and pad at the ready. The Ellisons and Ramona had already been led out of the building.

Molly gave clear, honest answers to every question asked. She'd stopped worrying about secrecy. She might lose her job, but she cared more about putting away Aldus and Ellison and keeping her family safe.

WHY I LOVE THE FRIENDS-TO-LOVERS STORYLINE

You know how you can go through your life not noticing something until it gets pointed out to you, and then suddenly it's everywhere? Like, I didn't even know Impalas were still on the road until I fell in love with the TV show Supernatural (and, of course, the Metallicar). Then every time I stopped at a traffic light, there was an Impala in front of me.

That's how I see the best-friends-to-lovers storyline, my favorite romance trope. I especially love when there's a twist to it. The first time I wrote one myself, the hero tells his best friend he's in love with her because he thinks he's dying. She says nuh-uh, no way. He moves on, but now she sees him completely differently…and it's too late. (That's Kira's Best Friend, in case you're wondering.)

In my newest book, Hearts Under Siege, I took a different tack. There's unrequited love of the standard sort—I didn't want to have Molly be in love with Brady already, but when he unknowingly shattered her heart at the end of the first chapter, I knew that was how it had to be.

But unrequited love plays a more active role in this story, too. Brady falls hard—love at first sight—for a woman who turns out to already be his brother's fiancée. He can't change how he feels, so he leaves and mostly stays away from his family—and Molly—for 12 years. Until his brother's death brings them all together and reveals some major secrets about all of them. Working with Molly opens Brady's eyes in a lot of ways.

I love this trope for a lot of reasons, but one of the biggest is the satisfaction of painful feelings turning into pleasurable ones. And if there's action-adventure thrown in, woo hoo! :)

So how about you? Do you like friends-to-lovers romances? Why or why not? If not, what's your favorite type of romantic storyline? I love to hear from readers, so hit me up on Twitter, Facebook, Goodreads, or my blog.

A Little Bit about Molly and Brady

When I started writing this book, I didn't know much about Molly. But as soon as she started playing her knees like a keyboard, I knew she was a serious musician. About which I know virtually nothing. I can't sing. You don't want to see me dance. And I can't play Rock Band at higher than medium on any instrument.

Enter Number Two, my younger daughter. She took viola starting in fourth grade (and continues) and did mallet percussion in fifth. Then she taught herself piano. Then guitar. Then ukulele! Musicians classically trained in those instruments will hear the flaws, but I get a definite thrill with every pass she takes through a new song. Anything I got right in this book is due to her. Anything I got wrong is my own fault.

Luckily, I write adventure plots, so Molly's musical training and skills didn't come into play very much. They served mainly as a cover for her real job. The story is obviously more about her and her friendship with Brady, and that kind of comes from me. Growing up, I had more male friends than females. My first best friend was a boy, the son of my mother's best friend, and he could be at least partly responsible for my career as a writer. We spent hours and hours pretending we were Steve Austin and Jaime Sommers (the Six Million Dollar Man and the Bionic Woman), acting out scenes and making up stories, while we made my little brother be Oscar Goldman. (He's still traumatized. Sorry, Andy!)

Anyway, Brady embodies all the traits I valued in my close male friends, none of whom turned into more (and I won't say which ones were the top candidates!). I hope you grew to love both him and Molly and, like me, were sorry when the story was over.

Thank you!

by Genie Davis and Linda Marr

Erotic romance writer Jenna Brooks lives an ordinary life in a quiet Oregon town, putting her sensual heart into her fiction rather than her everyday life. Deeply involved in her latest story about glamorous lovers on the run, she laughs off a carnival gypsy's prediction that she'll find everything she desires "between the sheets"—apparently those her DeskJet is printing. Because suddenly, Jenna finds herself drawn into her own stories, literally. When the seductive, mysterious Riley Stone rescues her from an attempted hit and run, she's plunged into a reckless, wild relationship unlike anything she's ever experienced—except on paper.

Meanwhile, Riley is feeling pretty upended himself. A specialist consultant with the FBI, he's on a mission to derail a drug king-pin whose wealth and extensive real estate is managed by Jenna's neighbor, he'd planned to ingratiate himself with Jenna just enough to gain access to her neighbor's apartment so he can keep a close eye on his comings and goings. Instead, he finds himself not only drawn to Jenna, but falling for her, hard. On the heels of this realization comes the discovery that her new neighbor didn't move in next door by chance: her father is the last hold-out against a drug-money fueled billion dollar development scheme and her neighbor plans to take and hold Jenna hostage until the necessary papers are signed.

As Riley struggles to keep Jenna safe, the romance they've woven could force them to pay the ultimate price: admitting they've fallen in love—for real.

RISKING IT ALL FOR HER BOSS

by Sharron McClellan (book 1 in the Heroes for Hire series)

Heroes for Hire: Big Risk. Big Reward. No Regrets.

When High Risk Securities (HRS) agent, Eva Torres, botches an undercover job by failing to rescue both of the kidnap victims she was sent to retrieve, Quinn Blackwood—her former lover and the man who broke her heart—pulls her and one of the victims out of harm's way. As a penalty for her sins, she's offered the dull job of escorting a former bio-chemical warfare scientist to London to reunite with his daughter. Much to her displeasure, the job of monitoring her assignment is given to Quinn Blackwood, her former lover and the man who broke her heart.

Quinn isn't thrilled with the situation either. He taught Eva everything he knew about secrets, sex, and lies—but the biggest lie of all was the one he'd told himself: that his missions for HRS were more important than anything, including his relationship with Eva. Because now that they're working together again, the urge to put his hands on her, to feel her beneath him again, is killing him.

Things only get worse when their current operation goes wrong and the scientist they're guarding is kidnapped mid-air. Now, Eva and Quinn have to work together to find him before he is forced to create a monstrous weapon that could destroy entire cities. A hard task made more difficult they find themselves fighting both the enemy and their building desire for each other. Can they work together for the sake of the mission without reigniting the passion between them—or will passion be the salvation of them all?

Made in the USA
Charleston, SC
06 October 2014